Nemesis from Burma

The Bamboo Murders

# Nemesis from Burma

*The Bamboo Murders*

Arthur F. Freer

The Pentland Press
Edinburgh – Cambridge – Durham – USA

© A. F. Freer, 2000

First published in 2000 by
The Pentland Press Ltd
1 Hutton Close,
South Church
Bishop Auckland
Durham

All rights reserved
Unauthorised duplication
contravenes existing laws

ISBN 1-85821-781-4

Typeset by Carnegie Publishing,
Carnegie House, Chatsworth Road, Lancaster
Printed and bound by Bookcraft Ltd (Bath)

To the memory of all
those who served with
the Armed Forces in
the 14th Army in
India and Burma
1942–1945

# Contents

| | | |
|---|---|---|
| | Author's Note | ix |
| | Acknowledgements | xiii |
| | Foreword | xv |
| | Personnel | xvii |
| | Preface | xviii |

| Chapter: | | Page |
|---|---|---|
| One | 1945 Rape and Retribution | 1 |
| Two | 1945 Cakes and Rubies | 15 |
| Three | 1982 Interrogation | 33 |
| Four | 1945 Ywathetgyi and Tina | 37 |
| Five | 1945 The Plan Matures | 50 |
| Six | 1945 Rubies Galore | 58 |
| Seven | 1982 The End of Our War | 70 |
| Eight | 1946 Peace-time Murder | 76 |
| Nine | 1947 Another Murder | 82 |
| Ten | 1948 And Another | 84 |
| Eleven | 1982 Ma Tina Mying | 89 |
| Twelve | 1982 A Vital Clue | 107 |
| Thirteen | 1982 Miller Identified | 110 |
| Fourteen | 1982 Future Plans | 115 |
| Fifteen | 1946 Transition | 119 |
| Sixteen | 1946 Justice? | 128 |
| Seventeen | 1947 Impulsive Action | 131 |

| | | |
|---|---|---|
| Eighteen | 1948 The Crossbow | 136 |
| Nineteen | 1982 The Final Caper | 142 |
| Twenty | 1982 Police Intelligence | 147 |
| Twenty-One | 1982 Media Manipulation | 153 |
| Twenty-Two | 1982 The Informer | 156 |
| Twenty-Three | 1982 Arrested | 165 |
| Twenty-Four | 1982 Trickcyclist | 168 |
| Twenty-Five | 1982 Another Volunteer | 175 |
| | Appendix | 178 |

# *Author's Note*

During World War II, the four troops in a squadron of cavalry were numbered 4, 5, 6 and 7 and these became part of their wireless call sign, e.g. Baker 4 etc. The numbers 1, 2 and 3 were used by three of the tanks in the Squadron HQ Troop. I have used the name of '2 Troop' to identify my villain so that no member of the Regimental Association will wake up in the small hours of the morning wondering if I am claiming that he was involved with such a murderous sergeant. This book is intended to be for interest and amusement only.

Since the publication of *NUNSHIGUM, On the Road to Mandalay* in 1995, I have been asked many times whether the murderous 'jogger' existed. Indeed, there was one shocking occasion, on the Cambridge Radio, when I was asked if I personally had such inclinations! Of course I denied both questions. The character is a creation of my own mind, since I know of the traumas that were experienced by soldiers spending months or years in action under appalling conditions, or even, more simply, through long service in 'kharab stations'. I believe that such a person could exist when I recall the training that was given to many thousands of decent civilised young men, turning them into very fit fighters who could kill an 'enemy' quickly and without hesitation.

I have tried to tell the light-hearted story of serving in the British and Indian Armies during the last days of the Raj, when Japan invaded the vast country of India as we knew it then. The serious philosophy came from Dusty Miller, who appeared to be able to envisage the future! There certainly were rumours of a rape carried out as described in the narrative, but I regret to say that there was no visit to Maymyo in order to use a 75mm AP shell to open a safe. And, therefore, no hoard of rubies.

In 1943 and 1944, the 14th Army, commanded by 'Uncle Bill Slim', grew to include mainly British, Indian and Gurkha troops, who were supported by Chinese/American forces from the north and local Burmese levies throughout the mountains and plains of Burma. Other support came from our colonies, including Africa, the Americas, and many thousands of labourers recruited locally. We proved that we had the determination to train our people and supply firepower that made the 'invincible' Japanese 15$^{th}$ Army reel in its rapid advance westwards, halt in its tracks around Imphal and Kohima and then turn and retreat back to annihilation in Burma in 1945.

During April 1998 I was privileged to visit Kohima and Imphal with a pilgrimage organised by the Royal British Legion. There were some changes to be noticed. The old Manipur had been split into two separate states. The northern mountainous area is now named Nagaland, with Kohima as the capital. The remainder of Manipur retains Imphal as its capital. A military presence is noticeable everywhere, including the crossing point on the Manipur Road. The old milestone markers can no longer be used to identify different locations, as the road now has only a few 'kilometre markers' showing the distances from each of the two capitals to the border.

When I asked to see the mountain of NUNSHIGUM, it was pointed out that it is really named NATUMCHING, meaning Natum's Hill. It appears that some British officer had misspelt and mispronounced the name when first highlighting it on his map. This would not be the only occasion of error, when we realise that Bombay and Rangoon have now reverted to their original pronunciation of Mumbai and Yungoan.

Following the end of World War II I returned to the UK during 1946, when the problems of Partition were tearing the sub-continent apart, and I tried, without success, to forget those four years spent there. I have enjoyed visits there during recent years and found that the colour, warmth and vitality which are so apparent have become part of my nature.

I recall the real joy that I experienced once when taking a swarm of bees from a bush in a back street garden in Bradford. The tenant told me that he had served with the Bombay Grenadiers in Burma and that he loved the Carabiniers.

Another old soldier, whom I also met in Bradford, told me that he served in the Indian Army.

"What regiment were you with?" I asked him.

"I was in the I.R.A., sir" he replied. I was rather puzzled.

"The I.R.A?" I repeated, "I don't think I know them. What was the name?"

"Oh yes sir, the I.R.A., the Iroyal Rindian Angineers," he said, very proudly.

And I am proud to have served with them.

AFF

## Author's Note

May I take this opportunity to correct an error in my first book about Burma, *NUNSHIGUM, On the Road the Mandalay*. On a few occasions I mention a Lieutenant Ken Ryman who was the Royal Engineers or 'Sapper' officer attached to B Squadron, 3rd Carabiniers, for the year spent fighting the Japanese in India and Burma.

We had all admired this amazing man, who would walk in front of our advancing tanks in order to make sure that the ground ahead was suitable for their safe progress. He did this firstly on our approach to the mountain of Nunshigum, when he continued his walk up the ridge until he came under fire from the Japanese snipers. He did this regularly in each successive battle, risking his life to help to ensure that the tanks were on the best route over rough ground and that the small bridges and culverts had not been previously mined by the enemy.

In my opinion he earned a number of Military Crosses in these many situations but I learned that his name was not recommended for a medal because 'he was his own senior officer'! Justice reigned eventually as I read his obituary in the press, recently, that he had been awarded two MC's for bravery in the later stages of the war in Burma. I learned that his name was really Kenneth Ryden, not the 'Ryman' from my faulty memory, and I was able to apologise to Mrs Ryden and her family when I met them at the opening of the new Regimental Museum in the Castle, Edinburgh.

AFF

# *Acknowledgements*

Once again, I am indebted to Major G. L. 'Dickie' Scott-Dickins, for reading the first draft and writing the Foreword. His advice and encouragement are greatly appreciated. His own experiences in action against the Japanese are recorded in the *Reminiscences of Four Members of C Squadron, Burma Campaign 1943–45*. These include the climbing of the Chocolate Staircase on the Tiddim Road, south from Imphal, when one tank was in action on the summit of Kennedy Peak. I believe that this was at the record height of 8870 feet above sea level.

I could not have completed the tale of the first cake without John Carver telling me of its hitting a tank at high speed, with no damage to either the tank or the cake. He also gave me detailed instruction on how to dig the four-seater latrine so that the users would be facing each other and being near enough to occupy themselves by playing cards.

John was the driver of the 7 Troop Leader's tank when Lt W. R. B. Allen (later, Commanding Officer of the Regiment) led his three General Lee tanks into action at Ninthoukhong, near Bishenpur on 5th June 1944. His tank was hit by a 47mm Japanese shell and burst into flames. They were both badly wounded but were able to return to the Squadron and continue the War. When the fighting had stopped and the Regiment moved up to the North-West Frontier of India, I had the pleasure of beating John into second place in the camel race on Christmas Day 1945.

My thanks go to the late Leonard Van Oppen and his wife Kathleen. Leonard was a civil pilot who spent much of 1937 and 1938 flying monotonously over the plains and jungles of Burma during an aerial survey. Some of his photographs of the Chindwin area came into my possession for intelligence purposes. I was able to look under the tree canopy on the river banks by viewing two prints with a stereoscopic viewer, and then recommend a possibly safe landing on the opposite shoreline where there were no buildings.

After I had married Kathleen's niece in 1950, we had many hilarious evenings in Menorca, during which she told us of her exploits with Leonard in Burma. These included her experience in Meiktila, hiding under a market stall when the town was overrun by dacoits.

A.F.F.

# *Foreword*

**By Major G. L Scott-Dickins, who was commanding C Squadron, 3rd Carabiners, during their last battle in the Arakan, April/May 1945.**

When I first read Arthur Freer's *Nunshigum, on the Road to Mandalay*, I could appreciate why his detailed stories of wartime experiences with B Squadron, 3rd Carabiners, is considered to be required reading for new recruits to the Regiment (now the Royal Scots Dragoon Guards). I must admit to being a little puzzled by the fictional first and last chapters. These introduced a bright detective inspector, Harry Bennet, and a suspected serial murderer known as 'the jogger'. Now, I understand!

After reading his new mystery novel, *Nemesis from Burma, the Bamboo Murders*, I realise that he was setting the scene for a 'whodunit' which I have found to be intriguing. The well structured plot opens with the first murder in the middle of an action against the Japanese in Burma. It then leads to an amazing robbery in a ruby mine, using a tank gun to break open a safe, and through to the early post-war years and up to the 1980s. Humour and pathos are there, together with the tale of two cakes, one of which proved to be shell-proof.

He shows the closeness of 'family life' in a tank crew, and in a squadron, but also indicates a possible effect of training our young men to become thoroughly efficient killers of enemies of the state. The majority of them were quite intelligent and this author develops the character of the 'jogger' to show how such a person could easily be identified with some of the people we read about in the press today as similar enemies in times of peace. Elimination of these people might appeal to him but he would be very much of a 'loner', always on his guard. The tension builds up to the point where a sudden twist to the plot caught me by surprise.

Arthur and I were both at the same school before the War. In fact, our paths had crossed a number of times before we grew to know each other during the last two decades. In 1943 we both served in the 26$^{th}$ Hussars and, in October of that year, were drafted to re-inforce the 3$^{rd}$ Carabiners, then stationed near Madras. The three sabre squadrons of that Regiment spent the next eighteen months, mostly under separate commands, in action in various parts of Assam and Burma. The Regiment was reunited in Rangoon in 1945 before moving to Ahmednagar in India. When they arrived on the North West frontier of India (now Pakistan), the Regiment was in a state of flux due to the arrival of reinforcements, leave, repatriation and some hospitalisation. it is good to see that at least one of us is able to apply his memory and creative ability to produce such a story fifty-five years later.

G. L. Scott-Dickins<br>April 2000

# *Personnel*

### 2 Troop Baker 2

i/c Lt Michael Dibble-Williams "Dub", "Double", for short. Double-barrelled.

### Crew of Baker 2 Able

Commander Sgt Andrew "Dusty" Miller, from Hull. Later Philip Anders.
37 Gunner John Kerr
37 Loader Les Bickerton
W/Operator Jimmy James
Driver Nick McGowan
75 Gunner Paddy Wills
75 Loader Blondie Benton later Eric "Tug" Wilson

### Crew of Baker 2 Baker

**Commander Corporal Kenny**

### Police

Barnsley
Detective Chief Inspector James Ackroyd
Detective Chief Superintendent Strachan
Detective Inspector Harry Bennet, "Flash Harry"

# *Preface*

When Detective Sergeant Harry Bennet was transferred from Sheffield to Barnsley and promoted to the rank of Detective Inspector, his reputation was transferred with him. Natural human jealousies of his quick brain and above-average success rate were implied in the soubriquet of "Flash Harry" – and he had never really objected to this. He had taken it as a compliment and as confirmation that the majority of his contacts realised that he was on track for steady promotion – that he had a real future in the Police Force. He tried not to appear to be arrogant but he knew that he had many advantages from being a graduate from Durham University, from having a high IQ and Mensa rating, and of usually being one step ahead in any group discussions on a case. His quick brain and fluent speech helped him to shine on many occasions.

They had certainly given him a good start when he began to investigate the murder of Vince Hallett, President of the Colliery Workers Union, in his office at the Grange in Field Lane, near the site of the old Greenfield Colliery. Although his 'governor', Detective Chief Inspector James Ackroyd, had accompanied him on the first visit to the scene of the crime, it was Harry Bennet who had identified a person known as 'the jogger' as the likely culprit.

Helen Fagin had seen an older man from her cottage in Field Lane on both the day of the murder and the day before. She had been puzzled by the fact that he had returned on 13th April, when he must have realised on the previous day that there was no easy exit for a walker or a jogger.

This had convinced the DI that he had a very good 'prospect'. Basic police work should soon trace the man. The really intriguing part of the investigation came when the murder weapon was identified as a bamboo dagger.

More surprises arose when Harry Bennet gained access to the new police computerised system, based in the Sheffield University. This was known by the near-acronym of Crusoe, Computer Record of Unresolved Serious Crime in Europe, and it gave the first opportunity to sort all the British and European police records by any selected aspect. Bennet had firstly fed in the requirement of 'bamboo', only to be given the fact that there had been more than forty killings in the past thirty-eight years where a bamboo weapon had been used. Even more surprising was the fact that thirty of these had occurred on 13$^{th}$ April.

He then fed into the computer his selection of the date of 13$^{th}$ April and took a printout of the result. This showed that there had been a killing of a controversial character on each of the thirty-six years since World War II, and that they all appeared to have been carried out by a single person. Victims had previously received adverse criticism of their activities in the press over a period of months before they were killed, and public opinion had swung against them.

Harry Bennet informed DCI Ackroyd of his findings and he became aware that his boss was looking at him with increasing puzzlement tinged with respect.

"You see, sir, this is the first time that we have been able to analyse the statistics from the whole of Europe in this way. I find it sufficiently convincing to believe that we have a murder on our patch carried out by a nutcase who has committed a similar crime on 13$^{th}$ April each year for 37 years, and that we have a description to work on. The previous 36 murders were spread all over the British Isles and had never been grouped together on a list similar to this one."

DCI Ackroyd was not going to let his protégé have all the stage. "You realise that this theoretical man of yours must be around sixty – and, he's probably thinking of taking retirement any time now? Will this be his last effort? Your main task now is to find this white-haired old jogger. I hope to get some background information for you from a contact who was in Burma in the War." He made a few phone calls and eventually arranged to see a friend of his brother who had been in the 14$^{th}$ Army.

That evening, in a long session with Alan Fenner, Ackroyd's contact, they learned more of the strong connection with Burma in 1944, the 14$^{th}$ Army and, possibly, a mechanised British cavalry regiment known as the 3$^{rd}$ Carabiniers.

## 16th April 1982

"Alan Fenner's story of life in a tank in the 14$^{th}$ Army has proved to be invaluable, sir. I've been in touch with the Carabiniers' Regimental Association and they have given me a few names." Harry Bennet was doing the necessary thing to keep his boss fully informed and to keep the case moving in the direction that he wanted. "I have already found a man called Jimmy James, who served with Alan Fenner in B Squadron, 3$^{rd}$ Carabiners, in Burma in the War. He has a hardware shop in Sheffield and he has agreed to come in here tomorrow, so I'll let you know the result." DCI Ackroyd nodded. "Yes, Harry, I want to be kept informed. You'll need to be very careful to avoid any hint of poaching on other patches. Don't rely too much on old contacts in Sheffield. Just keep in mind that you are going to resolve this local murder and don't bother yourself with trying to fit the other bamboo jobs into your theory. We can sort that later."

*Squadron Sergeant Major 'Bunny' Holmes with his crew on his Mark III General Lee tank after another successful attack on the retreating Japanese Army in Burma 1945*

*B Squadron 3rd Carabiners (now the Royal Scots Dragoon Guards)*

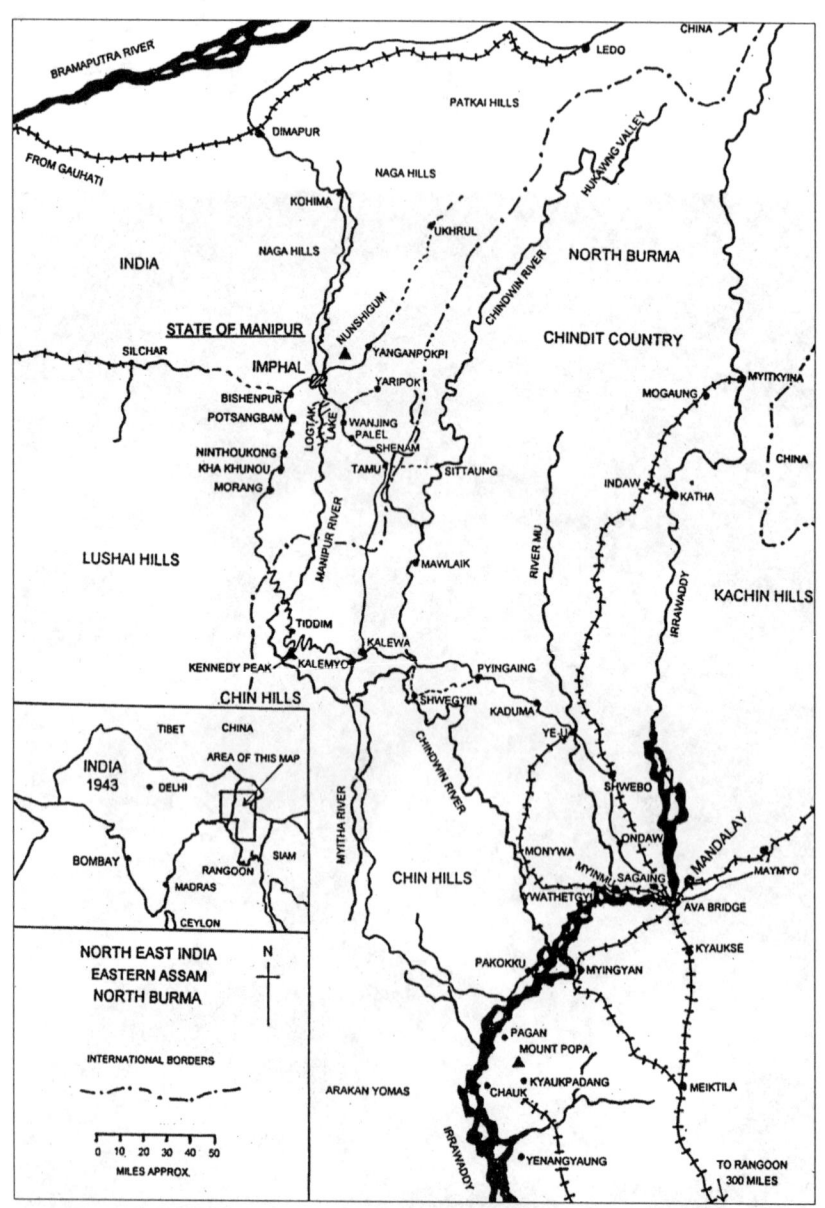

*Sketch map of the main area of India and Burma where the 14th Army engaged the Japanese invaders of India*

## Chapter One

# *January 1945*
# *Rape and Retribution*

"He's got to go", Sergeant Miller scowled, "even if I have to do it myself". I looked across at him. If he meant what I thought he meant, he was planning to kill the newest member of our tank crew. "Are you going to top him?" I asked, knowing he would give me an honest answer. He looked all around to make sure that no one else could hear.

"Yes, and you're going to help me!"

I had known Sergeant Dusty Miller for two years now, since January 1943, when he and I had arrived together to join the 26th Hussars at Secunderabad in central India. We had travelled by train from the Royal Armoured Corps training depot at Poona and had had a long discussion on the War situation as seen by the average British squaddy. We had agreed that the War would be won despite some of the officers that we suffered under and not because of them. We were two volunteers who were wanting to fight the enemy; whether they were German or Japanese, it didn't make any difference to us which we came up against. We were both troopers at that time but I had since seen Dusty climb the promotion ladder rapidly to the rank of corporal with the Hussars, until that Regiment had been disbanded and then, recently, to his third stripe during the fighting around Imphal with the 3rd Carabiniers.

This old British cavalry regiment, '3rd Carabiners (Prince of Wales's Dragoon Guards)', to give it its full name, had a history going back to the 18th century and it had done little to help the War effort until it had moved up to north-eastern India, to the State of Manipur. That was in October 1943, soon after the regiment had been equipped with 52 General Lee/Grant tanks and prior to the Japanese invasion of India from Burma in March 1944. The three sabre squadrons had each fought their own separate battles, supporting different infantry formations around Imphal, capital of Manipur. B Squadron had made a name for itself by climbing the ridge of Nunshigum, seven miles north of Imphal, where nearly 300 Japanese were dug in and overlooking our IVth Corps HQ. Together with the 1st Dogra Regiment, they had cleared the ridge of enemy with the loss of seven tank crew members, three officers and four other ranks – all shot through the head when they looked out of the turret. This was followed by weeks of close fighting amongst the villages to the south of Imphal, where most of us had been suffering from at least one tropical disease, to add to the problems of shortage of rations and water.

It was all different now. When the Japanese had been driven away from Imphal and Kohima and back over the Burmese border, we had expected to be withdrawn from any contact with them and to have a period of rest and re-training. Every man had certainly had two weeks leave in India and had returned to Imphal to find that the Regiment was busy preparing to drive east into Burma. We were told that we were going to lead the British 2nd Division down the Kabaw Valley and to cross the Chindwin River on the Burmese border. Our objective was to be the town of Shwebo, about 100 miles into central Burma. After that the Regiment was likely to return to India for a well-earned period of rest.

In the meantime our guns were silent and we started to return to the routine activity of a British Regiment in the Far East. This activity, including P.T., sports and swimming in the rivers, plus a return to an excess of bullshit, started a rash of applications for transfers to other units. There had been a notice on the orderly room board asking for volunteers to go to India for six weeks' training to be glider pilots, ready for the next Chindit expedition into Burma. Experience in gliding would be helpful. Very few of the other ranks did not apply. We were all given a personal interview and turned down. Despite my brief experience of watching some gliders at Sutton Bank, in Yorkshire, the Squadron Leader told me that I was not fit enough, at seven stones, to march hundreds of miles with an 80lb pack on my back. Oh yes, the pilots would fly the gliders into Burma, but they would then have to march and fight with the infantry. There was no return flight ticket. I readily agreed to have my application destroyed and to continue as a wireless operator in 2 Troop.

The inflow of new men created plenty of work for the NCOs. Training courses, sport and entertainment were all organised and put into effect. Frequent visits from senior officers kept everyone on their toes as we moved into December 1944. These included our GOC, General 'Uncle Bill Slim', an officer who was admired and respected by all those who served under him. When we set off to drive down the Kabaw Valley, we had already met and trained with each of the nine battalions of 2 Division and the orders were for one of the four troops of B Squadron, 3$^{rd}$ Carabiniers, to lead the column each day. Despite the tank troop and the infantry battalion being changed each day, Major Huntley-Wright had decided that his tank would be with the leading troop each day until we reached Shwebo. This was going to place extra strain on him and his crew.

But first we had to cross the Chindwin, a deep and fast-flowing river which the Engineers had just spanned at Kalewa with the longest Bailey Bridge built to date. It was decided that we would not use the bridge because of our weight, but instead we would be floated across on rafts made from sections of Bailey Bridge. This worked out well and we were all safely across, landing half a mile downstream at Shwegyin, in Burma, soon after sunset on 20$^{th}$ December 1944.

The last items to be loaded on to our tank were the alcoholic goodies for the Squadron for Christmas – six bottles of whisky for the officers and a keg of overproof rum for the other ranks. The Major put them into my charge, which was a mistake. He must have decided that I was a quiet, reliable and sober trooper so I stowed the whisky safely in one of the containers on the back of the tank and the keg of rum was wedged under a tarpaulin. When we halted for the night, I put the keg under a bush near my bed. During a flap in the night we were ordered to "mount, start up, and leave your kit where it is. We will return to have breakfast".

I should have learned by then not to believe everything that an officer told me. We did not return and we did not recover our bedding, cooking utensils or the rum! We set off that night to chase the Japanese stragglers for two hectic weeks through the jungle paths, until we came out into the central Burmese plain, as far as Shwebo. During the mad rush we lost our second Squadron Leader, Major Huntley-Wright, who was shot by a sniper whilst he was conferring with the infantry on 23$^{rd}$ December, and we all lost any desire to celebrate Christmas.

The next two weeks took us through a variety of hazards, including driving through the field kitchen of a Japanese Divisional HQ, clearing the town of Shwebo, which was left empty of enemy but well supplied with booby traps, driving over mine fields and into a number of ambushes. On 12$^{th}$ January our Squadron Orders stated: "Christmas Day 1944 will be 12$^{th}$ January 1945". We were to have a rest. We halted in a village named Chiba, only a few miles south of Shwebo, and started to clean up our bodies, our tanks, and a level patch of ground nearby for a football match in the afternoon. Our cooks had worked wonders and produced a chicken dinner with trimmings, a hot Christmas pudding, without rum sauce, and a bottle of beer for each of us. No one mentioned the missing rum.

The trouble started in the afternoon. Whilst most of the men were playing or watching football, one of my tank crew, a new man named Benton, who was being trained as the 75mm loader, decided that he needed some sexual relief. He was lucky to have the energy. Most of us still had the remains of some tropical bug or other and were debilitated by running to the latrines every hour or so. Some of the lads said we were still being given bromide in our tea, but this couldn't be right as we had been making our own brews for more than a year.

The story spread round the Squadron rapidly after the football match. It came from the village. A sahib with white hair had walked into the village that afternoon, accompanied by four Indian sepoys of the Bombay Grenadiers, and he had forced his way into the house of the headman. He had then ordered everyone out except the young daughter, a maiden aged 14 years, and he had raped her. The villagers had heard her screams but had been unable to go to her aid because they had been threatened by the Indian soldiers. It was a sickening story and I am not aware whether it reached the officers. Blondie Benton was known for his very fair hair and his constant talk of sexual needs, experiences and kinky fantasies. He did not deny that he was the one who had raped the girl and that he would do it again if the opportunity arose. He even admitted that he had persuaded the four Indians into going with him on the promise that he would let them take their turn afterwards. As it happened, they had all lost interest when they saw how distressed the villagers had been. They had each been hoping for a willing partner. Dusty Miller was not the only Carabinier who was very angry about the dirty business.

"You could end up by being topped yourself," I answered, "Is it worth it?" Dusty looked me straight in the eye. "What are you in this War for if it isn't to sort out the rotten bastards who take what they want when they want it? What do you think about the Germans and their death camps or the Japs and the way they treat their prisoners? You saw what they had done to that local in the last village before Shwebo, stringing him up to the tree with barbed wire before they gutted him. He had only told them the truth – that he had no rice in store. The other villagers told us that it was the truth. And you could see that they were all undernourished.

"Yes, I know I could be hung for it but I don't expect to survive this War anyway. After nearly a year in action, I know the odds against survival. I've seen off a lot of Japs and I hope to see off a lot more before I'm finished".

We had talked on this subject many times and had not always agreed. From my boyhood upwards I had had a strong aversion to killing anybody, but I had no difficulty in accepting that I had volunteered to join the Army in order to fight the enemy. This was a different matter. Benton had joined us in order to fight alongside us but I had to agree that he had gone beyond the pale. If I was not prepared to do the deed myself, I was certainly willing to keep quiet about this conversation, should Benton suddenly meet a sticky end. Perhaps that was the coward's way out.

"What do you have in mind?" I asked Dusty.

He spoke very quietly but clearly.

"During the next few days we will be chasing the Japs wherever we can find them and I will order him out of the tank when there is some shit flying about. That will be our chance. One of us will get him – with a grenade or gun, it doesn't matter which."

"What about the others?" I asked. "Let me handle them," he said, "the fewer who are in the know the better".

The rest of the crew were moving around the tank by now and we all carried on with the daily chores – cleaning our weapons, both the tank guns and our own side arms. My own Tommy gun had a problem of jamming when on automatic, and there were a number of possible causes. We all had trouble with dust and grit getting into the moving parts and, on two very unpleasant occasions, I had found that the jam was caused by the rim of the magazine being curled up due to rough handling over a period of weeks. That was discovered later, after the charging Japs had been stopped by fire from a nearby comrade. Most of our fighting was done from inside the tank, at a time and place of our choosing, but there were times when the Japs attacked us at night, when they thought they would have the advantage. That was the reason we stood to for half an hour at dusk and dawn. Part of the crew would be in their positions inside the tank. The two gunners and their loaders would be ready to fire at any targets selected by the commander, whilst the wireless operator, and perhaps the driver, would be in a slit trench at the side of the tank, ready to fire the dismounted Browning machine gun. This was taken from the front of the tank, where it was the responsibility of the wireless operator. I never knew whether I would feel more secure in the slit trench or in the tank. I usually wished that I were in the other place on the many occasions when we were attacked at night. There was something eerie about hearing an English-speaking Japanese officer calling out to us "Are you there, sergeant, can you come and help me? I've been wounded." The first man to answer him would have a grenade thrown at him, so we all ignored any such calls.

These maintenance jobs were part of our automatic routine for survival. The old hands never questioned the need and would jump on any of the reinforcements who took short cuts, whether they were troopers or even the troop officer. We were all interdependent and our lives could be forfeit if there were any shortcomings. Immediately after returning to our base for the night, however tired we might be, we cleaned and refuelled, ready for instant action if required. One of the checks was the fact that each crewman was trained to do every other job in the tank and was aware of all the requirements to be ready. Blondie Benton had been seen taking short cuts in loading ammunition a few times. He did not get away with it, and each of us had pointed it out to him at least once. He was not liked. "A clever bugger," Paddy Wills, the 75mm gunner, had called him. It had not been a good start for the new boy. No, he would not be missed if he disappeared.

# January 1945 Rape and Retribution

It was on 13th January 1945, after the morning stand to, as we were all busy eating our breakfast of canned bacon and beans, biscuits and hot char, squatting on our haunches in the usual Indian Army fashion, when Corporal Alan Fenner, Squadron wireless NCO, came up to me.

"Ah, Jimmy, we are going out today and here are the two frequencies to use. Squadron net at 0800 hrs." Then off he went to the next tank. It was all very laid back.

"Tank commanders!"

The call came from our troop leader, Lt. Michael Dibble-Williams, who had been with us since Imphal. He had proved himself to be a capable leader and had acquired the nickname of "Dub", an abbreviation of "Double" or "Double-barrelled". Any officer without a nickname had not really been accepted by the men under him and was viewed with suspicion by the other ranks. Respect had to be earned and it was not paid automatically.

Dusty walked over to the next tank, commanded by Corporal Kenny, and the two of them went to meet the troop leader for briefing on the programme for the day. I jumped into my seat in our tank and quickly netted the 19 Set to the carrier wave being sent out by Alan Fenner. It was a very smooth routine.

When Dusty Miller came back, he called the other six members of his crew and quickly told us the plan for the day.

"Right, chaps, we're going out with 3 Troop and the Major's tank to sort out a road block three miles due south of here. It's another routine job and we'll take it as we find it. To continue the crew training, the 37 gunner and loader will change places before we set off, until I tell them otherwise. Also, the 75 loader and wireless op will swap places. Apart from those changes, everything else is as usual. Are we netted, Jimmy?"

"O.K., Sarge," I replied.

Twenty minutes later, at 0830 hrs, came the order "Mount, start up!" and we were all quickly in our seats and away.

The Major's voice came over the set firmly and clearly.

"All stations Baker advance, Baker 2 leading and Baker 3 following number nine". That put the two HQ Troop tanks in the middle of the column.

There was no mention of the infantry and I presumed that we would be meeting them nearer the road block. Nothing to worry about.

The one sure fact about this War in Burma was that nothing was routine, nothing went smoothly. You could guarantee that if anything could go wrong, it would. And it did.

We were a mile from the position of the reported Jap road block when we came to a culvert where the road crossed a dried-up stream, and Corporal Kenny in Baker 2 Baker stopped his tank just before he reached the culvert. It was a wise move.

Two weeks earlier, both A and B Squadrons had each lost a complete tank and crew when crossing a culvert. There had been a Japanese soldier sitting on a large explosive device and prepared to commit suicide by hitting the detonator with a hammer when an enemy vehicle was crossing overhead. On each occasion, the tank had been blown into a scattered pile of scrap metal and the first on the scene had not been able find any recognisable bodies – only a few pieces of limbs and torn uniforms.

Since then we had all been very wary when approaching any possible position which could be booby-trapped. Japanese intelligence reports had confirmed that they would do anything to destroy a tank. Orders had been sent to their forward troops that they must be prepared to give their own lives if it meant that they could put a tank out of action. A Squadron had already suffered one such attack when a tank had stopped momentarily under a tree. A Japanese officer had dropped from a branch on to the tank and climbed into the turret, attacking the crew with his sword. After killing the commander and the 37mm loader, he was shot by the gunner with a few rounds from his pistol.

"Baker 2, what is the delay?" The Major's voice came over the wireless for everyone to hear.

Major E. S. P. Dorman had joined us on Christmas Day to become our third Squadron Leader in nine months. He was an Irishman with a cultured English voice and an assertive manner. He looked likely to be a survivor, and he had been told by the Colonel to keep his head down when in action. B Squadron were beginning to get a reputation for carelessness by losing too many officers.

"Baker 2, suspect booby trap in the culvert ahead and am dealing with it, over", replied Dub, showing that he also was competent. He waited a few seconds to give the Major the chance to reply, then he called his Corporal.

"Baker 2 Baker, give the target two rounds Howe Easy and then check, over."

"Wilco, Baker 2 Baker, out."

Corporal Kenny's tank moved to the right, dipped the barrel of the 75mm gun and immediately fired two rounds of high explosive at about ten yards range. It then moved back into the centre of the road and approached the culvert and, slowly, drove over the danger spot before the dust had settled. If there had been any suicide bomber under the road, he must have been put out of action by the shelling. The Corporal was, perhaps, a little too eager to move forward as he should have asked for a Sapper to check that there were no effective mines left in place. The advance continued.

Within five minutes we arrived at the map reference of the reported ambush and were immediately sprayed by machine gun fire. None of our infantry were to be seen but the Japs were obviously dug in and intending to hold the position.

We halted until all the other tanks came up and deployed into the paddy fields at either side of the road.

"Baker 2 to the left, Baker 3 to the right, advance and destroy the targets as seen, Baker 2 and 3 out". The Major gave his troop leaders a free rein and prepared to watch the action from his position on the road.

The Japanese had chosen a poor place for an ambush. The ground was quite flat at the bend in the road and the only cover for them was in a few clusters of bamboo along the roadside and the low bunds between the paddy fields. If they needed to move, they would be exposed to fire from all sides. It looked like another suicide party, whose objective was to attract the attention of our tanks and then to attempt to destroy us. We could almost feel sorry for them at this stage of the campaign, but we had memories of Imphal and Bishenpur that hardened our attitudes, and they still had plenty of fight left in them. It could possibly be another rabbit shoot. All we had to do was to keep our heads low (that was, the tank commanders) and we would clear them from the road.

It seemed strange to me that the Squadron Leader was going into an action without any infantry support. He had not even brought any of the Bombay Grenadiers with us. These 'tank guards' had been permanently attached to the Carabiniers for a year now and had saved many of our AFV's from the attention of enemy, who had got very close to the tanks, especially at night. We had rarely gone into action without them. They appeared to enjoy riding on the tops of the tanks as we moved towards the enemy, despite suffering many casualties in such an exposed position. Perhaps I was becoming too anxious as the War progressed.

2 Troop moved across the paddy field to within a few yards of the first bunker that we could see. Our Coax Browning machine gun sprayed the slit trench as we approached but the Japs continued to fire back with their own light guns and to throw hand grenades at the sides of the tank. It was noisy inside but that was normal.

Suddenly the wireless went very quiet. We could usually hear what was going on around the other tanks involved in the action, but now we could only hear Dusty's voice on the intercom. We all seemed to recognise the fact at the same time.

"Benton, what have you done to the wireless?" he asked.

"Nothing, Sarge". Benton seemed calm enough. He had been operating the wireless properly so far.

Dusty switched to me.

"What's happened, Jimmy?"

I had had this experience once before and recognised the problem.

"It sounds like the aerial has gone. If there is no reading on the variometer there must be a break in the circuit somewhere. Blondie can see through his port whether the aerial has been blown away and, if it is still in place, it means that the lead into the tank has been cut, probably by one of the grenades."

Benton cut in. "There's no reading on the set and I can see the aerial is still OK."

"Then you'd better get the tools together and go out and mend the lead," Dusty told him.

Looking across from behind the 75 gun, I could see Benton picking up some pliers and insulating tape ready to do the job. He asked on the intercom, "Can I climb out through the turret and keep on the safer side of the tank when I do the job, Sarge?"

"Sure, go ahead".

Dusty was getting what he wanted. Benton was going to be outside the tank and exposed to plenty of hot lead. He would be much more exposed if the tank were moved away from its present position, which was giving some protection. I tried to look into the turret to see what Dusty was doing but it had been rotated enough to block my view.

Listening on the intercom, I suddenly heard the voices of other tank commanders reporting their results to the Major, followed by his replies. The set was working again. Benton was not stupid. He had joined the two broken ends of the aerial lead and put us back in business. Just at that moment there were two more explosions close to the tank – this time on the port side, where Benton was probably tidying up the lead with some tape. I jumped and felt a cold shiver go down my spine. Were the explosions from Jap grenades or had Dusty dropped a couple of ours down the side to where Blondie was working?

"37 canister, straight ahead, fire!"

Dusty had seen a group of fanatical Japs running at us from in front. I could not see anything to the front, but Nick McGowan, our driver, told me later that there were about ten of the bastards, led by a sword-wielding officer, running at us with the obvious intention of doing us damage. Paddy Wills had also seen them because he fired the 75 at them without waiting for an order, using the high explosive that we kept 'up the spout' at times like this. Whether it was the HE or the canister shot that stopped them we will never know, but the Japs lost interest in hara kiri as they were all knocked out and probably already on their way to their heaven.

The reports to the Major all claimed complete success, with none of the enemy surviving. Our only loss was what I had suspected. Blondie Benton was found lying at the side of our tank, torn apart by grenades. He must have been killed instantly.

I climbed out of the hatch above my head and joined Dusty on the other side of the tank, where he was checking for any sign of life. Whatever wrong Benton had done recently, he had just lost his life obeying orders and ensuring that our tank was kept in operation and ready for further action. It had happened so many times in the past year to young men who had joined up "to help win the War". This was different. I had a niggling doubt whether the grenades that killed him were Japanese or British, whether he had been killed in action or murdered by my friend and tank commander.

"How did it happen, Dusty?" I asked, "How could the Japs have known he was there?"

He looked up at me. "They were using grenade launchers, like mortars, and dropping them all around the tanks, probably trying to drop some into the turrets, so this was the result of a near miss. Tough on the man."

We had become very used to the sudden death of comrades and his comment was not as callous as it sounds, but I still had a doubt. He must have realised this and added, "and you can forget what we were talking about earlier. No need to stir it up. No one in the Squadron will miss him."

The Troop Leader walked up at that point and asked what Benton had been doing out of the tank. Dusty's explanation was accepted without question and we were told to dig a grave at the side of the road. The remains were wrapped in a blanket, buried under a marker and reported by Dub for later removal. He would probably end up in a War Cemetery in Mandalay or Rangoon. The Squadron Leader would ensure that a suitable letter was sent to the next of kin.

That was the time when I began to wonder about Dusty Miller. There was absolutely nothing to prove that he was the cause of Benton's death – only the memory of a conversation in which he had apparently justified the right of one man to take another's life without any recourse to the legal processes that would normally apply. Perhaps he was reverting to a Stone Age philosophy, and I must admit that I could find a measure of logic in the idea of a vigilante, or do-it-yourself application of justice, especially when the law of the land appeared to be ineffective or was flouted so easily by so many. We had plenty of proof that there were many civilians who were taking advantage of the war conditions at home.

Stories of the black market were brought to us by each draft of reinforcements and each bag of mail contained some "Dear John" letters from wives and girl friends trying to explain why they were sleeping with someone else. The usual message was "He hasn't got anything that you haven't got, but he's got it here!"

This joke was hilarious for most of us, but it evoked a very different reaction from anyone receiving such a letter. Some men were so shocked after hearing this sort of news that they became incapable of carrying out their duties for some time. The wise officer watched his men after they had read their mail and could usually spot those in trouble.

I know that Dusty had been told that his wife had been playing around with an American soldier in Hull whilst he was fighting for his life in Imphal. He had gone berserk for 24 hours and the Squadron Leader had had him pulled out of the tank crew and put in B Echelon for two weeks. We had seen him bringing water and rations to the tanks.

The break must have helped him because he was soon back in the crew, taking his full part in the actions in the villages around Bishenpur, where we were sometimes in the tank for more than 24 hours, on one occasion for two and a half days and nights. This happened because we were involved in the fighting, very close to the enemy, and neither side was prepared to withdraw when it became impossible to fight at night. They stayed in their bunkers and we stayed inside our tanks, perhaps only ten yards apart. Our Bombay Grenadiers were dug in at the side of the tanks to prevent any closer contact, and we stayed put, trying to rest whilst eating whatever bits of rations were left over from that day. Tepid water was available for drinking but there were no ablutions. We stank. Some of us had the runs, needing to crap every hour or so, and we were able to open an escape hatch in the floor, under the 75 loader. The loader, poor sod, had no sleep because he was constantly having to move to let those with diarrhoea have access to the hole in the floor. It was not a happy time.

But eventually we were very successful.

During those two months there were three Victoria Crosses awarded to the infantry. Our Troop Leader was evacuated with serious wounds after his tank was hit by a shell. Sergeant Dusty Miller was told to take over as his successor (without being commissioned) and he remained our Troop Leader for another three weeks of action until some officer reinforcements had arrived. These new officers were introduced to the finer points of tank warfare by joining a tank crew as a gunner or wireless operator. After a few actions, this initiation was usually effective, and they would then be appointed to a troop requiring an officer.

Dusty had proved himself to be very capable and respected as a troop leader. Some of us who had fought under his command had agreed that he should have been commissioned "in the field", but we were not the ones to make the recommendation. Perhaps, if he had been from the landed gentry instead of a successful businessman, he would have been treated differently. Cavalry traditions would be maintained. After the Benton episode, our relationship appeared to be unchanged but I did have reservations. We were too busy continuing the War to complicate life with an examination of motives. Anyway, it was during the next week or so that I became aware of a chance to become very wealthy – and this meant remaining alive in order to benefit.

Chapter 2

# *1945*
# *Cakes and Rubies*

During the next few weeks B Squadron were employed in similar work, responding to requests from the nine different infantry battalions of 2nd Division for support in tackling pockets of Japanese resistance of varying strength.

Major Dorman would decide whether to order one or two troops into the action. Usually the fire power of three or six tanks would be sufficient to eliminate 30 or 40 well-armed enemy infantrymen, however well dug in they might be. We were often impressed by their determination to fight to the death despite being dressed in rags of uniforms and on the point of starvation. We were never complacent. We had received too many surprises. The worst shock was to arrive at a Jap ambush where there was a concealed field gun of heavy calibre. Some of these could fire two or three rounds at the leading tanks before we could return fire and often led to the loss of one or two tanks and some of the crews.

All this action took place in the Sagaing Bend, the large area of the central plain between the two rivers, the Chindwin and the Irrawaddy, on the other side of that river from Mandalay. We learned later that we were part of General Slim's strategic plan to make the Japanese think that he was going to make his main thrust against Mandalay by forcing a river crossing near the Ava Bridge. This was the only bridge across the Irrawaddy, built by British engineers before the War, and blown up by the retreating British Army in 1942. The feint was successful, tying up a large portion of the enemy forces in the North, whilst the reinforced and refreshed 4th Corps crossed the Irrawaddy further south to attack and capture Meiktila and block the Japanese escape route.

During this period the Squadron had acquired an addition to their strength. Corporal Alan Fenner walked up to me one morning after the Squadron net, accompanied by a young Asian wearing our green jungle battledress. "Ah, Jimmy, I want you to meet Saw Derry Pwe who has joined us as an interpreter. This is Jimmy James, my last remaining wireless operator in a tank crew since Imphal, last March." He said this looking at the man, who had a refreshing appearance of good health and honesty. "Derry speaks at least three local languages as well as very good English. He will be messing with my crew for rations but he will be available whenever we meet any locals."

I shook hands and made welcoming noises while Alan continued, "I'll leave him with you until tiffin so you can get to know each other and then he can rejoin me. O.K?"

I felt an instant liking for this man of about my own age. His skin was as white as mine but his hair was very black and cut short.

"Where did you learn to speak English so well?" I started, thinking that he sounded like any well spoken Englishman and surprised that there was no chi-chi /Welsh lilt such as we heard so often from Anglo-Indians.

"I'm BA Rangoon University," he replied, "We speak English there all the time and my family always spoke English at home." The use of the past tense and his sad tone made me ask about his home and family.

He told me that he was a Karen, born in Toungoo, just north of Rangoon. His family had been living there comfortably, with his father helping to run the railway, when the Japanese started to invade Burma from Siam in the south-east. He had been in Rangoon when he heard that his home had been bombed and all his family killed, including his parents and two sisters. That had been nearly three years ago. He had jumped on a train for Toungoo and found that he had been told the truth. There was little to salvage and he had continued the train journey further north to Mandalay to stay with his uncle until the War situation became clearer. His uncle had helped him to get a job as a clerk with the Maymyo Ruby Mines, where he had stayed until the company had closed down its operation a few months before.

"Rubies!" I said, "You'll have to tell me more about rubies when we have the time".

He smiled. "There are some wonderful opportunities in Maymyo, if only I can get back there before the management think about reopening the works. I would like to talk with you about it soon. Is there any chance of B Squadron going up there?"

"We won't know that until we are much nearer and after we've crossed the Irrawaddy," I replied, thinking that this could be the chance of a lifetime. "Have you been out in a tank yet? I mean have you seen any action from inside a tank? You could ride beside me when we go out in the next day or so. You could then see how we are helping to rid your country of the Japanese."

He was hesitant but only for a moment.

"Yes, I would like to see you in action. But, would I have to do anything? Would I have to fire the guns or use the wireless?"

"Of course not," I laughed, "you would be going for the ride, and to gain experience," I added, "I'll fix it with the Sergeant as soon as I see him."

He appeared to be quite excited at the prospect and I thought that it would be an opportunity to gain his confidence and trust. He then said that he should be returning to HQ Troop to join them for tiffin and promised to come round to our tank in the evening for a further chat.

Dusty Miller came back to the tank as the rest of the crew were finishing their tiffin.

"Listen, chaps, we are nearly ready to break out of this farting around with road blocks and the like. The Major has been told that we will be in one more big effort at a place on the river. It's called Ywathetgyi or something, and there's a Jap Division HQ well dug in with plenty of artillery. The Intelligence reports say that they are supplied by boat from across the river, so we might get a few shots at that. Where's my grub, I'm starving?" He took the mess tin full of warm meat and veg, tasted it and groaned, "cold as usual. We all have Squadron parade at 1400 hrs when the Major will go into detail. You, Paddy, will stay here on guard and we'll fill you in with the details later. And by the way, your new loader has arrived and he'll be over here this afternoon. He's called Wilson, straight from Poona Depot."

We made little comment about all this, preferring to wait for the full details from the Squadron Leader, and spent what time we had in re-checking the equipment on the tank ready to move at short notice. The mess tins and cooking utensils were rubbed with some of the sandy soil until they shone. They were clean enough to pass inspection by an officer (other than an MO, who would be more aware of hygiene) and were then stowed away ready for the next meal.

"Do I find Sergeant Miller here?" The high pitched voice made me think that a young girl was speaking to me until I looked around to see the biggest man I had ever seen who might try to get into a tank. About five feet six tall, he looked to be about the same measurement around the chest.

"There he is," I pointed across to Dusty, "are you joining us?"

He nodded and walked over to Dusty, who was checking the tension on the tracks.

"Trooper Wilson reporting for duty, Sergeant."

Dusty looked at him, his jaw dropped, and said, "If you're coming into my crew I want to see you get into the 75 loader's spot now!" The sergeant sounded as though he was prepared to reject this reinforcement because of his size, if he should appear to be a handicap. He was, of course, looking after the interests of the rest of the crew. A slow moving man of that size could be a real problem if we ever had to bale out in a hurry.

All the other crew members had been listening and they stopped what they were doing to watch. We all gasped as this man-mountain ran to the Lee tank. In one movement, he seemed to run up the side of it, around the turret, across the engine cover, lifted the heavy armoured plate cover above his position on the right side and slid down into the tank, closing the lid after himself.

Dusty Miller followed in the new man's path, slightly more slowly, lifted the 75 cover and looked down into the tank.

"You've done that before, haven't you?"

We could hear the reply from Wilson.

"Yes, Sarge, I was fully trained on Lees and others in Blighty and at Poona. Will I do?"

"Hop out, lad, you look strong enough to do your share of the chores. What were you in Civvy Street?"

"A chef, Sarge, hotel work mostly."

"Right, you are now tank chef and 75 loader but I'll give you plenty of training in the other crew jobs. Welcome to 2 Able. And

I like my food hot whenever I'm ready for it. Come out and meet the other lads."

They both climbed down and Dusty introduced him to the remaining five of us.

"The other tanks in the Squadron have cooks of some kind or other. 2 Able now has a chef. Meet Tug Wilson, our new 75 loader."

He gave a brief history of each man with the introduction, and at my turn he thanked me for my past cooking efforts saying, "you see we now have a professional."

"But Sarge, my name's Eric," he squeaked, "Nobody calls me Tug."

"We do now, Tug; all Wilsons are called Tug so you can get used to it."

I was glad to be relieved of the cooking duties, which included collecting the tank rations from the Squadron stores and struggling to make tasty dishes from such things as dehydrated mutton and mixed vegetables (sometimes when there was not sufficient water available to reconstitute them).

"I'm very pleased about it, Tug," I said, "perhaps we can have a cake one day?"

That was pressing things a bit for a new man, but Wilson nodded.

"No problem there," he said. "If we can find the ingredients and an oven, I'll bake you all a cake."

This was good news. We had been in action, close to the enemy, for almost twelve months and the only cake we had seen had been when we were on leave, just after the Japs had been driven from Imphal.

There was the never-to-be-forgotten occasion of an oven being designed, made and tested by our LAD Sergeant, Jock McDonald, during the rough few weeks in Bishenpur. He had used his technical skills to cut and assemble his oven from some ¼ inch armour plating, all beautifully welded, with a hinged door and efficient locking device. He had then asked the Squadron cook to prepare a cake mix using whatever was available. He had used some plain flour, eggs (found under a hut), and ghee (a local cooking fat). The mixture had been put in a mess tin and placed in this preheated oven on a petrol compression stove near a slit trench.

It was during those endless weeks in and around Bishenpur that the Japanese had shelled us on a daily basis. Their heaviest calibre field gun, a 150mm, was hidden in a trench on the left-hand side of the Silchar Track about 600ft above us. It was pulled forward by a young elephant each time that they wanted to fire it and immediately pulled back again after the firing. This saved the gun from damage by RAF bombing and from our tank 75's, which often fired up at the sight of the muzzle flash. The treatment must have had a bad effect on the elephant, which escaped and was captured by Corporal Alan Fenner. (That was another story, which is told elsewhere).

On the day of the test-bake in the new oven the men of B Squadron were going through the normal routines of maintenance and trying to find enough food to prepare for the next meal. They were surrounded by the delicious odour of a baking cake – something they had not enjoyed for many weeks, or even months. The comments from the nearby men were all envious of Sergeant MacD, who used his rank to confirm his authority during the operation. Disaster struck at that point. The daily shell from the Jap 150 came over without any warning and hit the oven that was, fortunately, the only casualty. This masterpiece of engineering and craftsmanship was now nothing but a pile of scrap metal in the mud. The cake, on the other hand, was blown on to the turret of a tank some twenty yards away and appeared to be unharmed. It was, admittedly, a little scorched on the crust but no one was surprised at that because the timing of the bake had been by trial and error. The comment by Paddy Coffee summed up the opinions of all of us. "If the bloody cake can stand a 150 shell and being blown that distance before it hit a bloody tank, then I don't want to break my teeth on it".

That seemed to have settled any desire to bake a cake – until now! Whilst our Mark 2 oven could only be described as 'makeshift', it was a practical proposition. We had obtained four tins of different sizes and fitted two of them inside the others so that there was a space between them to soften the heat that would be applied to the cake in the middle. There was no door to the oven as it was likely to be a 'one-off'. It seemed to be working because the aroma of newly baked cake was making our mouths water. It also attracted a few unwanted characters, mainly the CO, who was a huge man of 6feet 6inches with a hairy face. Lt. Col. F. J. S. Whetstone OBE had taken command of the Regiment before we left Imphal the previous

December and we had seen very little of him. The three sabre squadrons were all in action, under the command of their own squadron leaders, in different parts of Burma and the CO had overall responsibility for our welfare but not for our daily activities.

This surprise visit to B Squadron was obviously meant to cement his authority over us.

"What are you doing there?" His voice came from under his huge moustache, which was joined up to his sideboards. I looked up at this giant of a man, whose eyes had a friendly sparkle under his equally bushy eyebrows. He was leaning on his six-foot walking stick.

"I'm baking a cake, sir." This could have appeared to be a rather cheeky answer under the circumstances, for everyone else was getting their tank or themselves ready for immediate action. But the aroma was my alibi. It proved the point and had been the attraction for the officer, who asked for a taste.

"I believe it will be ready by now, sir," I said, turning down the flame of the burner. The rest of our crew and the CO watched as I used two pairs of pliers to pull the oven apart. Our driver, Nick McGowan, helped the operation by giving the odd tap on the tins with his 14lb hammer. At last, the oven was opened and we could all see the black lump of charcoal in the mess tin. "I think there has been too much heat for too long, sir." The CO nodded gravely, "But it smells so good," he replied.

I placed the burnt offering on a plate and tackled it with my knife and fork, cutting away about an inch of carbon from the outside. The remaining core of the sphere looked, smelled and tasted remarkably like a sponge cake and I was able to cut it into eight pieces worth eating, whilst we had a cup of freshly-brewed char. We all agreed that it was a treat and worth the effort and the Colonel was quietly surprised when I told him that the raising agent had been some sodium bicarbonate from the MI truck. He thanked us all very much for allowing him to share in our little treat, wished us well in the future and said that he was now going to visit A Squadron, who were some 30 miles away from us. None of us ever made another oven in the field and we were back in India within four months, testing the joys of Indian cooking.

The Major's situation report to the Squadron later that day was something of an anticlimax. The CO had been impressed with our state of readiness for action and with our morale (no doubt, the cake had helped) but he had been very critical of our lack of tidiness. The possible big attack on the Jap HQ at Ywathetgyi had been postponed because Intelligence reports had indicated another and larger Jap headquarters in a village much nearer to us. We would be making no move against them until they had been 'earthquaked' by the rapidly growing air forces supporting the 14$^{th}$ Army advance. This was a new word for us, as it referred to a heavy bombing. Most of us had experienced a natural earthquake during the past year, but we were all intrigued at the idea of a man-made shaking, especially for the enemy. It was to occur the next day.

That evening, after stand-to, I suddenly became aware of Derry Pwe standing beside me.

"Don't do that, Derry, I nearly gave you a burst from my Tommy gun," I ticked him off firmly; he had to learn. "I just wanted to have another word with you about Maymyo, Jimmy, it is important to us both that you know what I know."

"Then you'd better sit yourself down here and I'll just see if the Sergeant is free to join us." I walked over to where Dusty was checking the Browning tripod and its possible line of fire. "Dusty," I said, "Derry has come back for a confidential chat about his contacts at the Maymyo Ruby Mines. I think he is on to something and he wants us to help him if possible. Could be interesting?" Dusty looked up at me. "Get him into this slit trench and you sit on top, keeping an eye out for anyone else getting near." I beckoned Derry across in the dim light from the moon. "Jump in here and keep your voice down," I said.

He started. "I'm wanting to know if there is any chance of my getting back to Maymyo for a few hours when we get over the Irrawaddy? I left some valuables there when I left in a hurry." Dusty gave the impression of having serious thoughts. "That must be some 30 or 40 miles due east from Mandalay and up into the hills. It's all overrun by the Japs at present but we will be sorting them out during the next few weeks. Yes, there's a good chance that we can help you." He hesitated. "You will be at risk if you try to go there on your own. You know there will be dacoits as well as stray Japs running about? Is your property heavy?" I knew the way he was thinking and that he wanted to know exactly what the valuables were. Derry only hesitated for a moment and then poured out his worries to us both. "You two, Sergeant and Jimmy, are the first really honest men I have met for many months. I know that I can trust you and this is absolutely confidential." He wanted our confirmation and he got it.

"Call me Dusty. And carry on with your story." That convinced Derry.

"I believe that you all know that I worked at the ruby mines until the end of last year, when the management decided to close down until the fighting had stopped? The Japanese had only interfered with us to the point of buying all our output at a very low price and in the currency that they have been printing for us. That had been fair enough under the circumstances as they had been giving us security against the dacoits, who are a great trouble. These bad people have always come into the towns at times and done a lot of damage, robbery, rape and murder. Then, last November, the Japanese commander told us that he could no longer guarantee our safety and he withdrew the armed guards. He also took our complete stock of mined rubies. This action convinced the management that the Japanese had decided to withdraw because they knew they were losing the fight against the British. They then told all the workpeople that the business would be closed until it could be reopened in more peaceful times. I had the job of paying everyone with their last pay packet, including myself.

"This is where I come to the point of my wish to return to the mine soon, before any of the management does so. They do not know that I am aware of the fact that they tricked the Japanese. They had been keeping a separate set of books for them that recorded production volumes showing roughly 80% of the actual figures. The extra 20% had been secretly hoarded in a hidden safe so that they could be sold at some time in the future to help with the development of the company." Dusty quietly broke into the tale.

"Are you telling us that you know where this safe is hidden and do you know the value of the rubies?

Derry nodded gravely. "Yes. And do you know anything about rubies?" We all shook our heads and listened carefully. "To start with, they are formed from alumina, aluminium oxide, and are found in the limestone gravel and clays in various parts of the world. They are very hard indeed, second only to diamonds, and are the same chemical formula as sapphires. Their only difference is in the colour. The best rubies of a rich red colour are found in Burma and I know where to find them! The managing director's office is built up against a cliff in which there is a tunnel carved into the rock.

"In the tunnel there is a large safe and only the MD has the combination to open it. I saw all this one day when I walked into his office with some papers. He was very angry but he did not know that I had previously seen the secret books showing the 'reserve' stock of rubies. I know that this stock is hidden somewhere on the premises and the safe in the tunnel is the only possible place. And the value of the gems will be a few millions of pounds sterling, plenty for us all to take enough so that we do not need to work again! With the country in the state of turmoil that it is, there is no certainty that any of the company's management will have survived when the fighting has finished. I think we should take advantage of a 'once only' opportunity. Don't you agree?"

Dusty and I could hardly control our excitement. Dusty said, "We must find some way of helping you – and ourselves. What are your feelings, Jimmy?"

"Like you, I see this as a way of setting ourselves up for the future, when we get back to Blighty. It's very exciting, but we must look at every possible snag, and there are plenty of those already. One, there is no certainty that we can get up the road to Maymyo without a direct order from the Major. We can work on that one, but we mustn't be too obvious 'cos he's no fool. Two, we need to get there with the tank for our own safety, to carry all the loot away and especially I can see the need to have some explosives with us, perhaps in the form of AP shells, to help to open this big safe."

Dusty raised his eyebrows at this. "Good point, Jimmy. And we have to look after the rest of the crew when we pick up the rubies. A bag full for each of them will keep them quiet, but not a word to them or anyone else until we have the goodies in our hands. The whole Regiment will want to get a share if they get so much as an inkling. They'll call them 'the spoils of war'. No, we must all three agree here and now that we will not let any whisper of this leak out at all. Let's not even use the word 'ruby' even in our thoughts or dreams. We can still work towards success in Maymyo and, at the same time, get on with sorting out the Jap army. We need to do that before we can cross the Irrawaddy and capture Mandalay. Then we can work out how to get up to Maymyo."

We were all well trained in tactics but this talk on strategic lines came as a surprise to me. I had to agree with Dusty. The knowledge given to us by Derry could only be put to really practical use if we were able to organise a visit to a place that had not yet been mentioned to us as an objective. We had to be lucky, and I was feeling lucky.

Dusty shook Derry warmly by the hand and thanked him for his trust. "We'll not let you down, lad, you play straight with us and we will with you. Now, off you go for some kip and I'll try to arrange for you to spend the day in our tank tomorrow. It should be interesting. An 'earthquake' – never seen one before."

True to his word, Dusty had arranged, through our Troop leader, for Derry to join us immediately after stand-to the next morning. He was to travel with us inside the tank and learn something of what our lives had been like for the past year. He might possibly find it to be rather exciting to get within a few yards of an enemy who were desperate to kill us, but he would soon learn that such close contact is interspersed with frequent periods of boredom either from the waiting for orders to move, or else for some reaction from an enemy who might have slipped away unknown to us. We never knew what each day might bring.

On this day we were having a long drive on our tracks – some 20 miles – to be near the heavy bombing of the Jap HQ. Intelligence reports told us that they were well dug in in a village that we had cleared only three weeks ago. We remembered it well. It was a typical Burmese village on a small stream which was used as a source of drinking water, openly spread with the usual beautiful bamboo bashas. Each basha had its own productive vegetable garden with clusters of tall bamboo growing in the corners. Irrigation came from smaller tributaries of the stream and was controlled by high clay banks (or bunds), which gave the Japs easy cover for their bunkers and defensive systems. This was the southern village of two similar ones that were separated only by the road running east and west.

Just before we entered the northern village, reputedly free of enemy, we met the CO of the Lancashire Fusiliers from 4 Brigade of 2 Division, who were to be our infantry colleagues when we advanced after the 'earthquake'. We could see Major Dorman dismount from his tank and confer with the LF colonel. After about ten minutes the Major climbed back into his tank and his voice could then be heard over the wireless.

"All stations King, we will advance into the village as arranged and prepare for the night. If you meet any opposition, eliminate it and report when in position. Get what rest you can before dawn, All stations King, out." He had planned it all with the troop leaders and had not even required an acknowledgement. Any English-speaking Jap officers who had heard the transmission would not have learned anything from it. They would already have heard the noise of the tank engines and be in no doubt that we would be attacking them in the southern village in the morning.

I don't know whether the LF patrols had made only a casual search of the northern village or whether the Japs had withdrawn south on their approach, only to return to their prepared bunker positions later, but we were in for a shock.

2 and 3 Troops led the advance with a company of Lancashire Fusiliers spread behind us. It looked like a routine exercise with us all ready for any enemy fire but not really expecting any. As soon as we were amongst the bashas, the hidden Jap machine guns sprayed the infantry who dropped for cover and returned the fire.

"King 2, is that near you, over?" The Major was as cool as usual. It had happened so many times before.

"King 2, yes, we can handle it, over"

"King 2, go ahead, out."

Lt Dub now had the authority to attack the suspected Jap bunker positions and sort them. "King 2 Able, advance to your right. Can you get close to that maggie?" Dusty answered, "King 2 Able, yes, I am engaging, out." He switched to the intercom. "Nick, get as close to that bund as you can. The maggie seems to be dug in there. 75, Howe Easy, get ready for when I tell you. Coax spray the bamboo patch to your front." The sound of our Browning .300 being fired from the turret above my head was reassuring. John Kerr was a very competent gunner, ready to fire the machine gun or the 37mm when ordered. He had been known to fire without an order once, when he spotted a group of kamikaze Japs running at us with swords and bayonets. We could hear the distinctive noise of other tanks firing their Brownings as they tried to make the Japs keep their heads down and to relieve the pressure on our infantry. We could all hear the voices of the other tank commanders informing the Major of the location of Jap positions. Things were buzzing. Derry was hearing everything but he couldn't see anything outside the tank. He seemed to be enjoying it.

As I looked forward out of my roof periscope, I spotted the flash of fire from a machine gun immediately in front of us, about five yards ahead. Dusty must have seen the same flash.

"Driver, halt. 75, did you see that maggie? Fire when you can." Paddy Wills didn't bother to answer. He fired his 75, the recoil clanged the empty shell case into the receiver and our new loader, Tug Wilson, slid a new HE shell into the breech in one smooth movement. This closed the breech and we were ready for another target. The engine-operated fan was quickly extracting the fumes from the inside of the tank.

"Coax, traverse left. Bottom right corner of basha, engage maggie as soon as you see it." Dusty had been scanning the area and had seen some more flashes. We were very much aware of how the enemy sited their bunkers so that each was covered by fire from one or more other positions. Any infantry approaching a bunker could be attacked from other angles. Fighting on foot was a much more hazardous way of life than ours was, in the comparative safety behind our armour plating. The proven method of sending the tanks in ahead of the infantry was so much more effective than sending the infantry forward alone. And we could do much more damage at close quarters as long as we had some infantry near enough to deter the Japs from climbing on to the tanks. We were well practised at this type of attack and we continued to seek and destroy enemy bunkers for another two hours.

Eventually, B Squadron found themselves on the road separating the two villages. "All stations King, do not cross the tarmac road but ensure that you can prevent any one coming north from the other side of it. Number Nines report to me on foot in 30 minutes, all stations King, over." The four troop leaders acknowledged the order and then prepared their own troop to be well positioned for defence through the rapidly approaching night. Our faithful friends, the Bombay Grenadiers, started to dig their slit trenches. This job was completed before they began to eat their haversack rations. We also carried out our vital maintenance and replenishment of ammo stocks, when the 15cwt ammo truck came right up to the side of each tank and gave us whatever we required. Dusty and Nick checked the right track, which appeared to have slackened more than the left one. They made an adjustment using the heavy crowbar, the 14lb 'persuader', and plenty of strong language. Derry proved to be useful by helping to lift the 75 ammo into the tank storage racks.

Lt. Dub came back from the Major's conference with the news that we had now cleared the northern village and that our own casualties were nil, with one tank disabled on a mine. The LF's had had five men killed in the early fighting with fifteen wounded. The count of enemy killed, so far, was 75 and probably some more who had been buried in the bunkers.

We had been told to sleep the night inside our tank with the Bombay Grenadiers dug into their slit trenches just outside.

This was where Derry became something of a problem. He had been sitting on my right side, with our driver Nick on his right, and he had enjoyed the novelty of a ride in a tank trying to look out of my periscope to see the scenery. He had been very excited on the road journey when he thought that he had seen some enemy infantry tramping 'in line' on the horizon. He told Dusty, on the intercom, who then decided that he could not tell whether they were Japanese or on our side and hence took no action.

Derry became much more subdued when he realised that he had to share my seat for the whole of the night. And so did I. I had suffered from claustrophobia ever since being kept in the tank for most of three days and two very long nights in Potsangbam near Bishenpur in May the previous year. It had been made much worse then by the fact that two of us in that crew had had the runs all the time. We had struggled to climb over each other and had used the escape hatch under the 75 loader to relieve ourselves. The various BO's of the rest of the crew, who did not have enough water to drink each day, let alone wash, had diluted the revolting odours. I personally had not been able to stand my own smell, let alone that of the others in the tank. But that was all history. We now had better supplies of water and all of us had a strip wash almost every day, I only had to run to the latrine five or six times a day, so we did not expect too much trouble with a night 'inside'. Seven men could sit and work inside a Lee tank fairly easily but an eighth body could be an encumbrance. Dusty told us on the i/c that the heavy bombing was due to start at 0830 hrs and that we must on no account show any part of our bodies outside the tank until the Major gave us the order to advance when the bombing had stopped 30 minutes later.

We did not sleep much that night in King 2 Able. We all managed to eat some of the rations we had brought with us and our main need, in the humidity of the night, was to drink tepid water from our supplies in bottles. This kept us all going.

I must have dropped off to sleep leaning across the wireless set with my headphones on when I heard the Major's voice. "All stations King. Ensure you are well battened down and 'Grinders' three feet below the surface. Support on its way, out." It was just turned 0800 hrs and I had never slept later than 0600 hrs before. The crew started to stir and drink from their bottles. "The Grinders had better start digging quickly, I reckon, if they're not three feet under by now, poor bastards." This came over the wireless and it sounded like a comment intended as an aside to a tank crew on the intercom. This often happened, especially in the heat of battle, when an excited tank commander pressed the pressel switch on his microphone for transmission, when he should have only spoken into the instrument. We could all recognise the broad accents of Corporal Geordie Burn of 3 Troop and felt sorry for him. His comment would have been heard by the CO and also by the Major, who would know his identity. His chances of a third stripe would have faded, at least for a week or two. It was usually the new officers who dropped that sort of brick and not a hairy-arsed NCO with Geordie's experience. They never learn.

Soon after that we all heard the throb of the approaching bombers. "Bloody Hell! Look at that!" It was Dusty, looking upwards in his cupola periscope. He could see the first wave of heavy bombers flying in from the west. I could just see them through my own roof periscope, which I tilted to the maximum angle. I could see the first squadron of heavy bombers flying immediately above us in a tight square. One of the lads said "Liberators!" but I am no plane spotter.

All I know is that they were very big planes and they were about to drop their load very close indeed to where we were waiting. We had no direct wireless communication with the aircraft and could only hope that they had been correctly briefed with the fact that we were all on their side and the Japs were on the south of the road running east to west.

We did not have long to wait. As we looked across the road, the earth, bashas and bamboo clusters simply erupted and moved rapidly towards the sky in a cloud of dust. Immediately, we felt the tremendous increase in air pressure and the tank seemed to leap into the air before crashing down to the earth. Our mouths, ears and the tank interior were all invaded by a massive, roaring explosion and a dust cloud. I felt that I had been hit all over my body by a large sledge hammer and my ears were again whistling and singing louder that they had been before then. This was followed by a much quieter sound of debris hitting the roof of the tank. Some of it sounded to be metallic and some of it was more like a sack of potatoes dropping on to us from a great height. And this was only the start.

I could see another square of bombers following the first and at a similar height. Behind them came another and yet another. We were in for a pasting and we got it. For an endless 30 minutes we sat in our tank and went through the same shattering experience of saturation bombing, with explosions as near as 30/40 yards away. Fortunately, none of the bombs landed on our side of the road but the effect of this 'earthquake' was totally demoralising for us. For the Japanese it was terminal.

When it had stopped and the bombers had flown off back to their base in India or wherever they came from, the Major walked across the road and studied the terrain. We could see some of it through our periscopes. There were no recognisable buildings or trees in the south village. He came back to his tank and called the Squadron.

"All stations King, the ground is now unsuitable for us to advance and I have asked the footsloggers to proceed without our support. They will not require it. All number nines report any damage on foot to me now, out."

Our Troop Leader had then dismounted and walked across the road to study the bombed area. He returned after only a few minutes and told his troop to check for any damage and to tidy up and be ready to drive back to our base. He told us that the entire village had been pulverised and that the Lancashire Fusiliers would have difficulty in finding anything recognisable as a human being. The ground consisted of bomb craters inside bomb craters inside bomb craters.

We learned that evening, after we had returned to base, that the infantry had had great difficulty in walking over the ground and that they had not found any signs of life or anything of any use. All the tank crews involved in the bombing, including Derry, were given two full days of light duties in order to recover from the effects. B Squadron moved to another quiet village on the banks of the Chindwin, a few miles south of Monywa, where we extended the two days into four days of relaxation.

We enjoyed swimming in the river, eating the fresh fruit, which the locals had grown in abundance, and fishing in the nearby tributaries running into the Chindwin. After converting some of our wireless aerials into fishing rods, and finding that method of catching fish to be too slow, we reverted to the tried method of using hand grenades. Our excuse to the Sergeant Major was that our grenades were unreliable, that they were obviously old stock left over from the 1914/1918 War, and that they had been affected by poor storage conditions. It was a known fact that about 30% of them did not explode when they should have done so. It was easy to convince anyone in authority that we should test every new batch in order to assess reliability. We did this by throwing six grenades into a deep pool at the bend in a stream, counting the number of explosions, and then diving into the water and throwing any stunned fish on to the bank for later consumption. This method required proper supervision, which the NCO i/c should have supplied.

Despite the fact that the grenades were fused to detonate either 5 or 7 seconds after releasing the firing pin, we always waited at least 15 seconds after throwing the grenades into the water before anyone was permitted to dive in. I was present when three of us dived in once it was considered safe to do so. Yet a delay of 20 seconds occurred before the last grenade exploded in the water. My head had just broken through the surface and Ginger Whiteley, from Barnsley, was under the water. I felt as though I had been hammered all over my body, and poor old Ginger came to the surface arse first. We helped him out on to the bank and he was soon feeling able to walk back to the village. The fish did not escape and we had a good meal of fresh grilled fish that night.

Derry had been with us most of the time and he made himself very useful to the Squadron in general and to Dusty and me in particular. He was with us at every opportunity and there was the odd comment that we were the 'inseparables'. We did not object to this, as we wanted his presence in our tank to be accepted as the norm, ready for when we went to Maymyo, if and when that chance came for us.

Tug Wilson proved to be an excellent crew member and he had all the basic knowledge to do any of the other jobs in the tank. He was switched into the different positions during training and sometimes in action too, when he practised his skills as we all did. But, he was happiest when he was the 75 loader, probably because that position had the most space for his enormous girth. Nobody mentioned Blondie Benton and he rapidly faded into the dim past. I certainly did not raise his name with Dusty, believing that I would not get to the real truth about his death. We were all simply too busy and other, respected, pals in the Squadron were leaving us every week, killed in action or seriously wounded and evacuated.

We still appeared to be being used by Bill Slim to fool the enemy and give the impression that we intended to cross the Irrawaddy near Mandalay and attack that strong base. This was not to happen until we had cleared our previous target of the large village of Ywathetgyi, where we nearly lost the Major and his entire crew to fire from a Browning in the turret of a new, but over-eager, young officer.

# Chapter 3

# *May 1982*
# *Interrogation*

The inquisitor took off his spectacles, sighed quietly and looked me straight in the eye. "You are being very helpful and you've given me something of an insight into the conditions you lived under during the fighting in Burma. Can you tell me your honest opinion of whether Dusty Miller actually killed that man Benton or not? Take your time before you answer. You may have some real doubts, so drink your cup of tea if that will help you." He stood up and walked over to the loo door in the corner of the room. "I'll be back in a minute."

I took a drink of tea and wondered how I should answer the question. If I said that I believed Dusty had committed murder after he had ordered Benton out of the tank, I would be dropping him in it. Dusty had been a good friend to me during the many months that we had been together in the Carbs. We had saved each other's lives on a few occasions and I could never forget that fact. Dusty had used all his animal skills and wiles to get our tank sent up the road to Maymyo whilst the fighting had been going on around Mandalay. I simply could not say that I believed him to be guilty when I had never had any proof of his guilt, only a niggling doubt. I had never asked him point blank if he had done it, probably because I had thought it to be more than a possibility, and I did not want to know for sure.

This questioning at the Barnsley Police Station had been going on all day and I was feeling weary. I had been told only a little of what the police knew and suspected about the recent "headlines" murder of Vince Hallett, President of the Colliery Workers Union, on 13th April this year. He had been stabbed with a home-made bamboo dagger and this had eventually led to the police interviewing any wartime member of the 3rd Carabiniers that they could find.

Inspector Harry Bennet had used a new Police Computer Record of unresolved national crimes to search for those involving bamboo. He had made the surprising discovery, not only that there had been other murders involving bamboo, but that there had been a murder of a controversial figure on 13th April each year since the Second World War. Even more surprisingly, they had been carried out with either a handgun or a bamboo weapon and, apparently, by a lone operator.

They also had the theory that the date of 13th April had been selected to commemorate some traumatic occasion during the War. A lengthy search of the War histories of military units which were in the Far East at that time, and exposed to contact with bamboo weapons, had produced the date of 13th April 1944 for the Battle of Nunshigum, near Imphal.

This had taken place at the same time as the Battle of Kohima, when the 14th Army had brought the Japanese invasion of North East India to a halt, before finally driving them back into Burma and eventual annihilation.

After more than a year of continual fighting, many of the men were suffering from exhaustion arising from the loss of sleep, lack of food and often lack of water, plus a variety of debilitating tropical diseases. These would plague them for many years to come.

The weary 3rd Carabiniers were eventually to reach Rangoon just when the monsoons rains were becoming heavier and creating conditions in which it was impossible to operate once they left the tarmac roads. The tanks were left in the dock area of Rangoon and the men sailed to India for re-equipping with Sherman tanks, ready to invade Malaya and recapture Singapore. They were all very relieved when the dropping of the atom bombs caused the Japanese surrender.

Inspector Bennet came back into the room and sat down again. He was awaiting my answer to his question. "Well?"

"I can't give you the answer you want, Inspector. He never said he had done it and he never said he had not done it. I have had no contact with him for a long time and I don't know anyone who has seen him since the War. Have you tried the Old Comrades' Association?" I was passing the can back to him.

"Yes, we are working our way through the list of members and that is how we met you. Look, it's been a long day. Will you come back here tomorrow, as I would like to complete my records of your experiences in Burma, particularly with the background of your trip to Maymyo?"

I readily agreed, although my wife would not be very pleased to be left to run the business for a second day this week. It had been a very long day and there were a lot of decisions that I had to make before I was faced with more questions from this bright young officer. I was glad to get out of the building and set off for my home in Sheffield.

---

After Harry Bennet had seen Jimmy James leave the premises, he walked across to the office of Chief Inspector James Ackroyd to give a resumé of the afternoon's interview before the verbatim report was ready. The knock on the door brought the usual clear answer: "Come."

"Ah, Harry, any progress so far?"

"Yes, sir. This man James has a wealth of experience with the 3rd Carabiniers, with twelve months of frequent action, and he knew Miller."

"You mean the 'missing' Miller, the one who could have killed a member of his own crew?"

"That's right, sir. The Army Records list him as War Substantive Sergeant Andrew Miller, number 7945175, basic training carried out at the Royal Armoured Corps Depot, Catterick Camp, in 1941. He was demobbed with Group 42 in June 1946 and has not been in contact with Army Records or his Regiment since that date. James told me today that he had not seen or heard of Miller since the War. I'm not too sure that he was telling the complete truth about the man and there was some funny business that they were involved in with a Burmese lad near Mandalay or Maymyo. I will be probing into that tomorrow. Seems they acquired some rubies that were waiting to be lifted."

The Chief Inspector raised his eyebrows at this. "Could be the source of wealth that would support a life of crime; even one murder a year would need to be well funded. We might need to search for any reports of ruby thefts in our international records. Can we find a ruby expert who noticed a flood of Burmese rubies into the UK soon after the War? There are plenty of avenues to explore and we'll have to decide on priorities before we chase every one of them. What puzzles me is where has this Dusty Miller gone? We should have been able to find him from his civilian identity number, his Army number or his 'Z' Reserve address records. They're usually on the ball with that. We need to find out why he has not been issued with a ration book since he was demobbed. Failing all that, it seems to me that he could have switched identities with another man after James lost contact with him. That would make things more difficult, especially if the man he switched with had no living relatives. Think round that one, Harry, and get all you can tomorrow about the great ruby mystery. Will you see if your interview has been transcribed yet? I would like to read it now."

Harry accepted the dismissal and went back to his office.

After urging the speedy distribution of his interview report, he settled down to plan the second day of interviewing Jimmy James, with notes of questions to be answered.

1. What was the plan to take the rubies?

2. How was it carried out?

3. Did anyone else involved appear to be close to Dusty Miller?

4. Were any of the crew involved with women? Or with men?

5. Who was with Miller when he was demobbed and where did that happen?

6. Had Miller any other friends, before and after the fighting in Burma?

7. What happened to the Burmese lad when the Carabiniers left Burma?

He intended to continue his friendly attitude to James but he was going to probe into the old soldier's thinking during and after the War. He could provide much more background information into the mental state of all the survivors of the fighting in Burma. He was more and more convinced that his serial killer was one of them.

Chapter 4

# *1945*
# *Ywathetgyi and Tina*

The next morning James arrived at the Barnsley Police Station just before 10 o'clock as arranged. Harry Bennet was ready for him, waiting in the same interview room.

The ready smile and warm handshake made little impression on the old soldier, who was well used to the brash camaraderie of salesmen visiting him in his hardware shop in Sheffield. His first reaction was to wonder what the Inspector had cooked up for him since the day before.

"Come in and make yourself at home again, Jimmy. Did you have a good night?" Without waiting for a reply, he went on: "I'm hoping we can go through the rest of your fighting in Burma, including Mandalay, Maymyo and the journey to Rangoon. Can you include the planning of your visit to the ruby mines and how it was carried out? Also, I would like to have your impression of the relationships between the various members of your crew. Were any of them involved with women out there? Or with men? It is important to get the background of your pal Miller, if we are going to know where to look for him. See what you can recall."

James settled himself down in the hard chair and made a start.

---

I had told you of B Squadron waiting between the two rivers, the Chindwin and the Irrawaddy, where we attacked groups of retreating Japanese as and when we were given targets. This procedure became routine and we were very good at it. We continued to suffer casualties and we all had the odd scare that made us realise that we might not survive, but we were becoming a little more optimistic. And our health was beginning to improve. There were some new drugs sent out to the medical teams – possibly for the MO's to try out on us as guinea pigs? I had a very large dose of a 'sulpha' drug that stopped me running to the latrine for four days. It was very dramatic and very effective. I began to feel much better in health and had an appetite for food for the first time in a year. It was years later that I found that one of the side effects of sulphaguanadine was to require a daily dose of vitamin B Complex in order to stop my tongue bleeding. That is something I've lived with for more than thirty years now.

We had the occasional Intelligence report that gave us an insight into the problems being suffered by the enemy. We were well aware that nearly all of them were starved and ill, but some of the orders issued to them from their division and Army HQ's would have been laughed at if we had received any similar order. Some of these orders blamed the Japanese retreat from Imphal on the destructive power of the British tanks, and the Carabiniers were specifically mentioned. In Japanese eyes we were seen as the prize target – to be attacked at every opportunity, by any means available, and any soldier who lost his life whilst destroying a tank would be a hero and honoured throughout their nation. This explained the persistence of the Jap snipers, who were a continual problem. It also explained the occasional booby trap that we found at bridges and culverts.

It was early February 1945 when things seemed to be moving again. We had been briefed yet again to attack Ywathetgyi, on the banks of the Irrawaddy. Reports indicated that there was at least an enemy division based there, which secured a crossing point on the mile-wide river. Our job was to support the Royal Scots in their drive to clear the eastern half of the village in the first day.

It all seemed to be going according to plan except for the fact that each stage required twice the time allotted to it. The first objective was the area around a hill with a windmill on the highest point of the eastern half of the village. Major Dorman took the whole squadron of Lees up to the start line and ordered two troops to advance on his left and the other two troops on his right. The infantry had been waiting there for us and they followed the tanks forward at a steady pace. Sporadic firing of our Brownings showed where the leading tanks had come across a few Japs dug in on the way forward. HQ A Troop's four tanks started to follow the Royal Scots, ready to do any mopping up that became necessary. The Major liked to be in the action and his tanks usually fired as much ammunition as any other single troop. He had his chance again on this day.

"All stations Able, reduce speed of your advance. Our friends on foot cannot keep up with you and you are missing a few targets left behind in foxholes. I shall deal with those I can see. All stations Able, over." The replies all came clearly and we halted for a few minutes to have a better look around and to let some of the infantry join up with us.

In the meantime, as I learned later, the Major's tank crew had spotted a couple of Japs jumping into a slit trench just in front of them and he ordered his driver to get as close to them as possible. His wireless NCO, Corporal Alan Fenner, was told to look out of his porthole and to confirm that they were indeed Japanese and not British. "Definitely Jap helmets and there are two of them in the foxhole, sir." His open port measured about 3 inches by 4 inches and he had a good view of the two enemy only five feet below his eye level.

As he looked down he was astounded to see a Mills hand-grenade land on the ground a foot from the nearest domed steel helmet. It immediately exploded and the two Japs heaved up and then fell down into the trench. "You got them both, sir," said Alan, "and you nearly got me in the process." The hint of criticism went over the Major's head. "I hope that they really are Japs. Are you quite sure Fenner?" Having just seen a grenade detonate within five feet of his face, and feeling very shaken by the possibility of being hit by a splinter, Alan could only grunt, "Yes."

The Major then moved forward to catch up with the remainder of his troop, who were all engaged in mopping up the odd few stragglers. The wireless was busy with traffic as the other four troops were engaging some well-built bunker positions. These were reported back to the Major but he did not give any acknowledgement. The reason was that he had not heard any messages from the other troops since the grenade episode. His two grenades, dropped at the side of his tank, had cut the aerial lead, in exactly the same way as had happened to our tank before Benton was killed. In a similar way, Alan Fenner had diagnosed the problem and gone outside the tank to do the repairs. The only difference this time was that, at the very moment that he held the two damaged lead ends, his body completed the circuit and the Major realised that he had the power to transmit. This he did, switching to 'send' and putting 400amps through his wireless NCO. The shock galvanised Allan into action. He ran up the side of the tank, banged on the Major's helmet with his pair of pliers and told him not to electrocute him in that way, at least not until the set had been repaired and he had given the OK. The message went home.

The Major then resumed his control of the battle by asking for situation reports. These sitreps came back immediately and confirmed that the slow progress was continuing with a steady clearance of well-prepared dug-in defences. The Royal Scots had a good time working with the tanks. They made full use of the 'infantry boxes' on the rear engine doors, where each tank had an armoured box containing a spare headset and microphone to enable an outsider to talk with the crew inside the tank. We often heard the strange voice of an infantry NCO or officer. "Hello you in there, Sergeant McNabb here, we have a problem bunker over to your left. Can you help us with it if we fire a red Verey light at it?" This always brought co-operation from the tank commander and was usually followed by the complete destruction of the offending strong point.

The sporadic fighting continued through to the late afternoon. The crews took their food and water as and when they could, inside the tanks and between skirmishes. I could often see the Royal Scots men munching a biscuit or taking bully beef straight from the open tin with a knife whilst lying flat on the open ground between runs forward.

When it became known that the enemy had been cleared from the whole of the eastern half of the target area, the Major gave the order to collect together near the old windmill for the night. This was normal for us and we started to gather into a defensive box with the tanks facing outwards. Apparently, it was at that point that the Major decided he wanted to resolve the doubt that he had about the two men he had killed in the slit trench during the morning. He would not accept Alan Fenner's statement that they were definitely Japs and he ordered his driver to take the tank back about a quarter of a mile to where he could see the slit trench at the corner of a field.

When the tank stopped, perhaps 100 yards away, Major Dorman

told his crew to dismount with him and they walked with him to examine the two bodies. The tank was left unoccupied, with the engine switched off but the wireless still on the net. Alan lent down into the slit trench and pulled a helmet from one of the dead Japs. "Look, sir, there is no doubt about it, is there?" The Major nodded and grunted agreement whilst the remainder of the crew satisfied their curiosity by lifting the helmet off the other body. Both helmets had plastic wallets inside them containing personal documents and photographs of Japanese families and children. We had rarely been able to examine the damage we had carried out with our destructive weapons as the tanks usually pressed on to the next target and let the infantry complete the mopping up. They were then followed by trained men who searched all the bodies for information and documents.

It was at that point that a machine gun was heard firing at the Squadron Leader's crew, who threw themselves down to the ground. The firing continued, with spurts of dust being kicked up as the bullets were sprayed across the field.

"It's a Browning," cried Alan Fenner, "it's one of our tanks!"

The Major agreed.

"Then go and tell them to stop it, Corporal," he said testily, keeping his face well down in the dust.

Alan needed no more advice. He had always been a keen sprinter and he was up and running flat out across the field with a spray of Browning .300 rounds kicking up the ground behind him. He was fast. And he made it to the tank.

The first time that the Squadron knew what had happened was when those who had been listening to the traffic on the wireless net heard the voice of Lieutenant Ketton, 3 Troop Leader, commenting on his shooting.

"Able 3 Able, you appear to have got them all now but I think I can still see some of them showing signs of life. Advance with Able 3 Baker and make sure you destroy them. Able 3 Able and 3 Baker, over."

"Able 3 Able, wilco, out."

"Able 3 Baker, wilco, out."

There was an immediate transmission from the Major's tank in the well known voice of Alan Fenner. He sounded to be in a real panic.

"Able 3, if you have just been firing your maggie, cease firing. Able 3, over."

Lt. Ketton had only been with the Squadron for a week or so, but it was long enough for him to recognise the voice of the Squadron wireless NCO, and he was going to let everyone know that he, an officer, was not going to accept an order to cease firing from a mere corporal. Especially when he had spotted some Japanese who could threaten the squadron.

"Able 3, yes, we are engaging some escaping Japs, Able 3, out."

His curt put-down of a junior NCO was meant to show his senior position and authority. He hoped, quite correctly, that the Commanding Officer would still be listening to his own set back at RHQ. He intended to make a name for himself. He had done just that.

Alan was a little less breathless when he came back on the air. By now, the whole of the squadron net was alerted and listening.

"Able 3, I say again, cease firing. You are firing at number 9 and his entire crew who are dismounted. Able 3, confirm, over."

It was a much less arrogant lieutenant who replied.

"Able 3, Roger, wilco. Are they OK? Able 3, over."

"Able 3, I suggest that you find out. I am going back to do that. Able 3 out."

There was only a moment's break in transmission when the unmistakable voice of our Commanding Officer, Colonel Whetstone, came over very calmly.

"Able 3, this is 'top number 9' asking for your personal report on the condition of your own number 9 and his crew within minutes, Able 3 over."

Lt. Ketton must have become a very anxious person by this time. He literally squeaked. "Able 3, wilco, Able 3 out."

Alan knew that the CO was fully aware of the fix he was in and started to climb out of the tank to go and see if any of the crew had survived the machine gunning. Just as he put his head out of the turret, he was very relieved to hear the voice of the Major and to see the other six crew members walking back towards him. They all appeared to be safe.

The Squadron Leader, his crew and Lt. Ketton were all lucky to some degree. They were all still alive, but the CO was very much aware that they had all blundered in varying ways. The Major should not have left his tank exposed and empty. At least one crew member should have remained with it. The man who was exposed to the worst criticism would be Lt. Ketton. He had ordered his troop to fire at targets that he had not identified correctly as enemy. The whole Regiment would now know that he was an idiot who had tried to wipe out an entire crew, including his own 'officer commanding'. He was not likely to survive in the Carabiniers.

He did not and was sent back to India as a psychiatric case after breaking down in tears in front of the Colonel. I met him six months later when I was in the BGH at Poona. He was still being treated for his mental breakdown.

After this unusual episode, the Major took his tank back into the box for the night and we all had a decent sleep; most of us took the chance to kip down in our blankets on the soft earth. We were all on guard, 2 hours on, 4 hours off duty, but we took that as normal. At the end of a two-hour shift we had only to lie down and close our eyes to be asleep until we were called again. The Bombay Grenadiers were doing a similar guard duty in their slit trenches and keeping us safe from any Jap night patrols. We had a good night.

After standing to at dawn the next morning, we were able to cook a hot breakfast of canned bacon, beans and sausages washed down with a good mug of garum char. It put a lining to our stomachs and prepared us for yet another day of slaughter. This went on in a similar way to the day before.

We had a different battalion of infantry from 2 Division with us as the Royal Scots had been withdrawn, but the routine continued smoothly. The only excitement was when 3 Troop, with a new officer, reached the banks of the Irrawaddy and saw two sampans full of Japanese troops halfway across the river. They were loaded to the gunwales and would be desperate to reach the other side and possible safety. We all heard the orders from the new troop leader.

"Able 3, enemy boats ahead, two rounds Howe Easy, fire."

Within a few seconds the two boats erupted in flame and the passengers were in the water. The tanks sprayed them from their turret Brownings for a few minutes and it was unlikely that any of them reached the safety of a sandbank or the other side.

The village of Ywathetgyi was reported clear of the enemy at

1600 hours that day and we began to relax. The Major called a squadron parade immediately after stand-to the next morning.

"Stand easy, men. You have had a long and very successful ten weeks since we crossed the Chindwin and these past two days have been no exception. Congratulations to you all. The Commanding Officer has received many messages from higher echelons saying how successful the Regiment, and especially B Squadron, has been in helping to bring this campaign to its conclusion. To the south of us, 4$^{th}$ Corps, supported by C Squadron and other armoured regiments, has succeeded in clearing the district around Meiktila of Japanese and forming a very strong block to the Japanese forces who are trying to escape south from around Mandalay. All this is on the other side of the Irrawaddy and we shall be crossing to join them in the near future. We will do this on rafts at a point to be decided but, for the time being, we will be having a few days well-earned rest a few miles north of here. I am proud of you all. Enjoy the rest." There were a few cheers as we fell out and returned to our tanks.

"How about a pass to spend a few days in Chowringee, Sarge?" The flippant joke from Paddy Wills, our 75 gunner, brought a laugh from Dusty Miller.

"You'll be lucky. You would spend more than the few days in transit camps and never enjoy the delights of sleeping with all the cows in Cal. Anyway, if you could make it there, you'd find all the officers would be travelling with you to spend the time at their Tollygunge Club. We'll find somewhere else to spend some time polishing our brasses and painting our tanks, I'm sure. But, don't think that we have finished fighting, Paddy. They say that our objective is now Mandalay, last month it was Shwebo, and we passed that. When we get to Mandalay, I'll bet a pound to a penny that we will be aiming for Rangoon. That should see us on a troopship for India – or for Singapore. There is no end to it all. Don't be surprised if we are issued with some new colour of blanco. The Carbs have a reputation to keep up."

As it happened, we moved north for a few miles to make camp in a village on the outskirts of Kyaukse, on the banks of a tributary flowing into the Chindwin. It was heaven.

Minimal guards were on duty each night, so we all had plenty of sleep and a small amount of work during the days. Some of us went fishing again, with grenades, and we all did the routine maintenance on our tanks and sidearms. We had another new barrel fitted to our 75mm gun. A close examination of the old barrel showed that the rifling had been completely worn away with use and we were glad to have our main weapon back in peak condition, ready to hit a tree at one mile. Even as a smoothbore, it was deadly at close quarters, but the accuracy was not there at ranges of a few hundred yards. It was reassuring to know that we were ready for anything we might come up against in the future.

It was during these few days of rest that I met the most beautiful girl I could ever have imagined. I must admit that none of us had had any close contact with any civilised company during the past year. At Imphal the civilians had all been evacuated before the Japs invaded. We had seen a few WASBI's who came with their mobile shops with toiletries, but their time off duty had been fully occupied with the officers. They certainly had no interest in the other ranks.

When we moved into the village I had noticed that there were a few civilians living in the part that we did not occupy. Like all Burmese villagers, they were quietly going about their business of gathering and preparing food and fuel whilst we did the usual thing of cleaning our tanks, weapons and our own bodies and laundry. Most of us had acquired a small vocabulary of Urdu or Hindi but this was useless with most of the people we met in Burma. That was why we were so pleased to have Derry with us. He would be very useful under these conditions. It was whilst I was washing my spare jungle green battledress in the river that I heard the most delightful voice say, in perfect English, "Excuse me, sir, but do you happen to have any spare soap that you could let me have?"

I looked up into the loveliest pair of brown eyes I could ever have imagined. This small Burmese lady, dressed in the usual villager's longyi and waistcoat, was standing only a few feet away from me. I stood up, dropping the soap into the river and losing it, realised that I was stripped to the waist and I blushed. I was even more embarrassed when I realised that she was smiling at me for being so naïve.

"Hello, young lady, I seem to have lost my soap in the river. But how can you speak such good English? I've been trying to learn

Burmese for months now and can only remember three words. My name is Jimmy James by the way." She continued to give me that lovely smile, with dazzling white teeth highlighted by the soft brown skin.

"My name is Ma Tina Mying and I am a BA from Rangoon University, 1942. My brother and I are living with my uncle, who is the headman here. We came up north when the Japanese began to make life in Rangoon unpleasant for the civilians. We have had very little contact with them since we came here."

I simply did not know how to handle this situation. Despite being an experienced soldier, who had spent the past year obeying orders and helping to kill a large number of Japanese who had been trying to do the same to me, I had no close knowledge or experience of the opposite sex. I suppose you would say that I had had a sheltered life. But, most of my contemporaries from the thirties were in the same stage of life. We thought that we knew all the biological facts, and probably fantasised at times, but we were innocent babes when it came to understanding girls. I know that I was.

"Let me see if I have any more soap in my kit." I walked over to the tank and looked in my corner behind the wireless, where I kept my stock of spare tins and ammunition. "It's all Lifebuoy, I'm afraid, but you are welcome to a couple of tablets of that."

She was delighted. "We have had no soap for more than a year, now. Thank you very much, indeed." She was beaming with pleasure and I was beginning to wonder if there was any other way in which I could keep her smiling. I need not have worried.

"You are very kind to give me this. Can I, perhaps, return the kindness this evening? Would you like to join my family for some fresh food in my home?" I nodded, with a smile. "We will be having a meal at 6 o'clock and you will be very welcome." She pointed out which was the headman's bungalow and I told her how much I appreciated being invited into her home – the first time I had received such an invitation during the three years I had been in India.

The excitement of the invitation was soon transferred to the other members of the crew. They made a variety of jealous comments such as, "You lucky bastard," "She's far too good for you, let me take your place," and, "You'll get your leg over tonight, do you know how to do it?"

I ignored all the badinage and was rewarded by the rest of the crew searching amongst their own stores in order to give me a few tins of meat and vegetables and some cans of condensed milk. "Take these with you, Jimmy. You must impress them with your generosity." It was all meant to be kindly to my hosts. And it proved to be very effective.

That evening will be in my memory for ever. Tina's uncle, U Ba The, welcomed me to his bungalow, which was built from bamboo and had a thatched roof covering all the rooms and a spacious veranda. He was very polite but had little English and relied on Tina to translate his good wishes. He wanted me to know how relieved they all were that the end of the fighting was in sight and that the Japanese would soon be pushed out of Burma.

I was introduced also to Tina's brother, who was addressed as Tinka. An apt name, I thought, and I have always remembered him as 'Tinker'. He was full of fun, had no English at all, and his only contribution to the conversation was to play his battered old gramophone continually. Sadly, he had no more than one record, which was completely worn out, and I could only guess that it was of "Blaze Away". The point of the needle on the machine was rounded from over-use and it was just as effective if it was reversed. Thinking of the words of the song, I remember wishing we could make "a bonfire of our troubles" and put the old wreck on to it.

But he did not spoil the evening. Uncle sat with us for the meal, which was vegetarian, consisting of their home-grown produce, salad with tomatoes, radishes and other strange vegetables, and beautifully cooked rice with a curry. This was completed with a variety of fruits, which we peeled and ate with our fingers. It was delightful and quite satisfying. The conversation, with and through Tina, covered the dramatic events of the past three years: the Japanese control of Burma, from their originally polite and formal treatment of the population to the more recent brutal methods used to express themselves. Tina had fortunately completed her BA in Rangoon before the troubles started, and she had avoided many possible problems by being in the north and living the simple life.

After the meal Uncle made his excuses and went into the bungalow, whilst Tina, Tinka and I remained on the veranda in quiet conversation, both disturbed by the awful gramophone. Eventually,

Tina spoke a few words to her brother and he looked at her, made no comment but picked up his beloved machine and followed in his uncle's steps. We were alone at last.

I was excited, tingling all over and simply did not know how to tell her of my feelings.

"That was a delightful meal, thank you very much. It is so long since I had such a pleasant one." Tina smiled again.

"It is a pleasure to have your company."

I thought, "Why are we talking such a load of codswallop when there are more important things to say? Tomorrow morning I could be out in the tank, in action, and never see this gorgeous girl again.

I looked up into the night sky. "What a beautiful moon," I remarked and meant it. It really was a gorgeous sight. Tina laughed again.

"In Burma, that is what a young man says to a lady he admires; have you been told that before now?"

Again, I felt embarrassed. Had I put my foot in it and spoiled my chances? "No, Tina, I have never heard the expression before, but, it really is a huge moon. I have thought that many times when on guard duty." I paused. Here goes. I will take the chance.

"But I do admire you. You are the most beautiful girl I have ever seen and yet we are going to be parted so soon." She became very serious.

"It is so soon after our meeting. Is it not a little too soon to be so outspoken?" We were both rather quiet.

"Then may I see you tomorrow, after we have both had a little time to think about our feelings?" She seemed to be relieved that the pressure was reduced and changed the subject very easily.

"Yes, of course, we will see each other tomorrow. If your soldier friends would like to have supplies of fruit and vegetables, my uncle will be pleased to arrange for them. Could you let me know in the morning?"

After agreeing to this, I formally held her hand in a shake and thanked her for a delightful evening. Tinka, who had obviously been listening to the whole conversation from indoors, came out and also shook my hand.

That was the start to a long story. The Major was very willing to buy fresh supplies from the headman. The squadron was delighted to consume them after so many months of tinned and dehydrated foods. And I saw Tina every day of the next four days until we were moved south again to be ready to cross the Irrawaddy.

We were both very much in love with each other but we hesitated before taking that final step of consummation, probably because of our own Victorian upbringing. We had each been given a very strict childhood, controlled by very different religious ethics, and we believed that there was a future that was worth a long wait. Before we parted, we each assured the other that we would meet again as soon as possible after the War was finished, and be married. We would be together and live in either England or Burma. We had faith in a future of peace and joy.

That faith was tested to breaking point many times. But we won through in the end. In 1947, after many letters had been written and answered, I was able to sail out to Rangoon and we were reunited, married, and we are still happily together.

---

"You mean that you are both together here, in England?" the Detective Inspector broke into my story.

"Yes. Tina is holding the fort for me in our shop today. She is not too happy about all this enquiry business, the time it is taking and the bad memories being raised, and she is well aware of the conditions in Burma, both then and now."

"Did she ever meet Dusty Miller?" D.I. Bennet never missed a trick.

"Yes, of course. In the last few days that we were together near Kyaukse she met all my crew and many of the others in the squadron. It was accepted that I had found her (when she had really found me) and no one tried to break us up. Even the Major always had a smile and a word for her when he saw her. She usually goes with me to the Old Comrades' Reunions each year."

"I would like to meet your wife, Jimmy. Perhaps it will be more convenient for her if I call at the shop one day soon?"

I agreed reluctantly and continued with the story of the river crossing.

## Chapter 5

## *1945*

## *The Plan Matures*

During our stay at Tina's village, the three of us, Dusty, Derry and myself, spent some time planning the best way to arrange for us to be ordered to go to Maymyo. This was usually done on our occasional foot patrols, which were intended and designed to give us exercise. At the same time they kept us on our toes in case we were ever required to fight on foot outside the tank.

Dusty seemed to be the one with the most creative mind. On the first patrol he suddenly stopped. Then he drew us into the jungle at the side of the path and said, "Let's sit down here a minute, where we won't be seen or overheard."

After checking around a fallen tree, looking for snakes and scorpions, he sat down and continued, "If we're going to get to Maymyo without too many questions being asked, we need to arrange to be ordered to go there!" This was pretty obvious, but we couldn't leave it in the lap of the gods, and I said so.

"Of course not," he replied, "I think I have an idea that will create just what we want. Tell me, Derry, how are you getting on with the Major? Does he ever thank you or express any appreciation when you are interpreting for him? This is very important."

Derry, who was as enthusiastic as ever when taken into our confidence, smiled. "Yes, Dusty, only yesterday he thanked me very much after he had had a long conversation with U Ba The regarding the compensation he was prepared to give him for our stay in the village. He was ready to be more generous than the headman expected and I was able to arrange a compromise that they both thought to be excellent. They were both smiling and the Major told me afterwards that I had made his job very much easier since I joined the Squadron."

Dusty became very serious. "Do you ever have any casual chat with him about your private affairs, your family and what happened to them? Or your future, when all this is over and we go back to India?" Derry was quiet for a moment.

"That was when I first met Major Dorman. He interviewed me and I explained that my uncle and I are now the only living members of my family. He knows that my uncle will be in either Mandalay or Maymyo. That is what I believe, and I will not know for sure until I can make contact with someone who knows the facts after we cross the river."

"That's what we do, then. During the next few days, whenever you get the chance, and the Major's in a mellow mood, let him know that you have worries about the whereabouts of your uncle and that you will be pleased when the fighting is all over and you can be reunited with him. That is all you have to do at this stage. Simple, isn't it?" He looked at both of us with a smile.

Derry nodded, looking serious. I said, "It's always easy to remember telling the truth, and that seems to be true to me. As I see it, it will be necessary for Derry to tell him a lie after the crossing such as 'please, sir, I have just spoken to a man who has met my uncle in Mandalay and he has told me that he has gone back to Maymyo. Is there any possibility of the Squadron going up there to clear the Japanese from the town? I would really appreciate it if I can be sent up there.' That would sow the seed in the Major's mind that he might be able to help you to get there, but it is essential that he links you with our tank and that he sends this crew up the road. That is, if we still go ahead as we agreed before. You will need a tank to blow the cover off the safe before we blow the door off as well."

"We are not going to back down on this, any one of us." Dusty was deadly serious as he stared at each of us. "Derry can forget what you have just said, Jimmy, until we cross over. All he needs to do is what I have told him. Take it step by step and don't get too complicated. We will go to Maymyo together, even if I have to disappear with the tank and crew for a day. We will make it happen. And we will come out of this as very wealthy men, each one of us. Come on, let's get on with this patrol. We need to be back before tiffin. OK, Derry?"

We rarely mentioned the subject during the next few days as we prepared the tanks for another advance some days later. This time we went to the west bank of the Irrawaddy, about ten miles south of Ywathetgyi, which was now the HQ of a brigade of 2 Division. Once again, we were going to float downstream on board a Bailey Bridge raft, urged across the steadily moving water by a couple of DUKW's or motor boats. The maximum load on each raft was one General Lee tank and crew and we were told to sit in our usual seats in the tank during the crossing.

The crossing briefing included the statement that there were no identifiable Japanese units near the river on the opposite side, and that we could expect an unopposed landing, but we were advised to be ready for some sniper fire. "Too bloody vague for me," said Dusty, "if they sink us when we are floating downstream, we won't have time to get out and swim for it, not all of us. Half of you had better be dismounted and shelter behind the tank so that you can't be sniped from the bank. I'll stay in the turret with John and Les so we can reply if there is any trouble." He need not have bothered, as we had no enemy fire from the other side of the river, but that thinking was an example of how he had survived so long. He was thinking ahead, as usual, and watching every point that could affect his crew. We were all with him.

Apart from having to avoid the many sandbanks, the Sappers in charge of our raft found it quite easy to guide us to a small jetty on the eastern bank, where we drove off the raft and on to terra firma again. It was approaching dusk before all the squadron AFV's had arrived and we stood to inside the tanks, which faced outwards from our box. The next morning we moved a few miles to the east, nearer Mandalay, which we hoped to enter as the conquering army. But it was not to be so. At least, not for the whole of B Squadron.

We waited in our box for two days and during the second day Major Dorman went to a Brigade conference to be told of our future role. He was in a very bad frame of mind when he returned and he let us all know with an outburst of temper that we had not seen before. He called a squadron parade and told us that he had upset the Brigadier and that his own future was in jeopardy.

"You all know that we were given the ancient capital of Mandalay as our next objective whilst we were passing time going round in circles in the Sagaing Bend. I am very much aware also of how you have fought so many successful actions in the knowledge that they were leading up to the point where we are now, namely, ready to enter Mandalay and clear the Japs from there. The powers that be," and he almost spat the words, "have decided that A Squadron will represent the Regiment in the entry to Mandalay and that we will now proceed south to the oilfields, still with $2^{nd}$ Division. A Squadron has been very effective in the fighting near us in the Sagaing Bend and they are being honoured in this way.

"I told the Brigadier that I would not criticise their being given a well-earned reward but he must know that B Squadron had led $2^{nd}$ Division every day for nearly three months, with the given objectives firstly of Shwebo and then Mandalay. You all deserved the honour and this treatment could have a serious effect on your morale. That hit him on a raw spot and he blew his top. He put me in my place and I could be replaced any day.

"But it did have some effect on him. He relented marginally and said that I could send one token tank into Mandalay tomorrow. I accepted the offer and I will be commanding my own tank in order to represent the whole of B Squadron. You will all be able to say to your children, 'I was in B Squadron of the $3^{rd}$ Carabiniers when they helped to capture Mandalay from the Japanese in 1945.' No one can take that from you." He looked around the silent men who faced him.

There was some subdued murmuring. The only comment that I heard was not what the Major would have expected. "He can stuff Mandalay for me. I'd rather head south for Rangoon and India."

"What's that, Sergeant? What did you say?" He was as testy as ever we had seen him. Sergeant Kenny must have thought that he had meant him and gave the tactful answer.

"I think the general opinion is that we will be honoured to have you there in our name sir. They will not be able to keep us all out of Rangoon when we get there. And we must do that before the rains start."

"Quite right, quite right. Rangoon must be our final objective in Burma, but there will be plenty of tidying up to do as we travel south. That is all I can tell you at the moment. Lt. Dibble-Williams, remain here. Remainder of B Squadron, dismiss."

We broke up into small groups, mostly of complete tank crews, as we discussed what we had just been told. The general feeling was

"What the hell! Let's get on with it. We've had a long time in action and the sooner it's over the better." Despite our knowing that there was the best part of two Japanese divisions between Rangoon and us, we wanted to get to grips and wipe them out. Then we could get back to India and have some rest before we had to face the future again and whatever that held in store for us.

Lt. Dub came back to the troop with some very interesting news. He called us together. "Listen here, men. The Major has a job for us to do tomorrow whilst he is in Mandalay. A company of the Lancashire Fusiliers is going up the road towards Lashio, where some Japs are retreating east, and they have asked for tank support before they enter Maymyo, about 20 miles from Mandalay. It is an old hill station with a climate like England. In fact, many British people lived there for part of the year before the War. 2 Troop have been given the task so we will set off immediately after stand-down in the morning. Any questions?"

"Yes, sir." Dusty jumped in before anyone else could speak. "I would think that there will not be any British in Maymyo now, sir. It will be a great help to all of us if we can take young Derry with us, to interpret when necessary. He is used to fitting into our tank without causing any problems, and he will be welcome."

"Good thinking Sergeant. Yes, I'll ask the Major for him. Of course, he might want him to go to Mandalay in his tank. Any other questions?"

There were no more and Dusty crossed his fingers to me as we returned to our tank. "It's in the lap of the gods now; let's hope that Derry was able to sow the seed properly." Raising his voice to the rest of the crew, "OK, lads, let's make sure we are ready for an early start and you, Tug, check that we've got the full load of AP ammo."

"Expecting a tank battle, Sarge?" Tug Wilson was no fool.

"No, but we must be ready for anything. Carry on." He glanced at me and beckoned me over to his side with a tilt of the head.

"Right, Jimmy, we are going ahead with or without Derry. We know enough to be able to look for the safe once we can find the mines offices. It will be easier if he is with us but it won't stop us if he doesn't make it."

"When are you going to tell the rest of the crew?" I asked. "Only as and when it's necessary. And that might be only after we've got the rubies in our hands. They'll get a share anyway, just for being with us at the time. You, Derry and I will get the lion's share, no messing."

This was reassuring to me although I had always trusted Dusty to be straight with me. At the back of my mind there was a niggling query about the way that Benton had met his end. In every other way I had trusted him with my life, and I would do so again. I was sure that he would keep his word on the matter of money or the rubies. It was nearing the time for stand-to and the beginning of the night when Derry came up to me. "Can I sleep here with your crew tonight, Jimmy? The Major has told me to report to Dusty in time for morning stand-to as I will be spending tomorrow with you." He was more excited than I had seen him before.

"Sure, Derry. You can kip down here, next to me." I indicated a slight hollow in the soft earth. "As long as you don't snore." Snoring was always a problem. It kept others awake when they should have been having their beauty sleep but, worst of all, it could be heard from a distance and would sometimes attract attention from a passing Jap patrol. No one liked to be awakened from a deep sleep by the arrival of a few Jap mortars or hand grenades. On the few occasions that this had happened to me, I had awakened with an immediate and uncontrollable urge to go for a crap, which was not a wise move in the dark, especially during a Japanese attack. Anyone stumbling around a defensive box in the dark was asking to be shot by both sides. Snorers were usually smothered at the first sound.

"No, I don't snore," he smiled, " and I'm so excited that I doubt whether I will be able sleep at all. I must tell you that I really have met a man who knew my uncle when he was living in Mandalay. And he really told me that he had gone back to Maymyo two months ago. I could not have planned it any better. When I told the Major, he was very pleased for me, and he was willing to let me join 2 Troop for the move tomorrow so that I can go to Maymyo. We can go ahead with the plan and I might also be able to trace my uncle."

"Good for you," I replied, "but, you must stick with us and not go wandering off on your own. There are still some Japs hanging around there. We'll help you to find your uncle and you'll be safer inside the tank during the search. The first job will be for us to go to the mine offices and sort out that safe of yours. That is important to all three of us."

The air was warm and balmy in the moonlit clump of bamboos and the usual cacophony of night noises fell on deaf ears. The chirping, squeaking, rustling and snuffling had become a part of our lives and we only became aware of them if they suddenly stopped or were interrupted by any new or loud sounds, or if a snake or scorpion should move on to our bodies. I have seen big strong men become quivering wrecks when they had seen a poisonous snake sliding across their legs during a stand-to. If they had called out, even if only to swear at the creature, they would have endangered all their colleagues nearby and possibly been bitten or stung for their pains, if not shot by the Japs also.

We had a good night. Derry was wanting to chatter but I cooled him down by being firm with him. "You'd better try to get some sleep now, Derry. We all need a good kip to be fit for tomorrow and anyway, we both have to do a two-hour stag when we are called. I see you have been given a sidearm."

Derry patted his pistol holster proudly and began to settle down with his blankets. I suppose that we were not authorised to issue British weapons to a colonial civilian but the Major must have agreed and it was only right that this co-operative youngster should be able to defend himself in case of an attack. The Smith and Wesson .38 pistol was more of an ornament than a weapon. It had proved to be deadly at a few feet distance but, as a serious method of stopping an enemy, it could be discounted. I have seen a charging Japanese NCO, wielding a heavy, two-handed sword, receive five rounds from a .38 pistol, before the sixth, and last, round dropped him in his tracks. No, we all knew that the more effective pistol was the .45 calibre that was issued to the officers. One round from that would knock a man backwards and down to stay down.

In a crew of seven there were five .38 pistols issued, unless an officer commanded the tank and he would be issued with a .45 calibre. The wireless operator and the 75 loader each had a Thomson sub-machine gun, the 'Tommy gun' of the Chicago gangster films. These two lucky chaps had to carry ten magazines, each containing twenty rounds of rimless .45 calibre – a heavy load when added to the gun itself. Derry would be safe with his pistol as long as he remembered to empty the chambers before he cleaned it.

The night passed fairly quietly except for the attention of a small Jap patrol. I lost no sleep over their spraying the tanks with light machine gun fire and a few grenades, as I was already awake and on guard duty for two hours. After half an hour they faded into the distance. Reveille at 0600 hrs was helped by the distribution of mugs of hot sweet char at 0530 hrs. The last man on guard duty had been briefed by Dusty to boil the water in the bottom of a slit trench.

Again, this was contrary to all the rules but it had been tested many times when near the enemy and the benefits outweighed the risks. It was always better to have an alert crew setting off into action, possibly in the dark, than to have us trying to wake up with our hands on loaded heavy weapons or driving a 30 ton tank. A mug of 'gunfire' was a lifesaver. Cold food could easily be eaten inside the tank as we were driving towards our destination.

## Chapter 6

# *1945*
# *Rubies Galore*

At 0730 hrs we met up with the company of the Norfolks who would be supported by 2 Troop in their clearing of Maymyo. Their 3-tonners led the way east along the road to Lashio, closely followed by the three tanks in a cloud of dust. The troop travelled in line with Lt. Dub leading, followed by our tank and Corporal Kenny in the rear. Derry was seated beside me so as to be able to look over Nick McGowan's left shoulder and see the road ahead. He was smiling happily as we munched our cold bacon and biscuits. We maintained a steady 25mph and passed the turning on the left towards Mandalay. Soon after that we started to climb gently up the twisting road, leading firstly to Maymyo and then on towards Lashio and eventually to China.

The three tank commanders had their heads out of the turrets and they had all covered the lower part of their faces with a cloth to try to avoid swallowing the choking dust. The rest of us also suffered from the dust coming into the tank through the driver's visor, which needed to be kept open in order to see the road. As the road climbed higher up the mountain, it became more tortuous and the pace slowed to down nearer 10mph. We were moving at about 5mph when we hit the roadblock. It was in an obvious place on a bend, which was well wooded with branches from the deciduous trees meeting overhead above us. A nasty place for lorried infantry and tanks.

"Fox 2, take – – – ." The ominous, broken transmission, in Lt. Dub's well known voice, was heard throughout the three tanks as we each reacted to the sudden attack. I was looking forward through my own periscope and could clearly see the Troop Leader's tank a few yards ahead of us. Machine guns had opened fire on the infantry lorries still further ahead. It was bedlam. The 3-tonners swerved to either side of the road with men leaping out of them and landing in a variety of heaps on the roadside. At the same time I saw a Jap drop from the tree above the tank ahead, landing on the engine cover and leaning across to the turret. He appeared to drop something into the turret and then he lay down on the top of the tank. Within seconds there was the most enormous explosion and the tank was enveloped in a mass of flame. Our tank was physically moved backwards by the blast. We were all deafened by the noise.

I knew immediately what had happened. It was similar to what had happened to B Squadron before now, when Corporal Dinty Moore's tank and crew had been blown to smithereens soon after crossing the Chindwin.

That time it had been a booby trap with an aerial bomb in a culvert. This time it was a Jap dropping one or two grenades down the turret. It had blown up the full load of ammunition in the storage racks. No one could have survived, and that included the bomber himself. I looked behind me into our turret, and saw that Dusty had quickly closed his turret lid. Self-preservation is a strong motivator.

"Fox 2 Baker, over." Dusty was calling Corporal Kenny, who replied: "Fox 2 Baker, are you OK?"

"Fox 2 Baker, yes. We are on our own now. You move to cover the right side of the road and sort the bastards out. I will handle the left, out."

On the I/C: "Nick, move back and left so we can spray these trees. 37 and 75, fire when ordered, or when you see your own targets."

The Norfolks had sorted themselves out by now, mostly on the right side of the road, and were engaging the Jap bunkers in the undergrowth. Both tanks were soon firing their big guns and their Brownings added to the din. Within 20 minutes the firing had petered out. The Norfolks could be seen probing into the dark corners under the trees and their officer came across to our tank walking in the open with confidence. Dusty opened his turret cover to hear the report. "We seem to have cleared them. You've had tough luck with the tank, we've had four killed. Shall we have 20 minutes to bury them before we proceed?" Dusty replied, "Yes, sir. We'd better tidy things up before we press on," and he jumped down to join the officer.

Tug Wilson and I joined him and tried to find the remains of the seven men from Dub's tank, which had been opened like a sardine can. There were no identifiable parts of anyone that I knew. Tug and I dug a shallow grave just off the road and put into it all the pieces of scorched flesh that we could scrape together. Some of them could have been from the Jap kame kaze. Dusty fixed a cross and stuck it into the ground. Then he made a note of the map reference ready for his report, when he would indicate that there were the remains of the officer and six men buried there.

Whilst that was being completed, the infantry Major came across to Dusty.

"Are you the senior rank of the Carabiniers now? We must continue into the town and complete our orders."

"Yes, sir, I'm Sergeant Miller. We will give you all the support we can from the two tanks. May I suggest that I lead the column from now on so that we can spray any likely ambush point before your men are exposed? The second tank can continue to be behind your lorries."

"Thank you, Sergeant, agreed. But we will move forward dismounted from here. We are within two miles of the outskirts of Maymyo and we'll be ready for any further action. I believe that we will be passing the industrial area on the way and I want to ensure that that is clear before we go into the town."

"Right, sir, wilco." Dusty saluted the officer and we all mounted the tank ready to advance.

"Derry, did you say that your mine is in the industrial area, before we hit the town?" Derry was still in a state of shock after seeing the mess of the Troop Leader's tank. He was not yet hardened to seeing the bodies of friends who had been killed in action.

"Yes, Dusty. We will soon see the main office and the mine entrance on the right hand side of this road." And we did exactly that. We drove into the mine area, followed by the Norfolks on foot, and Derry guided Nick towards the main office buildings. There was no enemy fire and the infantry spread over the ground very smoothly. They were soon out of our sight and we moved up to the remains of the offices. Derry was back to his normal self again. "That's it! There's the office I told you about."

Dusty had obviously decided that he would let the rest of the crew know a little about what we were there for. "Right, lads. This is your big day. We are going to open that building in front of us and find out whether we are all going to become well off when we go back to Blighty." The office building was partly demolished. The front had obviously been hit by a shell or bomb and was just a mass of rubble. The rear wall was still standing and it was very close to the hillside, which had long been cut away in order to create another vertical wall of solid rock backing on to the building. There were immediate questions from the rest of the crew. "What did you mean? Tell us all about it."

"Relax and enjoy yourselves." Dusty was very confident and in full control. "Unknown to the infantry, we are lucky to have made a friend of young Derry here, and he knows that there is a fortune in rubies stashed in a safe hidden behind the rear of this building. It is up for grabs as long as the Japs have not found it already. We are about to find that out. Paddy," to the 75 gunner, "Howe Easy, rear wall ahead, fire."

The 14lb high explosive shell hit the rear wall near to a door which seemed to give entry to the steep hillside behind. The door and part of the wall collapsed in a cloud of dust. "Is that anywhere near it, Derry?" The young Burmese nodded gravely. "Yes. The safe was just to the right of the door. Can I go and have a look?" "We'll go together," replied Dusty, "Come on, out you get." The two dismounted and walked over the rubble-strewn ground.

The rest of us watched through the nearest periscopes and I told them, "Keep an eye out for any Norfolks coming back and sticking their noses into it. This is for our tank only. We will all get a share of any loot we find. Dusty will play fair, but we must keep it dead quiet or else we can lose the lot!"

We could see both Dusty and Derry coming back towards the tank. They were talking quite casually and then they mounted and climbed back into their seats. "Well, we've found the safe but it's locked and apparently quite sound. This is where your AP comes in, Paddy. Clear the breech, Tug, so we can look down the barrel and be sure to hit the target. You, Nick, climb us up and on to the office floor so that we are half a length from the rock wall." Nick revved the engine, engaged a low gear and started to climb over the rubble in front of us. Tug Wilson lowered the breech-locking mechanism and removed the HE shell that he had previously inserted, replacing it in its packing tube and into the rack behind him.

The tank rocked from side to side as it slowly climbed to the level of the office floor and across the broken bricks that covered it. We moved forward until we had almost entered the gap in the rear wall and were facing the front of a huge steel safe. "There you are, Paddy, you are now a locksmith. You need to blow the hinges, so that the door falls off. It's a precision job and you should line up your barrel and check the accuracy of the lay by looking through the barrel before you load with AP. Ask Nick to move the tank if necessary. OK?" "Roger, wilco," was Paddy's laconic reply.

I could see the 75mm gun being lined up with Paddy using the sights that would be slightly offset from the barrel. At normal ranges this discrepancy would not matter, but when we needed to fire accurately to break a safe hinge, the need to look down the barrel and see the exact spot to hit was vital. The two lads on the 75mm were in their element and highly excited. Paddy told Tug, "I can see the top of the hinge through the sights, but you must tell me where to move the gun so that you can see the hinge through the barrel." Tug peered down the 4inch wide, rifled bore. "You're almost spot on. Traverse a fraction to the left. Stop. A shade more. Stop. That is it. We can't miss, now."

"Right," said Dusty, "load AP and fire when ready." The 75 roared and when the dust settled we could see that the safe had been rocked in its foundations. The top right hinge was badly damaged but the door was still firmly closed. "That's good, do the same for the lower hinge now." And our amateur cracksmen, using this novel persuader, followed the same procedure.

Again the 75mm belched flame and noise with a 14lb armour piercing shell. And again we could see the damage it had done to the safe door and hinge. We could now see that both the hinges had been broken open but the door remained closed, held possibly by the catch on the left side of the door. It was a tough one. "Right, you two, see if you can sort out that latch. Have another go with AP." Paddy seemed to know what was required. It now looked as if the safe had been set in concrete in a specially cut hole in the rock face. This rough treatment had had the effect of loosening it in its setting and the door appeared to be very shaky. We only needed one more shell. The third shot was enough to sheer off the steel catch and open the door like a can of corned beef. "Everyone remain where you are. Derry come with me." Dusty was still keeping full control.

The two of them climbed out of the tank and stood at the front of the opened safe. As the dust was still settling around them, we could see Derry nod to Dusty and they both leaned forward with their hands going into the safe. They were both smiling as they pulled out a few leather bags with knotted thongs tied round the necks and placed them in a neat pile on the ground. "We're in luck," I told the rest of the crew, just as Dusty called out to me to join him outside. "Come here, Jimmy, and bring a couple of empty 75 tubes. Make it three, there's more in here."

I climbed out, carrying the three papier maché tubes, which had, until now, been holding the three AP shells that had been used. Dusty had opened one of the leather pouches and he showed me the contents. It was filled with the most beautiful, rich red rubies that I had been trying to imagine during the past few weeks. "Congratulations, Derry," I said, shaking him by the hand. "This is what you knew? It is good to know you!" I laughed with him. "Let's get them packed and into the tank." Just then, there was a burst of small arms fire. Not directly at us, but it sounded like Jap rifle fire from a few hundred yards away. We each grabbed a tube and stuffed the numerous filled leather pouches into them. I could only see a few papers left inside the broken safe before we climbed back into the tank. Dusty was on the ball as usual.

"Right, lads. Stow the tubes in the rack with the other ammunition and Nick, you pull us back about twenty yards, still facing the safe." This was soon done. "75, Howe Easy, target around the safe ahead, three rounds, fire."

The first high explosive shell exploded at the same time as we heard the bang from the firing. Two more followed very quickly and we saw the cliff wall break and crumble down on to the broken safe.

"Fox 2, are you having problems?" It was the voice of the Norfolk Major.

"Fox 2, small problem, now resolved, thank you. Are you OK?" Dusty had timed it all well and given the right answer. "Fox 2, yes, we have now cleared this area and are proceeding into the town. Are you ready to move with us?"

"Fox 2, yes, wilco. Fox 2 Baker, report. Fox 2 Baker, over."

Corporal Kenny replied instantly. "Fox 2 Baker, have been working with our friends and cleared five bunkers. All OK. Where are you now? Over." "Fox 2 Baker, am near the mine office. Join me here and we will advance with friends, over." "Fox 2 Baker. Wilco. Out."

He soon rejoined us as the Norfolks prepared to enter the town. They advanced in open order with fixed bayonets, confident that they had the measure of the retreating Japanese. We had become used to the idea that they never seemed to want to give themselves up as prisoners. If they had shown any sign of wanting to do so, we would have been very suspicious. In the early days at Imphal, there had been a few Japs who had walked towards us with their hands held high, apparently in surrender, only to throw grenades at the naïve young men who moved to accept their surrender. The lesson was quickly learned and any other volunteer 'prisoners' were treated as hostile. We had seen no such volunteers since we crossed into Burma.

The remainder of the day was spent in probing into the cantonment area and the town centre. The Norfolks worked very well with us. In fact, it was a case of mutual support. They prevented any odd Jap from trying to reach the two tanks and we were able to give heavy support when they came up against any bunker positions. There was very little action after we left the industrial area. The Major soon came to the conclusion that there had been only about 150 enemy acting as a rearguard, whilst the main force had continued up the road to Lashio. The much depleted population of Maymyo came out into the roads and made us welcome with local fruit, which was very well received by us all. One of them was Derry's uncle and they had an emotional reunion, chattering away in their own tongue.

Uncle Pwe had had a difficult time while at Mandalay, mainly because he had been required by the Japanese to organise supplies of food for a sick and starving mass of soldiery. There had been plenty of fruit available, but that had not been helpful for those who were sick with intestinal problems. Their main demands had been for rice, but that was in short supply. He had received rough treatment from both the Japanese and from the local population, who believed that he was working against their interests. The move to Maymyo had been both an escape from trouble and an opportunity to make a fresh start in business as soon as the fighting had finished.

Derry told us that he had been invited to remain with his uncle and to take a part in the business. He had explained that he was now in the British Army, showing him his pistol, and that he was a member of a tank crew which had helped to beat the Japanese in northern Burma. He did not mention the visit to his old office at the ruby mine. He assured the older man that he would return to Maymyo as soon as he was released from Army service. Dusty had raised an eyebrow when he heard Derry's exaggerated account of his position. As far as we knew, he was a 'civilian attached' and should not really have been armed nor should he have been in our tank in action. We were not going to raise any query over his status. It had been very much in our interests to have him with us. All we needed now was to survive the rest of the War, though that seemed to be endless.

"Fox 2, report my signals, Fox 2, over." I heard the weak but readable signal in the voice of Major Dorman, who would be in or near Mandalay. He must have told his wireless operator to net on to our frequency as well as on the one he would have been using all day. Alan Fenner could easily 'flick' over to ours when told to do so.

"Fox 2, strength three, Fox 2, over."

"Fox 2, put your number nine on, over."

"Fox 2, wilco. Please wait, out."

This was a nasty one. Dusty had not yet reported the loss of his Troop Leader's tank with seven dead. He had been too keen to press on to the mine for our own selfish reasons. Now he had to get out of this one. "Dusty," I called to him through my porthole, "Major Dorman is calling number nine. Will you take it?" He climbed up to the turret and picked up his headset, pressing the mike switch.

"Fox 2, over." The Major's voice came through immediately.

"Fox 2, where is your number nine, put him on, over." He sounded very testy.

"Fox 2, regret to report that number nine and his crew lost to kame kaze. No other casualties. Operation completed successfully otherwise. Fox 2, over."

"Fox 2, Roger. Ask number nine footsloggers to speak to me. Fox 2 out."

Dusty climbed down to the ground and walked over to the Norfolks Major.

"Excuse me, sir. My Squadron O/C, Major Dorman, is asking if you will speak to him. Will you take it on my set or your own?" He came over to our tank and held the headset to his ear.

"Fox 2, over." We could all hear Major Dorman's assertive voice in reply, "Fox 2, what is all this about losing a crew? Over."

The Norfolk Major gave a very brief report of the ambush and the result. He seemed to accept that there was a loss of security by giving his report on the wireless but he made some attempt to encode parts of the message. He finished with the comment, "Our job is completed and I propose to return with your support to our start-point this morning. Over." Our Squadron Leader obviously agreed. "Fox 2, roger. Will see you then. Fox 2 out."

He turned to Dusty. "You heard all that, Sergeant? We have eight wounded here. Can you help by giving them a lift as far as our trucks that are at the other side of the town?" This was readily agreed and the men were lifted on to the engine covers of the two tanks. A crew member stayed on the outside with them. Dusty's comment on the conversation between the two majors highlighted his cynical view of commissioned officers. "Dorman made it obvious what he thinks of a factual report from an experienced sergeant. A load of balls that has to be checked with another officer, preferably of equal rank." He had always questioned the way in which authority was used and abused. He had a very high IQ and this often showed up in cynical comment. Perhaps that was the reason he had not been put forward for a commission.

Within a few minutes the entire force were all reunited with their vehicles and mounted ready to go home for the night. Although we left Maymyo in the daylight, it was dark and well after the time for stand-to when we arrived back in our box. There was a hot meal awaiting the returning tankmen and we were soon bedded down for some sleep. 2 Troop was excused guard duties that night after the trauma of losing their Troop Leader and a third of their strength. The report of the Squadron Leader's day in Mandalay would have to wait until the next day. The secret of our success with the rubies remained with the seven men of Fox 2 Able.

This was locked into our minds after Dusty had had a talk to the other six men of his crew during the next morning.

"Right. This is vital to you all. The three tubes of goodies have been sealed and locked into the bottom of the 75 ammo rack. No one touches them, and that includes me, until I give the word. That will be when we get to Rangoon or when the tank has to be replaced because of damage. They are the property of Jimmy, Derry and me. There are five bags of rubies sealed into a separate, marked tube locked in the same place. They are for the rest of you, Nick, Paddy, Tug, John and Les. You will each have one bag, worth, I am told by Derry, about £1000. That should set you up for an easier life after the War. Now, this is the really important part: You will forget the word 'ruby'. If any one of you leaks any information about our little jaunt yesterday to any outsider, I will personally finish him off. And I mean that! It could result in us all losing what we have gained as well as being court-martialled. Any questions so far?"

Tug was the first to move. "Yes, Sarge. I agree with your threat to top anyone who splits on us. Will you tell us, did you kill Blondie Benton?"

Dusty turned towards him. "You will never know from me but you can be sure that I will stop any of you who even thinks about splitting on us. Any more?" The others were quiet so I added my halfpen'orth. "There is no benefit for any of us to leak the 'gen' but I will support any control to keep it quiet." Dusty burst in with, "Don't pussyfoot about, Jimmy, if you mean that you will help to sort anyone who blabs, then say so. You sound like a bloody schoolmaster!" I nodded and stayed silent.

During the morning we all attended a squadron parade where Major Dorman gave his opinion of the previous day's efforts.

"Stand at ease, men. Yesterday, B Squadron had some real success. My tank, which represented the Squadron, entered Mandalay where we were able to support the infantry in a number of actions. We fired 40 rounds of 75mm HE on to Japanese positions dug into Fort Dufferin and helped to clear that area. Then we had a request to help a company of Dogras who were moving to clear the Japanese from the civilian internment camp. When we arrived at the gate, the commandant had already refused to open the gates or release the internees, who were mostly Burmese ladies with babies. I was very pleased to accept the Dogra's invitation to persuade him to change his mind. This was done by the tank being driven up to the main gate and flattening it in front of the Japanese reception committee."

The silent men burst into cheers at this picture of the Major asserting himself.

"We then fired a burst of Browning over their heads and their weapons were thrown down. The waiting group of young and middle-aged ladies, some of mixed race, then started to walk to the gates. They smiled and waved to us all and slowly made their way into the town. Half of them were carrying babies. I was told by one of these ladies that they had been treated with courtesy throughout their stay in the camp, that their only real problem had been the lack of sufficient food, especially food suitable for the babies. Incidentally, the babies had been fathered by the husbands of the internees and not by the Japanese, as you might have imagined. They seem to have had respect for the married women and never molested them but they had treated single women as chattels. You all saw some of the so-called 'comforts girls' who escaped from them in Imphal.

"There was no more action where we could be of use so we turned for home. On the way we loaded up with fruit, which you will all be able to enjoy with your tiffin today. That was not paid for with Squadron funds. The local people had not yet reverted to the Old Burmese or Indian rupees which I offered. They would only accept the notes printed and issued by the Japanese."

This raised a laugh from the men. "So, you see, I had to spend a sackful of the money you looted from that Jap mint in Shwebo.

Now, we come to the other B Squadron action yesterday. 2 Troop went to Maymyo with the Norfolks and were very successful in helping to clear a substantial Jap rearguard who were dug in, with orders to delay our advance and destroy any armoured vehicles. Sadly, they did that when a suicide bomber dropped from a tree on to the top of Lt. Dibble-Williams's tank. You all know that the entire crew was lost and the padre will be here this afternoon to hold a short service, when we will thank God for their lives. Sergeant Miller took command of 2 Troop and continued with the action with outstanding success. That is exactly what I expect from him, and any one else in the same position, and I congratulate him on his achievement. He will continue to be Troop Leader until I have another officer ready for the position. That will take a little time. I hope to have a replacement tank and crew with us within 48 hours.

Our immediate orders are that we remain here for the time being.

When ready, we will move south towards the oil fields and clear any enemy that we can find in the central plain around Mount Popa. We can expect the first monsoon rains to start during the next few weeks, so you will see that there is a degree of urgency about our advance towards Rangoon. Unless we can clear the capital and open the port of Rangoon before the rains really start, there could be delays in getting the supplies that we require. We have not won yet! There will be a medical inspection for all of us after the church service. No exceptions. That is all."

# Chapter 7

# *1982*
# *The End of Our War*

The Detective Inspector interrupted. "Thank you for all you have told me so far. Before you go any further, will you tell me what you know about Miller's love life, if any, and whether any of the crew were involved with women, or men, if that was the case? I need all the background that I can find if I'm going to identify this killer."

---

It might seem strange to you, now in 1982, but we were not obsessed with sex in those days. During the War most of us were involved in occasional conversations about our love lives. We had either a wife or girl friend at home and would put a photograph at the head of our bed when in barracks, and we often dreaded the thought of having our bodies damaged enough to prevent any sex in the future. I know that some of the men had problems with their strong sex drives and would seek some form of relief. The few who were able to get close to a local bibi would usually regret it later when the MO confirmed that they had caught a 'packet'. They were rare enough to raise a question in the minds of their mates when they were sent to a hospital for treatment, which was described to us as being so horrific that we were put off the idea of casual sex for a very long time.

I have already told you that I met my wife in Burma but I was an 'innocent' in those days. I'm quite sure that Dusty Miller was not a homosexual and I have never heard him say that he had had any sexual encounters. You must remember that our attitudes were affected by many factors at that time. We might make jokes about 'poofters' but there was a strong law against any sexual activity between men. It was a chargeable offence. It was also an offence to catch VD, as it was considered to be a 'self-inflicted wound'. After a year in the Imphal area of eastern India and in northern Burma, we had all suffered from the poor conditions. No one seemed to avoid at least one debilitating disease, some had three or four, which reduced any desire for sex and could have had a permanent effect. The poor diet and living in the open air during the monsoons all added to the result. No, I am not aware of Dusty having any close relationships. I would say that I was probably the nearest to being classified as his friend when he was in the Carbs.

Our tank crew stayed together intact throughout the next few weeks. We seemed to be either in action or travelling south every day. All the tanks were showing signs of nearing the point of complete breakdown because of this. There were new engines and 37mm and 75mm gun barrels, all made available, ammunition and food supplies were dropped to us at a variety of 'dropping zones' on the route. Whenever possible, our tanks were moved on Diamond T transporters. This rested both the clapped-out old machines and the weary crews. 2 Troop received a replacement tank, with a corporal as tank commander pending the arrival of a trained officer, and Dusty stayed in command of the troop. No officer arrived in 2 Troop until after we had reached Rangoon.

We were involved in many small actions as we travelled the 300-odd miles south. I remember seeing Mount Popa, which is the granite core of an ancient volcano, sticking up out of the flat plain. The walls were sheer cliffs dotted with clumps of trees and were an ideal spot for a Japanese company to commit hara kiri. It was about half a mile round the base with a flat top, and was full of ready-made sites for machine guns. A frontal attack by our infantry would have been very expensive in casualties and half of B Squadron was placed round the hill. The tanks all faced inwards and spent a morning firing at any possible target. The return fire from Jap machine guns was reduced from being heavy to the point where it faded out completely. After another ten minutes of 75mm attention, the infantry moved towards the cliffs and stood in the open. Despite being obvious targets, there was no return fire and they started to climb up the cliffs. We heard the odd shot from small arms as they met some resistance but we saw them waving from the top of the hill an hour later.

Our next actions were around the oilfields of Yenanyaung. The retreating British Army had destroyed these in 1942 and they had not been of any use to the Japanese during the past three years. We saw very few Burmese in that area, which appeared to be desolate apart from groups of retreating enemy. The infantry seemed to be able to sort out most of these without our help. After Yenanyaung we continued to move south. It was a race against time as the rains were beginning. We might have an inch fall in an hour, turning the road into a bog. This would be followed by a few hours of brilliant sunshine, which returned the road into a dustbowl. As the days followed on, the rains became more frequent and prolonged until we arrived in Rangoon.

The reaction set in. More than a year of fighting had now come to an end. We drove to the docks, where we were told to strip the tanks of all our own kit. The guns were dismantled ready for disposal and we never saw the old Lees again. They had mostly been driven over rough ground for some 2000 miles on their own tracks. They had been our homes and our workshops for a long time. We would miss them. Their guns had been so very effective in action that we had many messages of congratulation and thanks from the higher echelons of the victorious 14$^{th}$ Army.

This was where we said farewell to our Burmese friend. Derry had copied Dusty and me in packing his load of rubies into a spare rucksack and fixing it to his army belt. Major Dorman paid him for the months that he had spent with us and thanked him personally on behalf of us all. He really had done a good job and deserved our congratulations. We were sorry to see him go but he had plans for his own future. He had told me that he was going to deposit his loot in a bank until the city returned to a more normal economic life. He was not going to join his uncle in Maymyo, as he expected that there would be some police enquiries when it was found that the mine had been robbed. He preferred to be able to leave the country at short notice if it became necessary.

B Squadron personnel were then put on to a troopship from Rangoon to Calcutta and entrained for a long journey to the Central Deccan. They arrived at the old cavalry barracks in Ahmednagar, where the remainder of the Regiment were collecting together for the first time since they left Madras in 1943. Many of them were overdue for repatriation and the camp was in a state of upheaval, with farewell parties, new arrivals from the Poona Depot, new Sherman tanks being prepared for training the new crews, and leave in India for all those who had been in Burma.

All our old crew were sent to Ootacamund for fourteen days leave. 'Ooty' was a hill station in the Nilgiri Hills, to the west of Madras. The old rack-and-pinion train chugged up the winding track, covering the coaches and passengers in sooty smoke as it slowly moved higher up the mountainside. It was such a delight to be in a climate similar to that of the UK after nearly four years of tropical heat. We all rapidly regained our appetites and the feeling of wellbeing was given a huge boost by our hearing the news that the first atom bomb had been dropped on Japan.

This meant that we would not be making a sea-borne invasion of Malaya after all. Nor would we have to fight our way across much of Asia until we could invade Japan. We could at last really believe that we had a good chance of survival and a return to 'civvy street'. Our host, Frank Leembruggen, a Dutch tea planter in Ooty, gave us all a wonderful celebration dinner, which was followed by a dance at the Ootacamund Club in the town. My only memory of that is the fact that I had missed the main group for the return to my bed and had to walk alone, at midnight, through two miles of forest where tigers had been reported only the previous week. I ran most of the way.

---

The Inspector butted in again. "Yes, I understand how you all must have felt when you heard the news of the end of hostilities, but what happened to Miller after that leave? When did he return to the UK? Did you see him again after he left the Regiment? Did you ever hear from him, with a Christmas card or anything? Surely someone must have bumped into him at some depot or transit camp before he was demobilised?"

---

He was still with B Squadron after the leave. In fact, I was still in his crew, helping to train the replacements to the Squadron. Nick McGowan had gone into hospital with malaria. Paddy Wills had gone in with dysentery and Tug Wilson had been moved to another tank. As the Shermans only needed a four-man-crew, there was a lot of sorting to be done. We were kept very busy and yet we found time for sport and recreation. The good food and water were no longer in short supply and the general air of well-being was obvious to all.

Soon after being re-equipped with Sherman tanks, the whole Regiment moved north to some Victorian barracks at Risalpur, North West Frontier Province. This was near the Khyber Pass, the historical area of fighting the wild tribes between the two Wars. We were back to blanco and bullshit. If it moves, polish it. If it doesn't, paint it. We spent Christmas 1945 at Risalpur and we all had a good old-fashioned Christmas dinner, served by the officers. This was followed by a camel race, which I won. I was helped by the fact that half the men taking part had drunk the extra pint of beer and were unable to make their camels sit down for them to mount them prior to racing them round the football pitch. I had had a few minutes training from a regular rider of the camels. He taught me how to make the secret hissing sound whilst pulling on the single rein of the standing creature. I was on to its back and away round the course before most of the others had found a ladder, or willing helpers, in order to mount the weird creatures. My prize was yet another pint of beer.

Despite the fun and games of that day, the newly applied disciplines and poor management from some of the new officers helped to create a critical attitude and it was sad to see the morale of the troops go so low. There was a lack of communication between the officers and men that came to a head when the other ranks refused to eat a main course of canned pilchards when it was offered for the fourteenth consecutive tiffin.

That was at the time when I went into hospital with a whole range of complaints, including rheumatism, stomach bugs and other nasties that had caught up with me. I was sent to the Poona BGH and I never rejoined the Regiment. Eventually I was put on to a ship going to Blighty. I was a hospital patient, excused all duties, and I was delighted to find that there were many of my old friends from the Carabiniers going home on repatriation, but Dusty Miller was not amongst them. He seemed to have disappeared from the face of the earth. I asked about him but he had not been seen by anyone since I went into hospital. When I got home, I wrote to him a few times but had no response. Sorry, I can't help you there.

---

"So what did you do after you were demobilised? You had a fortune in rubies. You would have had more money than you could spend in a lifetime. And now you are running a hardware shop. What happened?" The Inspector wanted to know everything.

"I had a shock after I had been home a few days and when I decided to open the rucksack full of rubies. I waited until I was alone in my room and my parents were out for the evening, then I opened the first bag. I can still feel the shock that I received when I found that the bag was full of sand. In a panic I opened the second bag and found the same sand. It looked as though it was from the Punjabi desert and I had eaten enough of that to recognise it. When the winds blew, it was impossible to avoid getting it into my clothes and food. In brief, all the bags were the same. I had been robbed.

"I guessed that it had happened when I was with the Regiment at Risalpur, but I had no proof. I can only think that someone who knew the whole story, probably one of the tank crew we had in Burma, had robbed me. Anyone else would have taken the rucksack and contents without trying to conceal the theft for me to find at a later date. I was sickened at the time but that was thirty-six years ago. After we were married in 1948, Tina and I started our hardware business and we have succeeded through sheer hard work and no help from anyone."

The Inspector nodded in sympathy. "I can imagine how you felt at the time. You might still have to explain to us whether you were entitled to own those rubies, but it was a long time ago. I'm more concerned in tracing your Dusty Miller and eliminating him from the list of suspects. We'll leave it there. If you think of anything more that could be helpful, please phone me. I might need to speak to you again, and your wife, so thank you for all your help to date."

# Chapter 8

# 13th April 1946
# *Peacetime Murder*

Despite the shortage of many staple foods and most consumer durables, the streets of Peterborough were busy with van deliveries and salesmen moving around the shopping area. Many of the agents and salesmen were wearing their demobilisation suits. It was a rare sight to see a well-groomed young man in a dark pinstriped suit, wearing a black homburg hat and carrying a well-used brief case and a rolled umbrella. He did not go unnoticed by the other reps, especially the two who were waiting outside the biggest sweetshop in Market Street, where they were enjoying the warming spring sunshine.

"See that, Mike?" said Fred Wilson of Mars, "I reckon he's an ex-officer, don't you?" The Cadbury's man, Mike Sturdy, grunted. "Probably. We've all got to make our name again after six years away from it all. As long as they keep sweet rationing, we will be all right with allocating our quotas. But I wouldn't guess what it is that he is selling." He shrugged his shoulders as if he couldn't care less. "There are times when I wish that I was back in the Regiment despite all the bull. It was a good life and you knew where you were all the time." Fred laughed at this. "But you were the one who was always saying 'roll on the boat' while we were waiting to come home. Come off it, Mike, you don't have Japs shooting at you here, now do you?"

"No," Mike admitted grudgingly, "but, if they increase the ration any more, I reckon that there will be some reaction from the public, like widows refusing to take their full ration and we'll have to start selling again." Fred laughed. "Don't be so bloody negative, Mike. I remember that we were paid better commissions before the War when we had to go out and sell hard. It's going to come back to that again, and soon."

They watched the homburg go into the estate agents' office on the opposite side of the road. They could see the 'ex-officer' speak to the receptionist at her desk and then sit down to wait.

"Isn't that the feller who was arrested for interfering with kids the other week?" Fred was only mildly curious. "I read something in the *Telegraph* about it. The estate agent, Fyle, I mean. Wasn't he released after a few days of questions? Lack of evidence, they said." Mike was still feeling negative. "I don't know," he replied. "I've no time for that sort of muck. He deserves all he gets." At that point the sweet salesman, who had been inside with the buyer, walked out of the shop and nodded to them both. "You're next, Fred."

Across the road, the receptionist was intrigued with the waiting representative. She had been in this job for only three months and had not yet learned to be the impassable dragon who could put up barriers between visitors and her boss. Perhaps she had been properly trained to help in the communications. "It's a lovely day to be out and about," she remarked pleasantly. "Do you often come to Peterborough, Mr – er Smith?" looking at the card he had given her. "No," he replied, "this is my first time. Will Mr Fyle be free soon? I have another appointment in town but I would like to resolve the housing problem first." The girl smiled again. "I'll just go in and let him know that you are still waiting."

She rose and went into the rear office, carefully closing the door after her. "Mr Fyle, Mr Smith is asking how long he will have to wait as he has another call to make in the town. I'm sorry, but I thought he was a sales rep but I now think he is looking for a house." The estate agent glanced up from the papers on his desk. "Right, Sally, you'd better show him in. Wait a minute. While he's in here, will you go to the café and get the sandwiches? I liked the ham we had last week. See if they have any more, will you?" She took the ten-shilling note from him and walked back to her desk. "You can see Mr Fyle now, Mr Smith," showing him through to the private office. One minute later she had slipped on a light coat and gone out of the front door.

"Good morning, Mr Smith, how can I help you?" Peter Fyle had switched into his selling mode, full of charm and assessing what price of house would interest this prospect.

"I'm moving into the Peterborough district, partly for business reasons, and I would like to find something suitable within ten miles of here. A family house with five or six beds in at least an acre of land would be possible. Can you show me what is available?"

The estate agent was mentally rubbing his hands together. Hot prospect! "What sort of price range are we thinking about?" The prospect shrugged his shoulders. "Price is not a problem. I'll pay the going rate for the right property. I'll know it when I see it." Peter Fyle actually began to rub his hands together until he stopped suddenly and applied some self-control. "You have picked a good time to come to Peterborough, Mr Smith. I have just received instructions on two such properties this week, and I can arrange to show them to you very soon. These brochures give most of the details, if you care to glance through them. I see that you live in Yorkshire. Are you down here for a few days? When would you like to view them?"

There was no hesitation once the prospective customer had had a brief look at the leaflets. "This afternoon. I'm only here until this evening, so time is of an essence. Let's go and see them after fifteen hundred hours." The military timing and decisive statement left no doubt that the client was tending to take control of the interview.

"Ah, well," thought Peter Fyle, "they are all good buying signals." "Of course, Mr Smith, if you can be here at 3pm, I'll be pleased to take you to see both of them. I have another appointment at lunchtime, otherwise I would take you to our local hotel for some refreshment."

"Not to bother, Mr Fyle, I have things to do but I will be here at 1500 hrs." They shook hands and he walked out of the premises, noting that Sally had not yet returned to her desk.

---

At 6 o'clock that evening the duty sergeant at the Bridge Street Police Station in Peterborough took a call from Sally Webster, secretary to Peter Fyle, estate agent, and the recent subject of enquiries about a sex offence. "But there must be something wrong, Sergeant. Mr Fyle assured me that he would be back in the office before 5 o'clock, when we close. He was only taking a client to see two houses near Wansford and he knows that I should have been away an hour ago. He has always phoned me if there has been any delay in getting back to the office before now." There was a plaintive raising of her voice. A touch of panic, thought Sergeant Meadows.

"It's a bit early to be getting too worried, young lady. I suggest that you lock up and take the keys home with you. If you give me your home address and phone number, I'll record it here in case your boss contacts us. What were the two houses he was going to see?" Sally gave him her details and the two addresses as Castor House and Sacrewell House, two well-known houses standing in their own grounds. They had both been empty and for sale for a few weeks. "He will probably contact you at your home later this evening. My guess is that he had got involved with a possible quick sale and forgotten that you will be anxious. Will you ring in here tomorrow morning, after you've opened the office, and let me know what has happened?" Sally murmured agreement and did as she had been advised.

## 14th April 1946

Sergeant Meadows was giving Inspector Deeping his verbal confirmation of the points in the previous day's desk report. "You see, sir, I would normally have sent her on her way when she reported a missing person who was overdue for only one hour. But I know that Peter Fyle had been questioned about the child abuse case, and even though he has been released, the records show that he could well have been guilty but that there is not enough evidence to charge him. Sally Webster has just phoned in to say that she has been to the office this morning but that she can't raise any sign of her boss. She is sure that he has not been there since she left to go home last night and she knows that his wife is away and nobody answers the phone at his home. Do you think it is worth visiting the two properties that he was going to show to his client yesterday?"

"I'll see to that," said the Inspector, "and let me know immediately if you hear anything more." He returned to his office and picked up the telephone.

One hour later Inspector Deeping received a call from the local constable who was based in the village of Castor. He had visited the two houses that were advertised for sale and had seen the legs of a man protruding from under a table in the kitchen of Sacrewell House. This was at the rear of the house and they might not have been seen from a casual glance into the window. "Shall I try to enter the property, sir?" he asked. "No. Stay there and wait until I join you." The inspector had the bit between his teeth. He still smarted under the fact that he had had to release Fyle when he was sure that he had been concealing some pertinent details about the child abuse case. The publicity had reached the national papers and he had been pressed for an explanation of his lack of success. This could open up the whole enquiry again, as well as the national interest.

After visiting Peter Fyle's office in order to collect a spare set of keys for Sacrewell House, the Inspector joined the waiting policeman and they were soon in the kitchen, looking at the body of a man lying on his back. A wooden knifehandle was protruding from his chest and bloodstained shirt. "No doubt who he is," grunted Inspector Deeping, who had interviewed Fyle over a period of days. "This is now a murder enquiry."

The team which was assembled to investigate the crime was full of enthusiasm and was given all the support they needed. They quickly traced the two confectionery salesmen, who confirmed Sally Webster's description of the Mr Smith in the homburg. His business card proved to have a fictitious address in Yorkshire. The only fingerprints on it were from the estate agent and his secretary. The murder weapon appeared to be a well-crafted handmade paperknife, cut from a single piece of bamboo. It had obviously been hand carved and sanded, with the skin of the bamboo made razor-sharp for the three inches from the tip of the blade.

The weapons expert had commented that it was the first time that he had seen such a knife in Britain. "There were plenty of them in the Burmese jungles. Made and used by the local levies who helped us in the 14th Army. They used to harden the sharp skin by drying it in the sun. Some chaps even tried to shave with them, but I never managed to do that. They used to make large quantities of them, between two and three feet long, called 'punjis', and stick the handles into the ground with the sharp end pointing up at an angle. They were used by both sides in the War. Anyone stepping on one in the night, on a jungle path, would be put out of action. They could penetrate the sole of a British army boot, so they were even more effective on men with bare feet or wearing the Japanese issue canvas boots. Nasty things. This one has been made as a dagger, with a definite handle. It looks like native Asian craftsmanship, but it might have been made by a Westerner who had studied the subject. It will be difficult, if not impossible, to trace."

That proved to be true.

After many weeks of enquiries into the death of the estate agent Peter Fyle, the coroner's report recorded "Murder by person or persons unknown". The file on the child sex abuse case remained open. The national and local press had a few days of headlines referring to the two cases, but the lack of any more news allowed them to fade into oblivion. Even the two sweet salesmen soon stopped referring to the murder when they met occasionally at the Market Street call. Mike Sturdy's comment on the case was typical of those heard in the local bars and cafés: "He deserved it and it's good riddance."

## Chapter 9

# April 1947
# Another Murder

Jock McFee knew that he was going to succeed when he addressed the meeting of his Union in Glasgow that Sunday. The local train from Motherwell would take him and his cronies to what was to be the most decisive evening of his career to date.

The national press had highlighted the likelihood of the Scottish Union of Transport Workers starting an indefinite strike in support of their claims for a shorter working week, two weeks' paid holiday and a high guaranteed wage. They had built the General Secretary, John McFee, up to be an ogre, an unstoppable force, who intended to create havoc throughout Scotland. Interviews with representatives of the employers' organisations had given the opinions of the majority of citizens. No one really wanted to see a return to the problems of the thirties, with strikes causing delays in the distribution of essential foodstuffs and materials, so necessary for the continuing growth of all the industry that had started with the end of the War. No one, that is, except the Moscow-trained Red Union activists.

"Stand clear of the rails." The voice on the tannoy warned all those standing on the platform that the express train from Edinburgh to Glasgow was about to rush non-stop through the Motherwell station. The whistle and noise of the rapidly approaching train had that high pitch which would lower as it passed, the 'Doppler effect'. Very few passengers took any notice of the tannoy and the majority continued to talk whilst remaining near the edge of the platform.

McFee and his fellow Union official, Andrew Reid, stopped their animated conversation about how they were going to rig the vote and waited until the train had passed and they would be able to hear each other again. Reid glanced up at the station clock to satisfy himself that the express was on time and he did not notice that a stranger, a man aged around twenty-five, had moved nearer to them and was standing with his back near McFee. It all happened so quickly. As the train came into the station at nearly 60mph the stranger bent down as if to tie his shoelace, his bottom hit McFee's right thigh and he was catapulted on to the track immediately in front of the engine. No one heard the scream. The Union man was killed instantly and his body whisked away from the platform by the express engine.

"Bloody Hell!" Andrew Reid had turned back towards his colleague just in time to see him cartwheeling off the platform to be smashed by the train.

In the crowd of waiting passengers there were a few who had been shocked by the same sight, and they moved forward to where McFee had been standing. The young man with the shoelace problem stood upright and, at the same time, took two paces forward and into the crowd. He had not been noticed. In the flap that followed the killing, he was able to drift to the rear of the melée whilst the railway officials reacted to the disaster. They noted the details of as many of the people on the platform as possible and these were later summoned to the official enquiry into the "accident".

Only two witnesses expressed the opinion that they thought that there had been three people standing and talking together and they could not give any description of the third man. Reid admitted that it was possible that a third man had been close to him and McFee, but he could not be certain. The doubts about this were sufficient for the coroner to give an open verdict and for the police, who were aware of earlier threats of violence to the victim, to record a possible murder. Despite widespread advertising for information about the 'third man', there was no useful information and the report was filed as unsolved.

# Chapter 10

# *April 1948 And Another*

Brigadier Charles McAlister Fitzburn was feeling rather pleased with himself. He had had a good day at the Chepstow races. He was feeling comfortable after having enjoyed a well planned and cooked pheasant dinner from his deep freezer accompanied with claret from his own pre-War cellar. It had been organised by his wife Felicity before she left to attend a function arranged by her pet charity in Chepstow. Even on the few occasions when they dined together alone, they enjoyed high standards, and his wife had always been able to confirm his view that he deserved to continue with the creature comforts that his station demanded.

Whilst the table was being cleared by Mabel, the elderly retainer, the Brigadier went for his usual stroll through the gardens of his country house, set in almost ten acres on the edge of Mynydd Bach, near the Chepstow racecourse. He drew on his cigar and relished the after-taste of the blend of flavours of tobacco, Courvoisier and coffee. It was a mild and pleasant evening.

At the age of 46 years, he could look back on a long period of achievement. He had enjoyed a good War, which had started when he was a major in the Intelligence Corps. No combat for him. His fluent French and German and quick wit had ensured his progress in the Army. For the first two years he had been occupied with the tracing and internment of potential spies and his long list of successes had helped with his steady promotion. He had gained the nick-name of 'Fritzburn' after he and his team had locked up more than twenty men and women with German relatives, whether there was any proof of disloyalty or not. His persistence and animal cunning had carried him through so many enquiries and investigations that he had begun to believe in his own invulnerability and he spent the remaining years of the War on counter-espionage and continuing to climb the ladder.

He and his team were quite relaxed when mixing among all levels of society. They were the 'ears' in the widespread advertisements saying "Walls Have Ears" and they were used in a number of ways to entrap careless talkers, mischief-makers and often tired and innocent little girls and older men and women working in armament factories or government offices. They could always justify their work by claiming that they were preventing the enemy from gaining information and punishing those who were guilty of weakness or disloyalty – even when it required a spot of seduction or bribery. The methods might not be anything to be proud about, but the results justified the means.

The Brigadier wandered down the winding path through the shrubbery to the place where he could see down towards the racecourse in the bright moonlight. It really was a glorious evening. He thought again about the most productive of his years in the Forces, his spell in Germany immediately after the cessation of hostilities. "A misnomer, if ever there was one", he thought to himself. "VE Day might well have marked the official end of the war in Europe but the hostilities have continued for years."

He had used that time in Germany to extend his control of a growing number of investigators who were looking firstly for the hierarchy of the Nazi government. They were then required to pursue the flow of leads into the black market activity of a host of minor criminals in the underworld where they had learned to operate. "It's a mass of opportunities," said one refugee, arrested for trying to sell some stolen gold artefacts.

The Brigadier had smiled wryly and mentally agreed with him. He had already started to accumulate stolen property in a warehouse, which was guarded by a section of a locally based British infantry battalion. His team had sorted these goods into piles according to their value, crated ready for disposal. He smiled with some pride in his own arrangements for the disposal of a large proportion of the gold and a few invaluable paintings. They were stored in another warehouse whilst in transit to Switzerland, where they remained in the name of Herr August Gruber. This had been his alias during another successful operation of spy-catching. It had been necessary to pay his WO2, Sergeant Major Bill Simpson, a large sum to turn a blind eye to the alterations in the records and that was his only mistake. The bribe had not been large enough. The Sergeant Major had then tried to siphon off his own pile of valuables, but he had been stopped by the Military Police when driving the full 3-tonner to his own private storeroom.

During the enquiries and subsequent court martial, Bill Simpson had tried to minimise his guilt by blaming the Brigadier for starting the rot, but he had quickly found that he could not prove his words. The Brigadier's hoard had already been sold on the thriving black market and the proceeds, in excess of one million pounds sterling, were safely in a numbered account in Switzerland. The warehouse records were correct and the only apparent losses were in the captured 3-tonner.

Fitzburn had certainly had a few moments of anxiety during the lengthy questioning before and during the court martial, but he had kept his nerve and admitted nothing. During one session he was pressured by the inquisitor, a fellow brigadier, to the point of being accused directly of "feathering his nest like all the others", but he had been in the dirty game of espionage for too long to be caught by this simple trap. He had used it too many times not to recognise it for what it was. "No," he thought, with a smug smile, "it was better to follow their advice and resign with a good name and a very comfortable income for life. I can live the life I want to and I don't have to answer to anyone. The only snag was the publicity in the press."

The media had certainly reported most of the questioning that he had experienced during the court martial, leaving no one in doubt that he was suspected of helping himself to a fortune in gold and that he still had that to enjoy. He had learned to accept that many of his fellow officers had dropped him from their invitation lists. The whole business had now started again when Simpson had been released after serving two years for his offence. The telephone had been ringing repeatedly during the past few days, with calls from most of the national papers. "It will soon settle down again, as it did the first time", he thought. "I just need to keep calm and not answer the phone."

He was just about to turn back towards the house when his animal instincts made him listen very carefully. The normal spring night sounds continued with the rustling, squeaking, and sighing of the wind, but there was something else. There was the sound of a dry twig cracking under pressure. He looked around and, for a split second, he could just make out the shape of a man standing under the laburnum and pointing something at him.

The heavy thud on his chest from the projectile knocked him backward into oblivion. Somewhere, on his way to the ground, one word escaped his lips: "God!" It could have been an involuntary reaction to the blow or possibly an expression of surprise at meeting his Maker when he was not prepared for it. The stranger reloaded his crossbow and walked carefully towards his victim. He waited with the weapon pointing down at him, looking for any sign of breathing. There was none. He then bent down and felt for a pulse on the wrist for another minute. Negative. His last move was to take hold of his first missile, rigid in the brigadier's chest, and snap it off close to the ribs. He then stood up and turned to walk away into the shrubbery.

Felicity Fitzburn arrived home by taxi at midnight after a successful evening with her friends and was surprised to find the dining room lights were still switched on. The table had been cleared and tidied. The kitchen showed that all the utensils had been washed and put away. Obviously Mabel had done her job and then retired to bed but where was Charles?

The next twenty minutes became a nightmare after she had awakened Mabel, to be told that her husband had enjoyed his dinner alone and then gone for his usual walk in the garden. "No, she had not seen or heard him return. Perhaps he had had a fall in the garden?" That settled it. Felicity Fitzburn slipped her feet into the gumboots and her arms into the Barbour coat at the kitchen door and ran down the path to look for her husband. Her torch had a new battery and made the path clear in the moonlight.

When she saw the crumpled figure on the ground near the laburnum tree, she assumed that he had had a heart attack and that the good life had caught up with him. She realised that she was wrong when the bleeding chest wound came to view in the light of the torch. His body was cold to the touch. Too late. Mabel had by that time decided to put some warm clothing on and follow her employer down the garden.

"Oh, ma'am," she wailed, "is he ill?"

The stiff upper lip of the Army wife came clearly to the fore, despite the heavy feeling within her. "No, he's dead, I'm afraid. We must get an ambulance and see a doctor. Will you go back to the house and phone for them, Mabel? I'll stay here with the Brigadier. Oh, and you'd better inform the police as well."

Three hours later the house and grounds were lit up, with police working through until the afternoon, searching the garden for a knife or something similar which could have caused the chest wound. Metal detectors were unsuccessful and it was only after the autopsy that the police realised that the piece of bamboo found embedded in the chest was a part of the fatal weapon. It had been skilfully pointed at the leading end and snapped off near the skin surface. The conclusion of the weapons expert, brought in to advise the police, was that they should be looking for a spear, arrow or knife made by a man who had some experience of making and using such primitive tools. "Someone who was in the jungles of the Far East," was his suggestion.

The thorough investigation over a period of months brought no useful facts. Ex-Sergeant Major Bill Simpson, recently released from gaol, was questioned at length but he was able to prove beyond any doubt that he had been in Newcastle on Tyne on the vital date of 13th April. Like the other "13th April murders", the facts were recorded as unsolved and a summary was included in the Crusoe files many years later.

Chapter 11

# *1982*
# *Ma Tina Mying*

Harry Bennet had a hunch that there was a lot more to be learned from Jimmy James. He had always believed that he should play any hunch that he received, whether it was weak or, like this one, irresistible. There were plenty of occasions in his life when he had been successful and his colleagues had said he was "lucky". He had been fully aware that he had merely listened to his "inner voice" and had acted upon the ideas that he had received. Past experience had convinced him that he would benefit from keeping a closer eye on the old soldier, although he did not really suspect him of having lied during the interviews. He simply felt that he should probe more deeply and that a little quiet observation might give him the clue that he needed. He would not repeat the earlier approach of asking him to come over to Barnsley again.

"JIMMY'S HARDWARE" was the sign over the double-fronted shop window, halfway down the Attercliffe Road. It was easy to spot and it brought home to the policeman some of the realities that Sheffield had been facing since the War. The post-war boom in the steel business had slowly been eroded by the cheaper imports of raw materials and this had been followed by the slow but steady closure of some of the smaller manufacturing firms. Family businesses, still run by the descendants of the founders, had been unable to adapt to the changes in marketing methods of design and distribution. Derelict premises were to be seen on either side of the hardware shop, which had only remained in business by supplying gardening and do-it-yourself tools and oddments for all the passing trade. Harry parked his old Ford 100 yards away from the shop, put an open newspaper across the steering wheel and slumped down in his seat. He could now observe without that fact being obvious to anyone who was passing.

He saw what he assumed was Jimmy James's old red Ford Cortina parked in front of the shop. That rang a bell. There had been a report of a "jogger" getting into a red Ford near some public toilets only a mile from the Hallett murder scene during mid-morning on 13$^{th}$ April. The model and number had not been noted but it was enough to make him retain Jimmy on his list of possibles, provided that this was his car. That fact was soon confirmed. The old soldier came out of the shop, got into the Ford and drove off towards the city centre.

Harry Bennet waited only a few minutes before he was out of his car and walking towards the hardware shop. He gave some attention to the window displays of tools and then climbed the two steps and entered. Opening the door triggered off the old-fashioned ringing bell and he realised the fact that Jimmy James had not moved with the times. Nostalgia might be all right in its place but there was a growing population of younger customers who would drift away from this type of supplier. He wandered up and down the aisles between the display stands, picking up and examining the odd tool and gadget. "Can I help you, sir?" The gentle voice from behind him had a very slight foreign lilt. Turning quickly, he found himself facing a round-faced lady whose warm smile made him feel welcome. Her smooth skin was only slightly coffee coloured but her beautiful brown eyes reminded him of the Asiatic slant that he had noticed among the growing number of Chinese who could be seen in any large town. Her black hair was showing only an odd few grey streaks and she appeared to be very relaxed and in charge of the business. Wearing a European dress that was covered by a khaki smock, buttoned down the front, she was comfortably plump without being fat. "Cuddly," he thought, and he could imagine her being an exquisite beauty in her teens and twenties. "Jimmy was a lucky man to find her!"

"Mrs James?" he asked, handing her a steel tape measure that he had picked from the stand behind him. "I'm here for two reasons. Firstly, I need this tape and secondly I want to introduce myself. Detective Inspector Harry Bennet from Barnsley Police. Your husband might have mentioned me?" Tina James took the tape measure from the policeman and moved back to the counter. "Yes," she said, "I have heard of you. I will wrap this for you," taking the proffered note from him and giving him the small brown bag and his change in return. "What do you want to know from me?" She seemed to be on the defensive and he hastened to help her to relax.

"Mrs James, I must make it clear from the start that I have no jurisdiction here in Sheffield, not since I was promoted and moved to Barnsley. I want you to know that I was intrigued by your husband's story of his experiences in Burma during the War. He really opened my eyes and he was also very helpful in giving me some of the background of the 14$^{th}$ Army and how he met you in your fascinating country. There are quite a few questions that I need to ask you so as to help me in the investigation into the Hallett murder and I don't think that this is the time or place to ask them. I'm wondering if you will be willing to come over to Barnsley during the next day or so, or whether you would prefer to go into the Sheffield office?" He hesitated. "That would mean that a complete stranger would question you, whereas you have already met me, if only briefly. And, what's more, the enquiry will continue under my control anyway, so we might need to meet again in the near future," putting on his most engaging smile, "and I will be kind to you." Tina did not even try to resist. "Of course, Inspector, I will be pleased to come to your office. How about tomorrow?"

This was quickly agreed and he returned to his car and drove back to Barnsley.

---

Harry Bennet spent the remainder of the day completing the paper work of other cases and delegating the jobs that he had planned previously. He intended to be at his best when Tina James came for interview. She had all that personal experience of the conditions during the war in Burma and she had met most of the members of 2 Troop, B Squadron, 3$^{rd}$ Carabiniers near the time of the suspected murder of Trooper Benson. It could be very interesting. He did not have a clue how surprising it would prove to be.

The DI soon realised that the first rule of interviewing, given to him during his initial training, was unshakeable. "Remember, you have one mouth and two ears, so listen for twice as long as you talk. The only person who learns anything when you are talking is the interviewee. That is not the main purpose of interviewing a suspect or a witness." The second rule that he remembered was "Listen and Learn". The third was to keep an eye on the interviewee, even by occasionally using a mirror to catch the unguarded reaction to the interviewer's statement. These skills had been honed with practice and he was aware that he learned some new refinement from each experience.

---

Tina James arrived on time wearing a bright green spring outfit, which Harry found to be very refreshing, and her hair was lightly waved and well brushed. She obviously intended to impress the DI Or did she hope to distract him? He didn't really mind.

He welcomed her into the interview room and made a start.

"You see, Mrs James, I am fascinated with Burma, from what I have learned from your husband and from an old colleague of his named Alan Fenner, and I have every intention of visiting the country on holiday as soon as I possibly can do so. At the moment I am making enquiries into the Hallett murder, which appears to have this connection with Burma. Another Old Carabinier named Miller seems to have disappeared at the end of the War and I am wondering if you remember him from those days when you first met your husband?"

Tina appeared to nod at that point.

"Perhaps we can cover that during our conversation. I would like you to begin with something of your background and home life both before and after the Japanese invasion of your country. I will keep quiet and you please go ahead in your own time."

"Thank you, Inspector. Alan Fenner is an old friend of ours and we have met him many times both in Sheffield and at the Regimental reunions. I might be able to help you with a few memories of Sergeant Miller from 1945, although I am not aware of where he is now. Perhaps I should start with a little of my earlier days."

---

Tina Mying was born in 1924 into a successful Christian family living in a large detached house in the more affluent suburbs of Rangoon. Her Father, U Pen Tha, had enjoyed all the benefits of being a graduate of the city's University and climbing the ladder of promotion in the Burmese civil service. Many of the senior positions were occupied by British expatriates, but he and his fellow Burmese were accepted by the colonial masters, both at work and socially. English was spoken on almost all occasions. Tina was raised in a happy home where she was encouraged to think and converse in this language.

It was a full century since their country had been conquered and "civilised" and there were no living persons who remembered the previous times. Oh, yes, there were frequent attempts to form groups of politically inclined people who would work for "freedom" but nothing came of this agitation until the Japanese invasion in 1941.

U Aung San had been very much involved in the growth of the Nationalist Party and he had welcomed the invaders as saviours. He had believed their presentation of a 'co-prosperity sphere' for all the Asian countries that they were in the process of capturing, without giving much thought to the plight of the Chinese, who had lost almost a third of their land. He did not believe that the Burmese would be treated badly if they welcomed the Japanese as friends. For a few months this policy seemed to work. The Japanese army obeyed the orders to respect the gentle way of life of the Buddhists. Women were not molested, unless they showed antagonism. Even the majority of female political prisoners were treated as well as possible, provided that they were married. Single girls were liable to be drafted into support groups for the army. This required them to nurse the sick and wounded, with limited medical supplies, cook and feed the active soldiers in the field, and not refuse to give any other physical services on demand. The term "comforts girl" should never be used to describe the innocent, friendly young girls who suffered many months of rape and abuse before being disposed of in any way that came to the mind of their co-prosperity masters.

Through 1941 and 1942 the Nationalist Party helped the Japanese to drive the British Army, together with thousands of civilians of other nationalities, north from Rangoon. Some of these travelled by boat up the Irrawaddy and some by train to near Mandalay, where the only bridge crossed the huge river at Ava. The majority walked the 400 miles to the bridge, harassed by the Japanese and the Burmese guerrillas. There were many tales of heroism and help to the sick and wounded, both from the retreating British Army and from the civilians of mixed races. The tanks of the 7th Hussars were in constant demand for breaking through the frequent roadblocks. Captain Ralph Younger, one of the squadron leaders, eventually reached India and later became the Commanding Officer of the 3rd Carabiniers, who were stationed near Madras. He was in command throughout the battle for the Imphal Plain in 1944, where the Japanese were turned back from their "March on Delhi", before he was promoted Brigadier commanding 255 Armoured Brigade for the return to Burma in 1945.

Life in Rangoon became very unpleasant soon after the Japanese consolidated their position. Tina recalled her happy and comfortable childhood, shared with her younger brother Tinka, who had always been full of fun. His favourite joke was to pretend that he could not understand a single word of English, especially when in the company of any British sahibs. "I learn a lot more from them that way," he told Tina. "I really hear the truth when they talk about us."

Her school days were spent at the St George's Girls' High School and the family were regular attenders at St George's Anglican Church at Mingladon and occasionally they went to a service at the Cathedral. She was a bright girl and became well qualified to read PPE at the Rangoon University. The increased freedom of movement and thought helped her to develop into a mature young lady who was at home with the growing political awareness of the undergraduates as much as with the philosophical discussions of her Buddhist friends. The presentation of her BA degree coincided with the period of increasing pressure from the Japanese invaders.

Whilst the few British who had been captured were usually put in a detention camp on the outskirts of the city, a few British ladies, who had been married to ethnic Burmese, were placed under house arrest. Some of the Burmese Christians were arrested. All of them were treated with callous disrespect and their houses and properties were confiscated. Her father's family home was taken over by a senior Japanese Army officer after they had been evicted and left to fend for themselves. Her parents were offered a room with some friends from the civil service and her father arranged for Tina and her brother to go north to stay with her uncle U Ba The in his village, south of Monywa, in the Sagaing bend of the Irrawaddy river. The journey of nearly 500 miles was completed over a period of a few days, using the river boats which were permitted to operate on the river. At Myingyan, she and her brother had to transfer to another boat which would transport them due north up the Chindwin to Monywa from where a bullock cart took them to their new home.

U Ba The had been the headman of the village of Myinga for the past ten years, and he had seen it decline from a prosperous self-supporting community of nearly 1000 inhabitants to the present count of less than 300. He blamed the state of the country under the Japanese since they invaded in 1941. There had been no fighting on the land that he controlled but the locals had been upset by the varied reports of activity over the whole of the country. Some families had moved away because of tales of their relatives being molested, and often killed, during vicious actions between the Japanese and the British. Others had gone because they believed that they would be safer or more secure with their relatives further north. In fact Myinga had proved to be as safe as he could wish. There had only been a few rare occasions when a Japanese patrol had entered the village, usually to rest for a night before pressing on the next morning. He had always been willing to sell them fresh fruit and vegetables and a little of the limited stocks of rice. The fact that he had been paid in the standard government printed rupee notes did not create any problem, except that caused by the rampant inflation, as he could usually exchange them for a small variety of useful goods when he visited Monywa each week.

Tina had been reassured by the fact that she saw a Japanese patrol only once during the three-years' stay with her uncle. She had seen them enter the village and she had then kept out of sight until they left the next day. The only real intruders, who were to affect her life for ever, came with B Squadron of the 3$^{rd}$ Carabiniers in March 1945. She heard and saw the noisy General Lee tanks, followed by a line of 3-tonner trucks, approach from the south. They halted at the entrance to the village and the accompanying cloud of dust continued to move forward before it settled on to the bamboo bashas and the waiting villagers.

Her first thoughts when she realised that the soldiers were British were that she would soon be able to speak English again within a comfortable circle of friends and acquaintances. Perhaps some of them would have recent issues of the *Tatler*, which she had missed so much in the last three years. She had met many senior officers of the British Army when she had accompanied her parents to different social functions in Rangoon, and she studied this group of strangely garbed soldiers as they went through the process of settling into another new camp site. Her uncle beckoned her to join him as he made himself available to the obvious leader of the group. She stood just behind him with a few of the elders who had heard the noise, ready to interpret as required.

An officer jumped down from the leading tank and confidently approached them. She could see that he had some insignia on his epaulets but he and the other soldiers were covered in dust and looked the colour of the dry ground. "Good morning," he started, "I am Major Dorman and I would like to speak to your headman." He had another young man beside him, dressed in a similar khaki uniform, who gave a rapid translation of the request into Burmese. Tina suddenly realised that her services as an interpreter were not required and she remained quiet. Her uncle spoke directly to the Burmese soldier, who explained that he was a Karen civilian named Saw Derry Pwe and that he was employed by the officer to be helpful in just these circumstances.

The negotiations went smoothly. The Major explained that he needed to rest his Squadron for perhaps four or five days and would like to have the facilities for all his men to sleep under a roof each night. They would spend their time resting and maintaining the vehicles and would not interfere with any of the residents. U Ba The was willing to make available at least twenty of the bashas at the southern end of the village. His offer to have them cleaned out and ready for occupation within an hour was declined. "No, no, my men will do that for themselves in much less time. Will you take me to this area and I will allocate each house as I inspect it." He called his Sergeant Major to come down from another tank and the party walked away whilst the main group of soldiers jumped out of their vehicles and started to smoke cigarettes and stretch their legs. Tina heard the Karen tell the officer that it would not be wise to discuss the price to be paid for the services that he had agreed until nearer the time of departure. "I can negotiate with this man better when we know that we are about to leave." The Major had simply nodded. She then decided to wait a little time before she approached any of the newcomers. She would study them from the stronger position of being able to understand what they were saying whilst appearing to be a simple village girl.

Listening to the men relaxing after their recent journey, she became rather puzzled. At first, she thought she had been wrong in believing that they were speaking English. It seemed to be a very rough mixture of Urdu and Arabic, cemented together by a crude form of English, containing many uncouth words that she imagined to be swear words. She was not wrong. It was certainly not the English language that she and her family had heard in Rangoon. Much of it was shouted from one man to another in a most aggressive way and yet the men did not seem to be upset during the conversations. It was all very strange and she felt very relieved that she had not approached any of them just yet.

As she was watching some of the tank crews from under her long lashes, she believed that she heard one of them shout to his friends, "Cor, dekho that fucking bint o'er there, betcher I slip her a length, tora peechhi." She blushed, as she knew that he was pointing to her and that he was making a very rude suggestion. She needed some time before she decided whether or not to speak to any of them and she then returned to her uncle's house in order to watch them from a distance. This was not the sort of company that she had imagined when she knew that the British Army was moving nearer. The noise made by the tankmen continued for a little time as they moved their vehicles and parked them near the bashas that had been allocated to the different groups (or troops, as she learned to call them later). She realised that she was at the beginning of a steep learning curve that was to affect her for the rest of her life.

Tina was beginning to accept the fact that she would be wiser to remain out of sight of the new arrivals when she heard approaching steps and a voice called out a greeting in Burmese. "Hello, anyone there?" Her uncle moved on to the veranda and she heard him talking in a friendly manner with the Army interpreter, Saw Derry Pwe. As she approached, her uncle nodded agreement to her moving nearer and joining in the conversation. She was delighted to learn that Derry Pwe had graduated from her university during her first year there, and she could now recognise him as one of the seniors who would have been treated with the greatest respect by the youngsters of her intake. They soon moved into the basha and Tina arranged some fruit drinks on the table. Her uncle plied Derry with questions about the conditions in the other parts of the country which he had visited recently, and showed his delight that there were all the signs of the Japanese being in full retreat to the south and the east.

When asked "How long will it take to remove the Japanese from our country?" Derry answered quite openly. "The British Army is now very strong and growing stronger every week, but that is creating its own problems. The forward troops are being supplied mostly by air, but that system can only continue as long as the weather remains good. It all depends on the timing of the start of the monsoons. Unless the road to Rangoon is cleared of the enemy before the rains start, there is a distinct possibility that the advance can literally become stuck in the mud. In the very near future we will have to send a strong column due south, and at high speed, in order to open the port of Rangoon and enable supplies to come in by sea. The Carabiniers fought all through the monsoons last year around Imphal and they know the difficulties of being supplied by airdrops during the rains. The planes either cannot fly, or, when they do take the chance of a break in the cloud cover and take off, they cannot find the dropping zone and worst still, too many of the planes fly straight into the hillsides.

"No, I understand from what I have heard, there has to be a crossing of the Irrawaddy very soon in order to attack and destroy the Japanese army's three or more strong divisions on the east of the river. It is not yet decided whether to cross north of Mandalay where the Japs are moving their men to the south, or whether to make the crossing much further to the south."

Derry knew very well that he should not be giving so much information to a stranger but he felt that he had known Tina for some time. He was confident that she and her uncle could be trusted and that his comments could not get into the possession of the Japanese. Come to think of it, he would not want his "leakage" to be reported to the Major either.

U Ba The asked a few more questions about the general economic situation. He particularly wanted to hear the latest news about U Aung San, as he had heard rumours that he had lost his previous belief in the invincibility of the Japanese Army and that he and his party were now actively helping the British. He, Ba The, was personally convinced that the War was steadily moving towards its conclusion as far as Burma was concerned. The problem of the Japanese nation was likely to take many more years for the Allies, but that was not his concern. He just wanted to start to rebuild his lovely village on the banks of the Chindwin and to encourage the missing villagers to return and resume their pleasant way of life.

He made his excuses to Derry, saying that he was welcome to stay a little longer in order to reminisce with his niece and that he should keep in touch with him throughout his stay in Myinga. The two young graduates were left alone to chatter about acquaintances from their Rangoon days. This soon led to the conditions under which they had met today.

"Tell me, Derry, what are these soldiers really like? I was frightened today when I heard one of them making crude suggestions about me. And why do they shout all the time? They sound so aggressive. I feel that I will be safer if I keep out of their sight, but that will be difficult if they are going to stay for a few days."

Derry did not answer immediately. He still remembered his own fears when he had joined the tankmen only a few weeks ago. "I am quite sure, Tina, that you are not in any danger from them. When I joined them in January I also was frightened. They seemed to be so offensive with each other, as well as with the Japanese, but I soon realised that it was the result of their spending the past year fighting an apparently invincible army. They had not only kept fighting throughout the monsoons, but they had also had to contend with a wide range of tropical diseases that they had not met before. Added to that, their supplies of food, water and ammunition could not be relied upon due to the problems of supplying them in all weathers. There was a steady loss of friends and other personnel caused by casualties from wounds and disease. Those of them who lost their tanks from enemy action lost, at the same time, all their personal treasures, such as letters from home and photographs of their wives and children. Their shouting all the time arose from their attempts to communicate with each other over the sound of the tank engines and gunfire. Most of them are now deaf and suffering from a whistling in the ears, which causes them to feel extremes of frustration. This rest period is the first recognisable break in the past few months of action, so perhaps we can expect them to be a little excited. The medical officer has assured them that the deafness and noises in the ear are only a temporary problem and that a week or two of leave in India later this year will make them fit and well for the coming invasion of Malaya and, eventually, for the attack on the Japanese islands. Firstly, they have to eliminate the enemy in Burma and reach Rangoon.

"I must tell you of my two special friends in 2 Troop. Sergeant Dusty Miller and Trooper Jimmy James have been very kind to me from the first day that I met them. We are planning to go into business together after the War and I trust them implicitly. Perhaps I can introduce them to you? I will certainly tell them of your anxieties after this morning's rudeness."

Tina smiled at her new friend. "You reassure me. Perhaps I have been living too long in a rural area. My uncle has been a real help to Tinka and me in giving us a home well away from the Japanese army, but he is so different from my father. He rarely uses any English and he still thinks in Burmese." She appeared to ponder on the situation. "Could we walk together a little nearer these new visitors, and I would appreciate it if you could point out your two friends so that I can recognise them in future?" This was easily agreed and the young couple started to walk slowly through the village.

The crew of 2 Able were going through the usual chores of vehicle and gun maintenance when Dusty Miller spotted Derry coming in his direction accompanied by the little Burmese girl he had seen with the headman when they arrived. "Derry's quick off the mark," he thought, "let's hope that he can find some similar crumpet for a few more of us." He turned to Jimmy James, who was cleaning the stripped Browning from the bow position. "Dekho Derry, Jimmy, he's got some lovely crumpet lined up already. He's more talented than I thought at first. We must persuade him to help find us some friendly locals." Jimmy nodded and carried on cleaning his gun. It was too soon after the Benton episode to get involved in chasing village girls. Anyway, he still had the runs, though not as badly as the previous year.

Tina thought that the two soldiers pointed out by Derry looked decent and trustworthy and she knew that she would recognise them again when she saw them. "Perhaps, you can introduce them to me during the next day or two, Derry? I really should go back now and prepare the evening meal."

They parted and Derry wandered over to the tank that he had learned to treat as his mobile home. "Hello, Dusty, I am wondering if I can spend the next few days here with you to be with my friends? The Major doesn't need me all day as long as he knows where I can be found." "Of course, Derry, you're very welcome. We have plenty to talk about, with our plans for Maymyo, and you can be helpful if we have any negotiations with the locals. You seem to be making good contacts already." With a wink, "Is the little lady willing?" Derry pretended to be shocked. "You noticed. I will introduce you tomorrow. Her name is Ma Tina Mying and she is the headman's niece. She was at Rangoon University at the same time that I was there so I must ask you to give her every consideration. Her English is as fluent as mine is and she has heard some of our friends making indecent suggestions about her. She was frightened today and I have tried to reassure her. She is a very good Christian lady and she is not used to the rough life that we have been experiencing lately. I very much doubt if there are any girls in the village who are "willing", as you say. That could be possible in Mandalay or Rangoon, but not in the country villages." He decided to change the subject. "How would you like me to take a few of the lads upstream tomorrow where we can do some fishing?" This raised a lot of interest from the rest of the crew as they worked on their weapons and tank.

"Can we borrow your aerial, Jimmy, and make a fishing rod?" came from Tug Wilson, whose ears were big and in proportion to the size of his body. Dusty jumped in with his reply. "Not worth it, Tug. We've tried it before. Welding the loops on to the rods is a dodgy business and anyway we've no decent line we can use. No, we'll use the usual method. Jimmy, go to the ammo truck and draw out a couple of crates of grenades, 'for testing', remember to ask."

The fishing expedition was voted a great success that afternoon. Dusty led five of his crew along a path going north of Myinga until it turned to the east, along a small tributary of the Chindwin. They relaxed in the holiday atmosphere at the start of three or four days' break from the routine of fighting. The warm sunshine created a balmy breeze as the path led them up a slight incline to a bend in the stream. The undergrowth opened up and they saw a deep pool in front of them. Paddy Wills and Les Bickerton were the first to strip naked and dive into the clear, cool water. The others quickly followed them. Dusty waited a minute before he called out to them, "Who told you to jump in? Aren't we on a fishing trip?" he was holding a grenade in each hand. He appeared to be about to throw them into the water when he relented, stripped off his own clothes and joined the laughing nudes in the pool.

Ten minutes later they had all crawled out on to the grassy bank and were drying themselves in the hot sun. "Let's give the fish a chance to get over their fright," laughed John Kerr, who rarely made any comment. Perhaps they were all beginning to benefit from the break in hostilities. "Jimmy should have been here with us to enjoy the fun," Nick McGowan added his two-pen'orth. "Silly sod, doing his dhobiing when he could easily have come with us. I reckon he might have got himself lined up for his oats by the time we are back."

Dusty jumped up at that point and organised the assault on any fish that were there. They each threw one grenade into the pool and counted the explosions. There were no duds with that lot. Roughly fifteen fish, of reasonable sizes, rose to the surface and floated there, waiting to be caught. The crew needed no telling to get in after them and in they jumped. There was a lot more laughter as each man tried to hold a fish whilst throwing it on to the bank. Only two landed safely. The remainder seemed to wake up as soon as they were touched, and escape out of the wet fingers back into the stream. Dusty decided that this pool was not likely to have any residents left that would be willing to be treated in the same manner and he gave the order to dress and move upstream.

As they continued along the path beside the stream, they passed a group of four men from the Squadron Leader's crew, led by Corporal Alan Fenner. They were carrying nearly two dozen medium sized fish strung together. "Alright, Alan," called Dusty, looking at the size of their catch. "You'll have a good meal tonight all right!" Alan and his men joined in the general laughter and commented on a near disaster they'd just had. "We had one grenade with a delayed fuse and it went off when we were all in the water. Ginger Whitely was below the surface and he came up arse first, but he's tikh abbhi." Dusty and his men continued up the path and soon found some more pools in the meandering stream. They followed the same procedures and spent the next two hours accumulating a large number of apparently edible fish to take back with them.

Jimmy James had decided to spend the afternoon washing and repairing his filthy and torn battledresses. The basha that he shared with his mates was very near to the bank of the Chindwin and he could look across its 600-yard width to see that the other side was covered with jungle. Further downstream he could see the smoke from a similar village.

Before he started on his chores, he stripped naked and walked into the wide river. He could feel the current pulling him out towards the main flow, which seemed to be moving at about ten knots. He was a strong swimmer and there were plenty of other Carabiniers doing their jobs along the bank. He felt quite safe and soon returned to dress himself in a spare pair of shorts ready for his laundering operation.

That was how Tina found him. She had decided to approach him and ask if he had any spare soap. All her life, up to three years ago, she had had the luxury of using scented toilet soap at home and it was the one thing that she missed more than anything else since she had come to Myinga. She could not help laughing at Jimmy when he jumped at the surprise of her arrival behind him. He dropped his own piece of soap into the river and blushed in embarrassment. They both saw the funny side and were soon laughing at the sheer joy of each other's company. Neither would admit it but they agreed, a few years later, that it could only be described as "love at first sight". Jimmy knew as soon as he saw this lovely Burmese girl that she was all that he wanted and that his only aim in life now was to survive and marry her. "Yes", he thought, "with or without the rubies. But, they would make our life together a lot easier."

As a result of this meeting Tina acquired two tablets of Lifebuoy soap and Jimmy was invited to visit her basha that evening to join the family in a light meal. He was glad that he had a newly washed and darned battledress to wear and he was able to take a few cans of luxuries with him. He was not too sure about Tina's brother Tinka, who refused to understand any English and played his battered old gramophone all evening. His one record and the needle were both so worn that no one could recognise the tune.

The memories of that evening remained with both of them as the start of a wonderful marriage based on love and companionship lasting for thirty-seven years so far. They had few secrets from each other. Tina admitted to having one secret going back to that first meeting, but she refused to tell the DI what it was until he had assured her that he would not record it or repeat it to her husband.

Jimmy had felt that he was floating above the ground as he walked back to the troop basha after the evening with the Burmese family. The entire Squadron seemed to have been made aware of his good fortune and comments were thrown at him in passing. His Troop Leader, Lt. Dibble-Williams, smiled knowingly. "Had a good evening, James?" Jimmy threw him a salute. "Yes, thank you, sir." Sergeant Jock McGregor from LAD passed him and called out: "you're a lucky bugger, young James," with a tinge of jealousy. His arrival in the basha started an enthusiastic uproar, with all his mates asking if he had or hadn't. "Don't tell us that you didn't get it away, Jimmy," was the essence of the questioning.

A sudden feeling of isolation hit Jimmy when he realised that his thoughts about his new friend were very different from those of this group of randy young men. "You don't understand, you filthy-minded sods, she is a very decent young girl and I intend to keep in touch with her when we leave here." "You are just wanting to keep her for yourself, Jimmy," broke in Nick McGowan, "come on, tell us what happened."

Dusty Miller made no comment as he listened to the crude but good-humoured banter that continued for a few minutes. He could see that Jimmy was starting to get angry and he decided that his wireless operator wanted to keep his good fortune to himself. He was quite right. What nobody realised was that Jimmy had fallen in love, with the purest of thoughts, and that he now found that the usual sexual banter of the soldiers was simply revolting. Jimmy went out into the bright moonlight and wandered down to the riverbank to sit on the ground and try to settle the turmoil in his mind. It was an hour later when he returned to his bed and turned in, glad that the others were settled down for the night.

Tina had also had her mind in a whirl as she retired in her own room. The full moon lit up the village and shone in through her open window. The evening breeze was pleasant and refreshing. She relived the experience of feeling that she had met the one and only love of her life. What would happen to her? Would she ever see Jimmy again after he and his Squadron drove away to resume their fight with the retreating Japanese? Would he survive the future actions against a still-strong enemy? The War might go on for a few more years before they were completely beaten. It was in the hands of God.

Perhaps she and Tinka would soon be able to rejoin their parents in Rangoon. She wondered whether Jimmy would still feel the same when they met again and whether he would propose marriage. He seemed to be an honourable young man and standards of behaviour in those days had not deteriorated to the state of those that have been seen in England since the sixties. Time would tell. She snuggled down on her single bed, feeling happy and secure.

She must have been asleep for almost half an hour when she awoke with a feeling of shock. Something had disturbed her. She became rigid and felt that she could hear her heart thumping much faster than usual. All the normal night sounds were there, croaking of frogs and chirping of insects, but there was something extra and new. She listened intently and then she heard it. There was the sound of stockinged feet on the veranda, just outside her window. She was just about to call out to her brother in the next room when the whisper from outside reached her ears. "Tina, are you in there?" She did not recognise the voice. Certainly, it was a man's voice and English.

She must find out whose it was before she wakened the whole household. "Who are you?" she asked very quietly, aware of the icy chill that had entered her chest.

"I'm Andrew Miller, a friend of Jimmy James. We've been close friends for more than a year now. Can I talk to you, please?" She was not going to get out of bed in order to speak to a strange man, especially whilst she was wearing her night attire. "Certainly not," she hissed. "It is possible that we will meet each other tomorrow, but I have retired to my bed. You must go away immediately". He was not going to be put off so easily. "But I understand from Jimmy that you are anxious to meet some English people, and I am his Sergeant and much more experienced in the ways of the world. You can have the pleasure of my friendship and I could help you to go to England, if that is what you would like. Won't you come out on to the veranda instead of us having to whisper like this?" Tina recognised that he was being very persistent and that she would need to assert herself if she were going to be rid of the man. "If you do not leave the house immediately, I will scream for help and you will be treated as a dacoit and probably killed by the men of the village. Go back to your tank, now." She was trembling uncontrollably, but she knew that she must be firm if she were to succeed in sending him away.

Dusty Miller now realised that he was getting nowhere with the girl, that she was not a frustrated nymphomaniac, and that Jimmy had probably been speaking the truth earlier that evening. As cheerfully as possible he called out, "All right, Tina, I'll see you then. Please don't worry Jimmy by telling him that I called to see you." She heard the soft sound of stockinged feet walking along the veranda and the night noises resumed control.

It was another twenty minutes before her pulse rate returned to normal but by then she had decided that she had escaped an intended seduction, possibly an attempted rape, and that she would need to be careful to avoid being alone with any of these English soldiers. Except, perhaps, Jimmy James. She felt safe and secure with him. Should she tell him? Should she tell Tinka? Her instincts told her that it would probably be wiser not to tell anyone at this stage. She could always inform them later but if she mentioned it to anyone now, she could not withdraw the knowledge from them if it proved to be better that they did not know of Sergeant Miller's temptation. That was the logic at the time, and this was the first time that she had mentioned the episode to any one.

True to her upbringing, she had slipped out of bed and gone on to her knees in prayer. With her elbows on the bed and her head in her hands, she had thanked her God for helping her to escape from a most unpleasant possibility.

# Chapter 12

# *1982*
# *A Vital Clue*

"So, you are quite sure that Sergeant Miller was hoping to seduce you on that night?" Harry Bennet had listened eagerly to Tina's story and had resisted the temptation to intrude before she had given him some new facts. This might possibly lead him to more light on the background of this missing suspect.

She quietly confirmed her answer with a nod of the head. "Please don't tell my husband. Nothing indecent happened. At the time I did not want to create any trouble between the tank people and the village, nor did I want to be the cause of Jimmy and Sergeant Miller having any tensions between them. As my mother used to say, 'least said, soonest mended'. I think she had heard it from some English friends."

"Well, thank you very much for being so helpful. I'll certainly not tell Jimmy what you have just told me about Dusty Miller. I am trying to find any avenue of enquiries that could lead me to his whereabouts. Can you tell me what happened after that unpleasant experience when he first came to your house? Did you get to know him any more?"

"Oh, yes, the Squadron was with us for another four days and I was able to meet and know many of the men. I think that the word was passed around that I was a 'good' girl. Jimmy had been very upset with some of his friends when he heard how they had made suggestive comments about me and he had threatened to thump anyone who misbehaved in future!"

"But did you meet Dusty Miller after that evening?"

"Yes. Derry took me into the tank lines the next morning and introduced me to all of 2 Troop, including Mr Dibble-Williams. He was a lovely man, a perfect gentleman. His end was so sad. Sergeant Miller made no reference to his own bad behaviour and he acted correctly whenever I met him in the village. He appeared not to know me when I met him again last week. Perhaps thirty-seven years is a little too long for his memory."

"You met him again last week?" Harry Bennet could hardly restrain himself as he burst into her statement. "How did that happen, and where?"

Was this the breakthrough that he needed? After having spent many man-hours with his men probing all possible sources for post-war records of Miller, Army, National Insurance and employment channels, he had been prepared to accept that the man had changed his name at the end of the War and developed as an entirely different personality. An element of luck had been required, and this could be it.

"Last Monday, when I visited the wholesaler to resolve a few account queries, I was in the reception area, waiting for the accountant to come out to see me when Mr Miller walked in. My back was towards him at the time and he would not see my face as he spoke to the receptionist."

"Did he recognise you?"

"I don't think so. I saw his face sideways and I instantly recognised him. He didn't look so much older after all those years Perhaps his hair was a little greyer. He simply gave his card to the girl and, without any hesitation, he was told to go into the office. I did not hear the name he gave but he did say that he was from the Post Office and that he had called in order to check the postal records. It appeared to me that this was a normal routine and there were no security checks at all. I went into a side office with the accountant and completed what was necessary. Mr Miller could have left during that time or he might still have been in the main office. Anyway, I did not see him again".

Harry asked Tina for the details of the wholesaler's name, address and the names of her contacts there. This looked to be the most promising lead so far.

"I can't tell you how important it is for you to let me know immediately if you see or hear anything of Miller again. You will realise, I'm sure, that you could be in serious danger if he believes that you have seen him and that you are likely to inform the police? I believe that he is responsible for a record number of murders since the War and also that he might have been the murderer of one of his tank crew in Burma. That was just before he met you in Myinga. It is quite possible that he lives somewhere near Sheffield and that you could come across him any time. Thank you again for all your help today. I think that you should discuss it all with your husband. If either of you happen to see Miller, or whatever he calls himself now, it will be much safer for you both if you contact me as soon as you can. Please don't go up to him or make any enquiries about him. If he is the man I believe him to be, he is very intelligent and extremely dangerous."

This stressing of the risks involved was disturbing to the gentle Burmese lady but she understood the policeman's warnings and assured him that she would do as he asked. Harry saw her off the premises and went to report to his governor.

Chapter 13

# *1982*
# *Miller Identified*

Philip Anders felt the hairs on the back of his neck stand up when he was about to leave the general office of Williamsons (Wholesalers) Ltd in Sheffield.

In his capacity as a private investigator, he had used his well-tested technique of posing as a postal services representative in order to gain access to the main office. It was a simple ruse, which he had learned from a sales rep for a firm selling postage meters. Apparently there was a fifty-year history, in this highly specialised market, of there being only two suppliers of franking machines and the fact that they manufactured and supplied the machines for all types of offices under licence from the General Post Office. The licence gave the sales representatives and engineers the right of access to the machines, and therefore to the offices in which they were used, during normal working hours, for the purposes of maintenance and the checking of the records of usage volumes. This gave the manufacturers the opportunity to notice any abuse of the system or the machine and it was a simple matter to assess when a business had grown to the point where the volume of outgoing mail demanded a larger machine to handle it efficiently. It also helped the salesmen to find more business for their mailing machines. Access was limited to the machines of their own make. It did not apply to those of the competitor. On the other hand, representatives of the controlling Post Office, firstly a Government Department and later to be independent, were able to have access to the postage meters of any manufacture.

Philip Anders had learned that some unscrupulous salesman, who was desperate to find a prospect for the sale of his own machines, had cleverly implied that he was a visitor from the Post Office as opposed to being a supplier's representative. He had then been able to gain access to the general office and check the records of the firms who used competitors' machines. This required a confident entry and approach to the receptionist and, when asked "Can I help you?" a rather disdainful "Yes. John Smith (or whatever name he liked to use), Post Office. Can I go through?" If the ruse worked, he would gain some valuable information and quickly make himself scarce.

Lady receptionists are a breed of their own. Many of them believed that their main purpose in life was to prevent the majority of callers from being able to speak to the management. This applied particularly to any unrecognised, casual visitor who might even be trying to sell something. It did not apply to a visitor from the Post Office. Some of them would use their natural disbelief in a statement by a stranger and ask to see his business card. If the man were a rogue, or a genuine P. O. representative, he would have prepared himself with a suitable card and not be caught out by this question.

Anders, who did not consider himself a rogue, had often used this ruse to gain access to business premises and he was well prepared for any simple questioning. He had a stock of illegally printed cards endorsed: "James Kerr, Postal Services Representative", including the address and telephone number of the Head Post Office of the city in which he happened to be working. They had proved to be invaluable to him during his official occupation as a "private eye", giving him easy access to business houses where he needed to obtain information about an individual who worked there. He had not needed to use a card during this visit to Williamsons.

He had been pursuing a divorce enquiry and merely wanted to see if there was any truth in a report that the male head clerk was more than normally friendly with the computer operator. By involving them both in conversation on a matter concerning security of the company postal costs, he believed that he could make a fair assessment of their relationship. That part of the job was simple. The problem that now arose was that his sixth sense had alerted him to danger when he was giving his name to the receptionist.

He had been aware, on arrival, of a woman of medium height with greying black hair standing well away from the desk and apparently reading something on the notice board. The girl behind the desk had immediately asked him if she could help and he had given the prepared statement, "Jim Kerr, Post Office, just to check the postage meter", preparing to go through into the office. As expected, he was told to go through. He did this without taking another look at the woman standing near the wall, but he was very much aware of the tingling sensation in his neck and spine. This was beginning to fade slightly and he knew that it had been caused by the presence of the other person in the reception area. He must be ready for her if she came into the office whilst he was working there.

Anders had entered the general office, where he had gone through the usual procedure of asking the girl working her computer for the postage meter record card and commenting, "postage check", with a smile. It always worked. He accepted the buff card from her and pretended to be reading the amounts of postal credit that had been entered and the dates of the visits from the engineer. This was followed by a brief look at the machine, lifting the ink cover with an experienced flick of the finger, all the time wearing a confident and worldly expression of semi-boredom. It took only a few minutes and he turned back to the girl, who had been watching him with interest. "Could I have a quick word with Mr Jones, please?"

She turned to call across the room. "Trevor. Do you have a minute?" The office manager looked up from his desk, put his ballpoint pen down and walked across. "What is it, Jenny?" She waved a hand towards the pseudo-Post Office man, who spoke up immediately.

"I have just checked your records and everything appears to be in order. Are you aware of any problems?" The look of puzzlement on his face made Anders smile inwardly. "No. Should I be?" Trevor Jones turned to the girl. "Have you had any?" The warmth in his voice and the friendly smile on both their faces told Anders all he needed to be convinced that there was a close relationship between the two, closer that he would expect to find in the usual office. He had enough to help him prepare his report for Mrs Trevor Jones. The conversation was quickly brought to a close with: "Thank you both very much. I will call again next year."

As he moved towards the door leading to the reception area and exit, a well-dressed man pushed ahead of him, calling out to someone at the rear of the office, "I'll be with you in a minute. I'm just going to see Mrs James now. She is waiting in reception." Anders stood aside to let this man go ahead of him and, in doing so, he saw Tina James' face as she turned to meet the accountant. He knew. His instinct had not let him down. The immediate reaction was to let the door close, keeping him in the general office, giving the accountant time to greet Tina and take her into the side room. He bent down and gained another minute by retying his shoelace and standing up again.

The conversation in the outer office subsided as Tina and the accountant moved into the side office. Anders took his chance and walked out, nodding to the receptionist as he went through the swing doors and into the street. He quickly found his car, which was parked down the side road, and drove off. "A close shave," he thought. But he was far from happy. After more than 35 years since he had seen the Burmese girl in Myinga, he had come face to face with her and recognised her instantly. And she had done the same. He was quite sure. Jimmy James had been "crackers" about the lass and it sounded as though he had not only married her but that they were living somewhere in the Sheffield area. He must trace them and then decide what to do with them. This could be very dangerous for him.

One of the basic rules that Anders lived by was to act immediately on any hunch that came to him. He applied that rule now. Turning the pages of the local telephone directory to 'James', he tried to remember Jimmy James' first name, to fix the initial, but his memory failed to help him. He knew that 'Jimmy' was only a nickname, probably given to him on his first day in the Army. He should know his given name. He had been his Troop Sergeant and he had kept the proper records required by the Carabiniers, but he simply could not recall the man other than as "Jimmy James". 'I'm getting too bloody old for this lark," he mused. "It's time that I retired and started to take life more easily, but there are still a few more on the list." Luck was with him today. At the top of the list of "James" he spotted "A. James, Jimmy's Hardware, 150, Attercliffe Road, Sheffield." This could be the one. Tina James was obviously doing some business at the wholesale hardware office, probably paying an account or settling a problem. Easily checked.

He drove to the address and parked nearby at a point where he could see anyone leaving or going to the shop. He was quickly proved to be right. A blue van with "Jimmy's Hardware" on the side was driven to the front of the shop and he saw Tina get out and go into the shop. A few minutes later, Jimmy himself came out and opened the van rear doors, lifting a heavy carton out and taking it inside. Like Tina, Jimmy was heavier and older but still recognisable. Philip Anders had all he wanted. He turned his car and drove away before anyone could come outside again. He would give this some serious thought once he was well away from Sheffield.

It was possible that he should be planning a complete reappraisal of his activities. He had had a good run of thirty-five years or so without even being suspected and now he knew that the Barnsley police were aware of his existence, even if they did not have his description. If they once got on to the James's, they would get that and it could then be only a matter of time before they were asking him the questions. He must make a quick decision on whether to eliminate them, and soon.

## Chapter 14

# *1982*
# *Future Plans*

Philip Anders had become a successful solitary man, who did not feel the need for the company of another person. He never set himself a task that was not achievable and he had never failed to reach a satisfactory end result. He supposed that his life had been unusual. He had always learned from the few mistakes that he had made, and long before now he had decided that nostalgia was not for him.

He rarely looked back to his past but the recent encounter with Tina James had reminded him, very forcibly, of the time when he was known as "Dusty" Miller.

He had left the Hull Grammar School in 1938 when Europe was in a state of turmoil. His achievements were above average and he had been noted for his quick brain and practical attitude to any problem that he was given to solve. Work had not been easy to find recently but the situation was improving as more and more businesses were able to expand with the demand for materials needed for the defence of the threatened nation. His father had asked him to join his wholesale tobacco and confectionery business and he had been an enthusiastic addition to the staff. Within the first year he had proved to his father that he was a useful salesman and willing to work all hours in order to help the customers, who were spread over most of the East Riding of Yorkshire. That was soon to end with his volunteering for the Royal Armoured Corps in 1941. After the German air raids on Hull, with disturbed nights and many casualties, he found the Army to be a haven of peace at the RAC Depot at Catterick.

Old 1914/1918 comrades of his father had often given him the advice, "Never ever volunteer", as the secret of keeping out of trouble in the Armed Forces. They had said it with a knowing smile on their faces and he had accepted it as a standing joke and ignored it. As a result of doing exactly the opposite, he had been sent to various armoured regiments in the UK, North Africa and, eventually to India in 1943. After a couple of weeks at the RAC Depot at Poona, he was posted to a newly formed cavalry regiment, the 26th Hussars, based at Secunderabad, near Hyderabad, Deccan, in central India. It was at Poona that he first met Jimmy James. They had both been together on a draft of men being sent to reinforce the 26th Hussars, ready to defend India against any possible invasion. The two troopers had stayed together when the draft was being allocated to the three sabre squadrons. They had decided that they would probably be in the same troop, or even the same tank, when the 26th Hussars went into action against the Japanese, who were presently invading Burma. The 26th Hussars appeared to be an ideal regiment from the point of view of the two men. Morale was high. The officers all knew their business. They ensured that the men were trained and trained to the point where they were all eager to be tested in battle. If only they had had the tanks. That was the rub.

The other active tank regiments in India at that time were the 3rd Carabiniers and their daughter regiment, the 25th Dragoons. There were only enough American General Lee Mark 3 Medium tanks to equip those two regiments and this was done, much to the chagrin of the 26th Hussars. To compound the imagined insult, it was said that the 3rd Carbs, as they were known, was overloaded with time-expired men who would soon have to be sent back to Blighty without having fired a shot in anger. To the simple minds of the men of the 26th Hussars, and possibly to the less simple minds of their officers, the logical answer to the situation would have been to equip the 26th with the tanks of the 3rd Carbs and send the whole of that 'spit and polish' regiment wherever they liked. This would have resulted in producing a battle-ready tank regiment that was 'raring' to go into action. Life was not so simple amongst the planners of Whitehall. A war-time regiment like the 26th Hussars, with a life measured in months, could not possibly have any claim to the equipment of a regular regiment with 300 years of history. Oh, no! The simple and most expensive answer to the problem would be to dismantle the 26th Hussars and ship all the tank crews to the Carabiniers, who were somewhere near Madras. The remaining men of the 26th were sent as infantry reinforcements to the Long Range Penetration Groups, the Chindits, never to be heard of again.

It took only a few months of adjustment, training and travelling together before the old Hussars became fully integrated with the residue of Carabiniers and they thought and fought as one regiment. Thanks for that were due to the Commanding Officer, Lt. Col. R. Younger, who had been with the 7$^{th}$ Hussars during their retreat from Burma the previous year.

Both Andrew Miller and Jimmy James had survived the next twelve months, which started with their introduction to action in the well-reported Battle of Nunshigum. They had stayed together throughout the clearing of the Japanese 15$^{th}$ Army from the Indian plain at Imphal, the chasing of the defeated Japanese into Burma, the wiping of them out in their attempts to escape to the south, and the eventual ending of the War after the dropping of the two atom bombs on Japan. They had trusted each other in every possible way. The fun and games at the ruby mines at Maymyo had been a great success, apart from the bloody Japs blowing up the tank and killing the crew of seven men. That was war. It had paid off well. He had had no financial worries ever since the war. His only problem had been that of feeding the market with a few rubies at a time in order not to spoil the price. He had sometimes wondered whether Jimmy or the others would spoil things by dumping all their rubies at one time. He was a little surprised to find that Jimmy was running a shop when he should have been better placed than that. Perhaps he had lost his money in some way.

Dusty Miller had had more than his share of good luck throughout his life. The twelve months of action against the Japanese had been testing enough in a regiment that experienced more than 100% casualties, but he was sure that the gods had been with him on many occasions when he might easily have been crippled or killed. He had been able to take his tank to Maymyo, with full control over his actions, at the right time to take advantage of Derry's secret knowledge of the full safe and make all his crew rich men for life. All this had enabled him to carry out his long-term plan to eliminate a list of 'impossibles', men who had proved to the world that they were so selfish that they did not deserve to enjoy their lives at the expense of others. 'Idealist' he might be, but the authorities of government were not able to create the laws to stop the rot, which had survived the War and was increasing every year. He did not pretend that he would be able to stop it either, but he had the satisfaction of having had a long run of success. And there were many more prospects for his attention.

That news tycoon had been in the news himself recently. Philip was currently in the process of assessing how much could have been stolen from the companies' pension funds in order to cover up some of his pathetic speculation. The man was an idiot who was bright enough, or tough enough, to hide his self-help system from his senior management. Some of them could be involved in the cover-up and were remaining quiet because of their own guilt, or else were being bullied and blackmailed into silence. It was a messy one. When the news broke, the City and Parliament would be staggered by the number of so-called 'respectable' people who would be affected by the rumours and reports. Worse than that, there were hundreds of thousands of people reaching the end of their working lives who would find that their pensions had evaporated. All because one arrogant bullyboy had decided to make his own laws about the ownership of pension funds. The man was going to have a shock. As soon as it could be organised, he was going to have an accident. He could fall off one of his yachts or out of his penthouse suite window one dark night. He deserved something dramatic that would hit the headlines of all his newspapers for a few weeks or months. That was all in the future.

Chapter 15

# *1946*
# *Transition*

Another stroke of luck for Dusty Miller was meeting that chap from the Merchant Navy on the way home from India.

Like most of the men who had been through the Burma campaign, Dusty had suffered a variety of diseases and had been kept with the Squadron, helped by some of the new drugs which had been sent out from the UK. This treatment had raised many comments from the Other Ranks: "They're trying them out on us." "We're nowt but guinea pigs." All this scepticism was normal and could be expected, and it would have raised serious doubts amongst the senior officers if it had been absent. Most of the men had had their moments of weakness and had been glad to try anything that might make them feel better. Good food was perhaps the best way to make a start to rebuild themselves and this was becoming available more often than not.

The attitude of the regimental medical staff was much more relaxed at Risalpur after the fighting had apparently stopped with the Japanese surrender, and no man was likely to be accused of 'skiving' if he reported sick, even with fairly trivial problems such as back ache or haemorrhoids. Dusty had reported sick with continuing diarrhoea. After a week of taking some of the new 'sulpha' drugs, without any signs of success, he had been sent to the nearest BGH, where another two weeks of tests had convinced the specialist that he should be sent back to the UK. "This man had better be put on the next ship available for patients. With his service history he will be sent soon in any case for demobilisation. Better to go in some sort of comfort. All right, Sergeant?" That part had been easy. He had to make sure that he could keep his kit with him. He was not going to lose his rubies after all the effort he had made to get them.

The major problem that he saw was the need for him to disappear and take a new personality. There was no need to return to his home in Hull. Megan had run off to Newcastle with her boyfriend and he hoped never to see her again. His parents had both died in the last year and the business had slipped into oblivion during their illnesses. He did not need any money from their estate, now that he had the rubies. No one would miss him. It was always possible that the Regiment would try to make contact with him when they returned to Blighty. Otherwise, if he really intended to carry out his plan to sort some of the bastards who had benefited from the War, he needed to start a new life under a new name.

The opportunity came when he did not expect it. He and a small group of "walking" patients were taken by train and ambulance to a new medical transit camp on the outskirts of Bombay. It was staffed in the usual way with QA nurses, orderlies and sufficient medical supplies for their daily needs, but the holiday spirit reigned throughout. They were all well enough to be going home. Some of them had been overseas for more than the four years, which was the recently lowered maximum. There was even a bottle of export Guinness with the evening meal. That brought a smile to many a jaundiced face. Dusty turned to the man in the next bed, who did not appear to have any uniform with him.

"Have you lost all your kit, mate?"

"No, cocker, I'm a civvy. Tim's the name. Tim Smith. Merchant Navy. There's hundreds of us. Been wrecked and on the way back home. What have you been up to?"

This was a new world for Dusty. He had had only the slightest contact with any of the other forces and the Merchant Navy was a closed book to him. He gave the briefest information he could without being rude to the man.

"Dusty Miller. I've had four years out here with the tanks and am now going home as a hospital patient, graded Z, for discharge. Can't get there fast enough. And you? How were you sunk?"

"That was months ago. On the *Connaught Bay*. The Japs sank us off Singapore and I've been shore-based in Kandy ever since sorting the papers and records for all the other shipwrecked mariners. Cushy job but it couldn't last. I caught malaria and can't shake it off. Now I'm hoping to get better before I land in Southampton and find another ship."

This rang a bell with Dusty.

"What happens when a ship's crew survive a sinking and eventually get back to a friendly port? If they've lost their ship and all their personal papers, how do they prove who they are?"

"That's easy. That was my job at Kandy, sorting out just that problem. First of all I would arrange a meal, a medical examination and then I'd start getting all the necessary papers together for each man. He would tell me which ship he had been on, his 'line', so that I could advise his employer, and possibly arrange for some cash to be sent to him. He would, most likely, then go back to whichever port they needed him at. We would arrange his passage and he'd have a very comfortable return trip to his home. If he didn't want to return to sea, I would issue the necessary form for him to get a civilian identity number, and, of course, he'd need another form to get a ration book. It's all paper – 'coggage', they call it out here. But, you'll know that."

Dusty was very quiet for the rest of that day. He wanted to ask Tim Smith more about the forms involved in confirming a man's identity under those circumstances, but he did not want to rush it or raise the man's curiosity. He need not have worried. Tim was an extrovert who liked the sound of his own voice and wanted to be the life and the soul of the party.

"Do you think that there is a market for those forms I was telling you about, Dusty? I helped myself to a stack of them all in case I could sell them some time. Could you use any of them?"

It could not have been easier.

After a few moments of thought, and apparently not really bothered to show much interest, Dusty quietly said, "It is always possible that I could meet someone with a need to use that sort of thing. Are you short of cash?"

"Not desperate, but I can always use a few extras chips. You can get beer here most days, if you have the necessary."

"Very well. I'll have a few sets from you. How about five chips for five sets?" Dusty had his tongue in his cheek as he said that. He had no idea how many sets the sailor had for sale. He only wanted two sets, in case he spoiled one set.

"Not on your Nelly. I want five chips each set. Tell you what. I'll let you have three sets for ten. How about that?"

"Done". Dusty had no hesitation. He had what he wanted and

pulled out a ten-rupee note. They soon made the exchange and Tim Smith went into the detail of what was required on each form for a person to register his presence officially back in the UK. He would need a permanent address before he started to present the completed forms at the various offices of local government. Within a week of landing at a British port, a man could be swallowed into the economic life of the country. He would receive a ration book and be required to pay his taxes. He would need to register with a doctor for any medical advice and treatment. He could then become a perfectly respectable citizen, as long as he did not meet anyone who knew him by his previous name. It seemed to be the ideal solution to Dusty's problems. They shook hands on the deal.

"Thanks, Tim. I may be able to make a bit if I can sell these three sets at around five chips each. Good luck to you".

He was relieved to learn that evening that Tim Smith had been found a passage on a hospital ship that was sailing the next day, so there was a rush of packing and movement. Tim had had a tendency to ask very probing questions but he had managed to deflect them into other aspects of his life. When Dusty sailed from Bombay a few days later, he had already decided on the information he was going to put on the documents that he would use. Within two weeks of landing at Southampton he would become a shipwrecked mariner, Philip Anders, of the Ellerman Wilson Line, Hull. He would need and take a month's holiday in Scotland and then decide not to go to sea again.

---

Three months after the holiday, Philip Anders was living in a small flat over an empty shop in Wilmslow, Cheshire, and was about to start his own business as a private investigator. He could not have made a better choice of career. The Manchester area was populated by a growing number of ex-servicemen and women who had returned home from the forces to find that their trusted spouses had missed them during the War. They had missed the comforts and joys of married life, so much so that they had begun to look for those pleasures elsewhere. And they had found them.

A talented "private eye", who could produce results that held up in court, became a necessity for the divorce solicitors of the area. Phil Anders made his own 'luck' with long hours of hard work. He was not distracted by having a wife. His own experience of marriage had given him a cynical attitude to the whole business and, on the rare occasions when he became aware of the need for female company, there was no shortage of willing partners. His solitary life made the ideal cover for his fixation on the need to strike back at the blatant rogues who always seemed to get away with their rotten ways of life. He heard nothing from the Ellerman Wilson Line. They would have enough problems dealing with the records of all their current serving employees, without trying to trace those who had not shown any interest in renewing their contracts after the trauma of sailing under their flag during the War.

The first post-war 'elimination' was easily planned and executed. He had first spotted the articles in the press about the estate agent, Peter Fyle, in January, soon after he had landed in Southampton, and he had decided that he would make a start to his hobby. The national and local press were becoming very much aware that they faced a number of new challenges since the end of hostilities and the returning servicemen, who had been on the staff before the War, had now to be found jobs by their old employers. Some of them, who had been office juniors when they joined the forces, returned with ranks such as major, lieutenant-colonel or squadron leader. They expected to be offered positions that were more in keeping with that experience and the result was that the country appeared to be flooded with trainee journalists who were anxious to prove their abilities.

The excessive coverage of the sexual abuse of two boys in Peterborough had raised the awareness of the general public of the fact that they were interested in a variation of smut and innuendo as a change from reading of battlegrounds and the destruction of German and Japanese cities. It produced a new type of hate pattern. Many of the readers of the articles became incensed by reports of innocent young boys being enticed into secluded corners by some pervert. The fact that Peter Fyle had been "helping the police with their enquiries" was soon public knowledge and his reputation was ruined overnight. Anders had been affected, like all the others who wrote to the newspapers to condemn someone who had not even been charged, let alone been found guilty.

"No time like the present," he decided, "and it will be good practice".

His choice of weapon was simple. He had spent many hours, whilst in hospital in the North West Frontier Province, whittling away on a piece of fresh-cut green bamboo and the result had been a very practical carved paper knife. With a strong handle and a sharply pointed blade, it became a perfect weapon in the hands of a fit young man who had been trained in all the arts both of unarmed and armed combat. At last, he could put all that training to good use. And it could not be traced back to him.

He well remembered the lecture from that Guards WO2 on the training course at Ahmednagar. "You must realise that there will be times when you have to make your own decisions about your next action. You will not always have an officer there to do it for you and a quick decision by an NCO can save the day and the battle. Use your loaf and keep planning ahead."

Well, he had been using his loaf for a long time through all his years in the Army. And he wasn't the only one. All that bellyaching he had heard in the ranks had been a sure sign that the mass of Other Ranks would put up with a lot of waffle and inefficiency from some of the officers for some of the time, but there was a limit to what they would stand. Especially when it came to profiteering and corruption by those who had managed to avoid serving their country in that War. Now this dirty sod was using his money and position to bugger about with ignorant little lads who didn't know any better. It was time for him to find out that he had it coming to him for a change. He would learn what it was all about before he snuffed it.

Preparation for the project included printing a few business cards on a small press that he had acquired for his private eye work. They read "William C. Smith, Property Development," and gave a false address and telephone number in Hull. They would only be used if absolutely necessary and as a last resort. He then visited Peterborough on 6$^{th}$ April, using his own car, which he parked in Leicester before travelling by bus to his destination. An hour after arriving he was on his way back to Leicester on the return bus. The time had been well spent with a reconnaissance of the area around Fyle's office and the purchase of a pre-war street map of Peterborough. Anders did not think that anyone had looked at him in any curious way; he was dressed as untidily as possible without attracting attention from anyone in authority.

On his next visit to Peterborough, on 13$^{th}$ April, he was dressed in an old business suit and wearing a well used black homburg hat. He expected to be seen as, and he wanted to be remembered as, a reasonably tidy businessman. He had stolen a black Morris 8 Series E from a street park in Leicester and driven it to a back street park behind the Town Hall in Peterborough. There were a number of cars of a similar type, probably belonging to visiting salesmen, and he felt sure it would be safe until he needed it after the job was done.

Phil Anders had never been on the stage. He was a natural. No doubt the talent was beginning to develop because of the nature of his job as a private investigator, but he felt quite relaxed as he slipped into the mode of a businessman looking for an opportunity to use his abilities in the Peterborough area.

He could tell that the receptionist was a trainee as he handed his business card to her. She was too polite and too interested. A seasoned girl would have been far more disdainful. No matter. Once he saw the victim, he knew that greed would make his job very easy. His indication that price was no problem and that time was the controlling factor soon had the estate agent getting into top gear. Sacrewell House was the selected property and he was at the office at 3pm, climbing into Peter Fyle's car on time.

The estate agent was in good form as they drove along the Leicester Road through Longthorpe and Castor towards the Great North Road. The sun was shining as they enjoyed the scenery, including the thatched cottages and the views of the River Nene. Five miles from the office they arrived at Sacrewell House.

"Do you have any family, Mr Smith?" Peter Fyle did not like a long silence.

"Yes, but they will not be coming to Peterborough immediately. I've need to get the business started before I think about the domestic arrangements."

After a quick look of appraisal at the surroundings, Anders suggested that they moved indoors, which they did. No one had seen them arrive and he felt safe to give this man the surprise of his life. They moved from the hall entrance into the large kitchen. "This is promising", he remarked as he fitted the brass knuckle-duster on to his left hand. The estate agent had been leading the way and he turned around at the words to face Anders.

As he did so, the whole weight of Anders' twelve stones behind the brass hit him in the solar plexus. The gasp was quite loud and he hit the floor with his mouth opening and closing like a goldfish in search of food. The man was winded and speechless except for some feeble attempts to say "Why? Why?"

"I'll tell you why." The ex-soldier was icily calm. He was aware that the adrenaline was running in his veins but he felt very sure of himself. He was going to do it, and soon. "I want you to know why, before you go to sleep. The whole country is well aware that you think you have got away with your dirty habit of buggering little boys but you have not. Even the police know that you are the one they have been looking for, but they can't prosecute because there is not sufficient evidence. So I'm doing the prosecuting and the sentencing and the punishment." He gave a wry smile as he pulled his bamboo knife out of his right pocket.

"You don't deserve to live and enjoy this world of ours. You'll have a long time now when you can think about all your bad habits and all the lives you've blighted." Leaning over the distraught man on the floor he lunged downwards, with the weight of his body behind his rigid arms. His two hands were clasped around the weapon, which cut through the clothes and entered the heart.

The loud gasp was followed by a jerk of the body. The handle of the knife was pulled from his grasp as Anders stood up and watched the last few pulsations. He felt the satisfaction of a job well done.

The first one, Blondie Benton, had been more remote and the killing had been done by a hand grenade. This one, the first of the post-War years, had been much more personal. But both were successful. Now he had to be sure that he was not around when the body was found. He leaned over again and removed the keys from the body, leaving the bamboo knife where it was. He then checked his clothes for any blood and found that he was in the clear.

After he had locked the door to the house, he drove Fyle's car carefully to Peterborough and parked it behind the Town Hall, leaving all the keys in the car. Being a careful assassin, he walked away from it and around the block of shops and offices, including the Town Hall, before he returned to the part of the park where his stolen Morris 8 was waiting. He was soon driving west along the Leicester Road and away from the area. He made a similar exchange of vehicles in Leicester before continuing to drive to the west and on to his flat in Wilmslow. It was only after he arrived there that he removed the medical rubber gloves that he had worn throughout the caper.

## Chapter 16

# *1946*
# *Justice?*

Throughout the remainder of 1946 Phil Anders relaxed and consolidated his position as a successful private investigator. He looked back on the Peterborough job as both an achievement and proof that his planning had paid off. The splash of publicity did not last very long, mainly due to the complete lack of clues that could lead to any progress. The police admitted that they were up against a brick wall. There were many other items of news that would help to sell the papers.

He found that his work was interesting and satisfying. It certainly demanded long hours of concentration but he had an enquiring mind and he soon found that he could adapt to fit into any social stratum. Perhaps, his 'ordinariness' had something to do with it. He had no outstanding features or characteristics that stayed in the minds of those he met. He was simply remembered for his efficiency and the quiet way in which he asked questions to provide him with the information that he needed. Apart from an occasional advertisement in the local press and specialist legal magazines, he did not need to take any special action to maintain the flow of enquiries for his services. Life was full. Exercise was organised on a solitary arrangement of going for lengthy runs early each morning. Anders dressed the part in running shorts and a light shirt, bringing his army running shoes back into use. He was not the only one to do this and he often passed other ex-servicemen keeping themselves fit in this way. As the years passed, 'jogging' became a recognised method of exercising the body at convenient times.

He had decided that he would continue with his hobby of 'elimination'. The law might not be exactly 'an ass', but he found that most of the lawyers and policemen that he met through his work were simply very busy handling their own tiny aspect of life. The worst example was when a barrister, knowing full well that his client was a rogue and guilty as charged, would stand up in court and present a compelling case for dismissal of the charges. "Agreed," said one of them. "But, every suspect is entitled to being defended competently and it is better that ten guilty men go free than that one innocent should be condemned." This was before the days when the public became aware of the occasional faking of evidence against the accused, in cases in which the police were convinced of their guilt. This considerate attitude to the defendants created a deep and growing anger amongst the victims and their friends, especially when many of the freed criminals re-offended.

Anders also became disillusioned with the world of politics. Both local and national politicians were often in the news after some misdemeanour. "They seem to be obsessed with the law rather than with justice" came to his mind regularly. "Who said that the only honest man to enter parliament was named Guy Fawkes?" Yes, there was a real need for some organisation to apply justice in this world of ours. He had taken an oath to defend his country. He had volunteered for the armed forces, where he had been trained to become an efficient killer, and he would volunteer to eliminate a few of the rogues who did not deserve to enjoy this delightful country. There was no shortage of prospects. Their names and photographs were on the front of some newspapers almost every day.

Perhaps it was a good thing that he had not been granted a commission. If he had been an officer, he would have been expected to obey the law at all times. He often thought of Smudger Smith 162.

There was a lad, an old soldier of the old school. Smudger had never been impressed with his officers and he often took a chance to put them in their place. His favourite and most successful trick was to offer to be helpful to any new or untrained charwallah.

"Listen to me, Sher Khan," he would say, "you must learn to salute properly every time you see an officer-sahib. You've seen the other sahibs saluting, haven't you?" "Achcha, Sahib," he would reply. "Then I'll show you how to salute. You jump to attention, malum, then the right arm goes out, ooper, do, teen, then straight nichchi, ek, do, teen, – *up two three, down two three*, malum?" The man would shake his head sideways, which perversely meant 'yes'.

"Then you must greet the officer properly, every time you see him. And I'll teach you what to say to make him like you." The trainee tea-seller's eyes would gleam with delight that a sahib should be going to such lengths to help him be a success. "Achcha, sahib".

"When you have given him his cup of hot tea, you give him the regimental salute that I've just shown you, and immediately say loudly and clearly, 'And up your pipe, burra sahib'. That is an expression of both respect and admiration. He will appreciate it". These instructions were given to the naïve Punjabi in a mixture of Urdu and cockney rhyming slang that was intelligible only to the older, pre-war regular soldiers. The new re-enforcements, listening to such an expert, were desperate to learn to talk like that. Smudger was usually given a mug of tea and a large sugary cake by the appreciative charwallah. A lot depended on the reaction of the future officer victims as to whether the appreciation and benefits would continue for any length of time. It certainly caused some merriment amongst the other lads.

Chapter 17

## *1947*
## *Impulsive Action*

Phil Anders had been a trusting soul when he volunteered to fight for his king and country. He had believed all he was told by his parents, teachers and the officers under whom he served in the training depots. Some of the last, despite being commissioned, were not really recognised as 'officers'; not, that is, in the sense that he was likely to meet and fight the enemy whilst under their command. Such officers, whom he learned to mistrust totally and on sight, were those who gave the periodic lectures on 'the situation'.

They were introduced to the groups of Other Ranks as 'education officers'. Most of them lacked a military bearing and had such a casual approach in their presentations that they made some of the recruits wonder exactly what was going to happen to the war effort. The majority of them had cultured accents, dropped the word 'Oxbridge' into their talks, and left no one in any doubt about their superiority. They knew it all. There was an answer ready for any question, however biased or probing it might be. Dusty Miller, as he was then known, was like many of the volunteers and conscripts listening to these talks. He was not an idiot. They had one short word for it all: Balls.

After being raised in a conservative home, where there was a strong sense of self-determination with the need to help the less fortunate, he had a built-in aversion to communism as practised in Russia. Most of his comic books of childhood had contained stories of bearded spies prowling around the cities whilst carrying black spheres from which smoke was escaping. Why should anyone want to bomb innocent civilians in London? But he believed that there were such people.

He could hardly believe his ears when one education officer told the group of recruits that "we are now the allies of Russia. We have a common enemy in Germany and that vast group of countries known as the Union of Soviet Socialist Republics will commit all its resources to help us win." There were cries of 'Good old Uncle Joe' and 'Joe for King'. No more was heard of the horrors of the Revolution. "That was all propaganda," said the officer.

The nation could not afford to have divided loyalties and all the powers of a strong government were applied to prevent any criticism. In the Army occasional fights broke out between the odd Communist and a Mosley blackshirt. This would result in one of them being sent to another unit to prevent a recurrence. It was only in 1946 that a few stories of the Russian excesses leaked into the press. Reports of massacres in Poland were hushed up and ignored. It was going to take many years before anyone believed the truth about the graves at Katyn.

Phil Anders had further doubts about the stories that were handed out to the Forces when he landed back in Blighty early in 1946. He then heard, for the first time, that the southern part of the country had been bombarded with German high explosive, sent from across the Channel by means of the V1 and V2 secret weapons. It had been going on in 1944 and 1945, when he and his friends had been fighting for the defence of India at Imphal and during the successful invasion of Burma in 1944 and 1945. The ban on releasing the information in India was totally effective. Servicemen whose families had been wiped out with a 'buzz bomb' were quietly sent back to the UK on compassionate grounds. They were not even allowed to tell their mates the reason for their departure. There had been too many secrets. The established government had used the excuse "that it could help the enemy," and had continued to keep the simple soldiery in ignorance. Perhaps they feared that the bad news would undermine the morale of the troops. Anders had always believed that "every action created a reaction," and he had made up his own mind now. The Russians obviously intended to destroy the British way of life and were using their own net of spies, planted in important positions, to do just that.

In the last few weeks of 1946 there had been plenty of press coverage of the antics of the General Secretary of the Scottish Transport Union. 'Jock' McFee had been reported as being the leader of the group that intended to bring the country to a halt. "Instructions From Moscow?" were the headlines of the *Glasgow Herald*. This quickly convinced Anders that McFee was an obvious target for his attentions. He kept up to date with the daily reports in the *Telegraph* and the *Mail* and was surprised when McFee appeared to be slowing down in his activities. Perhaps he had received instructions from his bosses in Moscow to hold his position for a few weeks. It was possible that the grand plan was to organise more than one of the Communist-controlled Unions to go on strike at the same time. It could be more effective in maximising the damage done to the economy. Whatever the reason for the hesitation, the harsh Scottish voice was heard more and more on the radio and his ranting was read in the papers during February and March 1947.

"This is it," thought Anders.

He had decided to take time to assess the situation and to act when and where the opportunity might arise. He was well aware that McFee had received more than a few death threats, an indication that he was not the only one to believe that the world would be a better place without the man. It might have put him on his guard against any approach and made him wary of strangers. The press had supplied a lot of background information, which was very helpful to a potential assassin. This included his home address in Motherwell and the fact that the Union man would be travelling to Glasgow by train on 13$^{th}$ April in order to attend a meeting of all the Union members gathered there that evening.

Sitting outside the entrance to the flats in a stolen car with false numberplates was routine work for the private eye. He broke the boredom of two hours waiting by walking down the street and then returning to the café near the car and enjoying a hot cup of tea. The window seat gave him the same coverage of the flats. And his patience was then rewarded.

An old Jowett was driven up to the entrance. Anders recognised Andrew Reid from recent photographs in the press and knew things were beginning to move. Reid went into the flats and returned five minutes later with Jock McFee carrying his overnight bag. Both men were talking and appeared to be very excited. Today was going to be their day, or so they thought. Anders followed them in his car until they drove into a car park near the station. He parked his car well away from them and let them get ahead of him. He knew their destination and bought his own ticket to Glasgow without seeing them. He had no firm plans for finalising McFee but he only wanted to learn more about the man as he walked down the full length of the platform. Then he spotted the two Union men. They were standing together close to the edge, ready to be amongst the first to clamber aboard when the train stopped. He moved nearer until he was standing almost shoulder to shoulder with Andrew Reid. McFee was saying "and the Engineers and the M&GWU will be with us," when the growing sound of an approaching express train made it impossible for any conversation to continue.

"Human nature doesn't change very much," thought Anders. The piercing scream of the train caused the usual reaction. Everyone on the packed platform stopped their chatter and turned to look towards the entrance of the station. Turning his back to McFee, he quickly bent down as if to tie his shoelace. Half the weight of his body was moving sharply towards the Union man just when Anders' bottom struck him on the right hip.

It was all done on the spur of the moment. Unprepared for such a blow, McFee was caught off balance and he shot off the edge of the platform, to be struck instantly by the front of the express engine. As gasps of horror came from the onlookers, who all turned to look at the passing train, Anders moved away from his position and put a small group of passengers between himself and Andrew Reid. Without any apparent urgency, he moved slowly but surely to the edge of the crowd. He waited there for a few minutes until the Glasgow train arrived and halted. The two railway policemen who had arrived on the platform were unable to take control of the situation before the disembarking passengers had surged out of the train and towards the exit. The assassin went with them, handing in a platform ticket to the collector.

After reaching his car and relaxing into the seat, Anders realised that this had been the first time that he had acted on impulse. He usually weighed up the pros and cons before he took any vital action but this time he had acted quickly and with determination on what could only have been a whim. He knew that he could easily have done the wrong thing at the time and been spotted by any of the people around him, but it had not happened. "It was a gamble," he thought, "but it worked." A shiver went down his spine. "I must be mad to take a chance like that. Never again."

It was a simple matter to drive to Glasgow and catch the next train to Manchester, after dumping the car in a park near the shopping area. He waited to read the reports of McFee's death but there was no immediate suggestion that the man had been murdered. "Tragic Accident to Union Leader" was the most common headline. It was only after a week that some bright newshound asked the question, "A Convenient Accident?"

McFee's death prevented his speech being given to his Union on 14th April and his deputy was the first to wonder if he had been killed in order to stop that speech. The shock certainly gave many of those involved some serious thoughts about the possible repercussions of agitating for a strike. Some of them were aware of the lengths to which their Moscow bosses would go and the question was asked whether an undercover group had been formed by the UK government to use similar methods in order to counter the 'subversion'.

There were some organisations formed by the right wing of the political front in order to give talks to foremen and workmen on the shop floor with the intention of countering the 'red menace'. No doubt these could include a few extremists who would resort to violence to stop these damaging strikes before they started. No one gave a clear answer to these probing questions. No one suggested that there could be a lone operator such as Phil Anders. He continued to feel secure. He earned sufficient income from his work to live as well as he wished and he kept his stock of rubies hoarded for 'a rainy day'.

# Chapter 18

# *1948*
# *The Crossbow*

The third caper was more satisfactory and much better planned.

During his many hours of observing a variety of people to get information about their activities, Phil Anders would often use a nearby antiques shop as a place where he could spend time browsing without raising any questions in the minds of those who could be watching him. He had a quite genuine interest in the wide range of *objets d'art* and paintings that were jumbled together in these often dark but fascinating shops. The proprietors would rarely press him to state his interest as he wandered around. He could usually take the opportunity to observe his target across the street and leave with only a murmur of thanks if it was necessary to move quickly.

It was on one of these visits that he was attracted to an old crossbow on a shelf. The bow was made of willow with a mahogany shaft and butt. The greased string and brass fittings made it obvious to him that it had been made by an expert and had been well cared for throughout its life. It was a thing of beauty. Anders knew that he must have it to keep as a treasure long before he realised that it was an accurate weapon that he could perhaps use in the future. He was shown how to tension the bow and use the trigger mechanism whilst holding it to his shoulder and aiming at a target. There were only two bolts with the antique, and he used that fact to negotiate a fair price for it. Both he and the dealer were satisfied when he walked out of the shop with his prize.

During the next few weeks he was able to fire the weapon many times at a target in his garage, well hidden from any prying eyes. It was surprisingly quiet and accurate. He began to think that it could be a very useful means of despatching future prospects. The only snag was that he would have to obtain or make a supply of projectiles. He quickly decided that he would need to make them himself. Asking around possible suppliers would highlight the fact that he was involved in the use of crossbows and someone would recall his enquiries. The problem was quickly resolved. He found that he could easily make a few very effective bolts from a length of half-inch metal rod. After drilling into the leading end of the cut length, he fitted a piece of sharpened bamboo for the point of the projectile and another piece of flat bamboo in the trailing end to act as flight feathers. Testing these proved that they were as accurate as the two manufactured bolts.

He was delighted with his new toy, despite finding that the bamboo point could shatter when it hit a hard object. He knew that a well-aimed shot would knock a man to the ground if it hit his ribcage. He would be ready with a knife if necessary. The only other change he made was to alter the locking device which fixed the bow to the shaft and stock, so that it was more easily fastened with a wing nut and no longer required a spanner. This enabled him to disassemble and carry the little engine in a small bag or rucksack.

He then practised jogging in the mornings with the crossbow inside the rucksack and he soon became proficient at fixing the weapon so that it did not move or press on his spine. With its weight held against his waist it became unnoticeable, whether he was running gently or in bursts of speed. He also found that he could assemble the crossbow ready for firing within twenty-five seconds of stopping his running and sitting under a bush in the woods. It was certainly worth testing out on his next prospect.

There was no shortage of characters being reported in the newspapers for embezzlement, rape and general crimes of greed. One of the 'Sundays' had plugged away with articles about Brigadier Fitzburn and, over a period of weeks, had implied that the man had been a rogue throughout his term of service in the Intelligence Corps. The indications were that he had used his position in post-war Germany to fill a warehouse repeatedly with Nazi loot after he had arrested the culprits involved and seen them sent to gaol. He worked on a percentage basis – 50% for the Government and 50% for himself. In this way there was a steady flow of recaptured valuables being photographed and listed, with the intention of either tracing the original owners or selling them in the open market, the proceeds being held in trust until some bright person made a decision for disposal. His own half of the loot was shipped to a warehouse in Switzerland and held in one of his undercover names before being sold quietly on the black market.

Fitzburn's only mistake was in not paying his assistant sufficiently well. It was a stupid mistake. Sergeant Major Bill Simpson was an efficient administrator but he had expensive habits. In those days, when fraternisation was an offence, the WO2 had installed a lovely but hungry fraulein in a small flat near his billets. She had a few equally hungry relatives, who pressed her to plead for extra rations for themselves. They all liked to drown their sorrows in whatever spirits could be obtained and Simpson had many nights of alcoholic excess, which put him even more under their control. Knowing what he did about the Brigadier's private business, he did an 'Oliver'. The request to his boss, "Please sir, I want some more," put Fitzburn into a difficult position. He paid the man double the previously agreed sum but he was not yet aware that Simpson had learned most of the finer details of the scam. He knew the sort of a mess that was about to be exposed when the Sergeant Major was stopped by a Military Police patrol as he was driving three tons of loot to his own private warehouse.

In the ensuing court-martial Simpson tried to blame his boss, only to find that the Brigadier was too experienced in assertive questioning to be trapped by the prosecuting officer. Fitzburn had himself done it all before many times. All his records were correct, perhaps too correct. There was no proof of any fault other than the truckload of goodies which the WO2 admitted taking for his own benefit. The result was swift. Simpson went to gaol for three years, but was released after serving two years. Fitzburn was admonished for not keeping a better control of his staff and quietly told that his future in the Army was not going to be as pleasant as it had been. He was advised to apply for discharge so that he could receive all the benefits of a retiring officer. After a week of being ostracised by his regular drinking friends in the mess, he applied for a quick release from service.

Within the first year of retirement he had established himself comfortably in the Lawns, a delightful early 19$^{th}$ century stone mansion near Mynydd Bach, overlooking the Chepstow racecourse. His wife Felicity was delighted to have him around the place for a few days each week. She was very impressed with her husband's apparent affluence but she did not ask him for too much detail as to his finances. With a small staff, the house was a joy, which gave her a base for the standard of living to which she was rapidly becoming accustomed. She was soon deeply involved in a number of local charities and did not complain when Charles disappeared for two or three days at a time. "Checking on the investments", was his usual explanation.

This was perfectly true. He found it was necessary to make the occasional clandestine trip to Switzerland in order to turn some of the valuables into cash. He was a past master at disguising himself and slipping across the Channel without any of the officials knowing that he had left the country. His stock of varied and blank passports would last a long time and he thought, "Well, they taught me how to move around Europe without being noticed. I might as well use the training".

He was dining alone at home on 13$^{th}$ April 1948.

Phil Anders had spent the first week of April observing his target as he moved about the local area enjoying his good fortune. The Brigadier appeared to be in the best of health and he was treated with the usual respect given to the wealthy gentry in the country. Anders had jogged his way around the outskirts of the Lawns and was confident that he knew the geography of the place. There was plenty of cover in the gardens and shrubbery, which would enable him to come close to the house and possibly get a shot at Fitzburn through a window. During one evening spell of observation of the house he noticed that the Brigadier went out into the garden immediately after the meal, smoking his cigar whilst the housekeeper cleared the table. The younger lady, almost certainly the Brigadier's wife, stayed in the room and moved a few items from the table to the sideboard before going upstairs.

The routine was confirmed by another two evening visits. The garden was the best area for the job, after the evening meal. He would be able to confront the man and he might have the chance to tell him why he was doing this to him. No matter. As long as he was dining at home on 13$^{th}$ April, that would be the day.

On that day Anders followed Fitzburn to the Chepstow races and he felt sure that he would be returning to the Lawns to dine with his wife. He went ahead with all the preparations that he had planned in such detail. His own car was parked in Newport and he returned to Mynydd Bach in a stolen Ford, dressed for the job in his black shirt, trousers and running shoes. The rucksack containing the crossbow and a knitted balaclava helmet was over his shoulders as he slipped into the grounds of the Lawns. He was soon positioned in the bushes, watching the lighted window of the dining room with the weapon loaded and ready in his hands. There were no hiccups. After an hour of watching the couple enjoy their meal, he saw the Brigadier stand up and leave the room. He took up a position at the rear door within a few minutes, standing under the outside light as he lit his cigar and puffed away in sheer enjoyment.

Anders moved very quietly away from the house and went down the path towards the end of the shrubbery, where Fitzburn was in the habit of standing to enjoy the scene down towards Chepstow. He positioned himself under a mature laburnum and waited for his quarry to come to him. The previous reconnaissance had paid off. Army training again. Never go into action without first doing the fullest possible recce.

Knowing that he wanted the man to be within two or three yards and facing him, Anders had prepared a dry twig placed across a stone near his feet and he patiently waited and watched as Fitzburn enjoyed his last view of the evening countryside. After waiting a minute or two, Anders pressed his toe on to the twig and the crack of it breaking made the target turn towards the silent killer. There was no hesitation. The twang of the crossbow, the thud of the projectile hitting the man in the chest and the gasp from the falling body were one continuous flow of sound. Then silence.

Anders waited, listening for anything unusual, but the night noises continued and his speeding pulse began to quieten. He had reloaded the crossbow in case the first shot had not killed the man but it was not required. Walking over to the body, which was lying on its back, he could see no sign of life. A full minute searching for a pulse in the wrist found nothing, so he grasped the metal projectile in the man's chest and snapped it off, leaving the bamboo point imbedded in the heart. That would give them something to puzzle over.

That was it. The darkening night swallowed him up as he slipped away to recover the borrowed car for the drive back to Newport and his own vehicle. He had learned a lot from this, his third effort in Blighty. And he liked the crossbow as a weapon, although he had already decided that he must use it very sparingly.

The unusual projectile could create clues if too many of them were to be used. He had also decided to ration himself to only one obliteration per year in future. They were very exciting and very satisfying, but they were time-consuming and he needed to keep on with his growing business as a private eye. The stimulus from the hobby certainly helped to keep his thinking process in good trim.

Chapter 19

# April 1982
# The Final Caper

Anders had believed from the start that he would eventually be caught out. He accepted this possibility without being too worried. Perhaps he deserved it. He now realised that the caper on 13th April this year had had a few warning signs.

The choice of victim had been too easy. It looked like a repeat of the one deleted in 1947, when Jock McFee, the Union man who had declared that he was going to bring down the Government in that year, had been seen off without any real difficulty.

Now, another bigheaded Union leader, Vince Hallett, of the Colliery Workers Union, was intending to do the same thing. He had been reported in the national press to be acting on instructions from Moscow. "How on earth can these little people get such big heads that they believe they can disrupt the country in this way?" he wondered. "If they are so convinced that that is what they can do, then they don't deserve to exist, let alone be in a position where they can create so much disruption for the majority of the population. I would have thought that there were a few members of the same Union who could see that their General Secretary was leading them down the path of no return. Surely they could alert their colleagues to the situation that many of them would lose their jobs when alternative sources of power are exploited?"

Everyone else seemed to know that Maggie Thatcher had been sufficiently aware of his intentions to plan ahead in order to scupper the Union's activities. The Tory Government had organised a build-up of coal stocks that would ensure that the NCB customers' orders would be met in full for more than a year, without a single new ton being mined by the Union members. Hallett preferred to ignore this fact. He and his Russian advisers could not see the logic of the fact that the Union would be bankrupt after only a few months on strike. Surely the Russians had not promised to help with the finances?

Phil Anders had decided that Hallett must go.

The essential facts were easily obtained. The office of the CWU was situated at the Grange, Field Lane, Greenfields, Barnsley. This large country house had been built for the colliery owner prior to nationalisation and had been acquired by the Union soon after vesting day. He checked by telephone that Hallett would be at his office for the whole of the week. Hallett's secretary confirmed this quite readily when Anders pretended to be the representative of the company supplying the Union's printed stationery.

The reconnaissance was carried out on 12$^{th}$ April, when he drove to Barnsley dressed in his navy-blue jogging clothes.

Leaving his car in an almost-full car park in the centre of the town, he slipped out down some quiet streets and headed south towards the suburb of Greenfields. His pre-War Ordnance Survey map had indicated that he had only four miles to run from the town centre to the Grange and he soon settled into a steady pace that he could keep up for hours if necessary. Forty minutes later he turned right off the main road into the clearly marked Field Lane and was soon jogging past a row of terraced colliery cottages on his left. The six-foot-high stone wall on his right was the southern boundary of the target estate, the Grange.

As he went past the cottages, there appeared to be no sign of life but years of experience had taught him not to assume that he had not been observed. He continued up the lane, paused momentarily at the open gates to the Grange, and then continued up the lane for another fifty yards. He was in a cul de sac. The lane became a narrow path through the thick wooded slopes ahead of him. That was worth knowing. He needed to have an alternative escape route that went more directly to the north – perhaps it would be across the Grange land. He would recheck the possibilities as he jogged on his return journey down the lane.

Pausing again at the gates to the Grange, he could now see the house less than a hundred yards away. There appeared to be a brass plate fixed to the side of the open front door. There was a lot of cover available from trees and shrubs, which had been planted when the house was built more than a hundred years before. Anders continued to run down the lane and mentally noted the face of a woman who was watching him from the top of a downstairs sash window in one of the cottages. "Drat, she might remember seeing me when the proverbial hits the fan." He carried on with his exercise for the few miles back to Barnsley and his car. He was satisfied with his effort and decided to carry out his plans the next day. He would take his crossbow in the rucksack and a very sharp green bamboo dagger, just in case he should need it. He stayed that night at his usual small commercial hotel in Nether Edge, Sheffield.

## 13th April 1982

After an early breakfast at the hotel, Anders went to his car in the multi-storey park and quickly changed into his navy blue jogging kit. He took a wire clothes hanger and soon opened the door of a red Cortina on the same level. Within a minute he had shorted the wiring for the ignition and was driving down the ramp and northwards towards his destination.

Vince Hallett was already seated at his desk with the incoming mail read and cleared to his secretary, Molly White, who had gone back to her own room ready to start typing the replies. He was getting down to the job of writing his next speech for publication when his door opened without any knock and a man walked in with his eyes fixed on Hallett's face.

"Who the hell are you?"

He was not used to having people barge into his sanctum like this. None of his staff would dare to do it and any visiting Union member would have made an appointment to see him before coming the distance from Barnsley. He looked like an oldish man, perhaps nearly sixty, dressed for running or walking in a blue outfit and wearing a dark rucksack over his shoulders. Perhaps he had lost his way and had come into the Grange for advice.

"My name doesn't matter. I'm here to tell you that the decent people of this country are sick of you trying to disrupt their lives. You are leading your own members up the garden path with your promises of more and more pay with longer holidays. You must know that your methods will lead only to more pit closures and loss of jobs – your own included."

By this time the union man's face was puce and he was about to shout out at the intruder, but he stopped when he saw the automatic pistol in his right hand. He was struck with fear as the man moved nearer until the gun was only a few inches from his face. He was not aware that the intruder's left hand was held behind him and out of sight. Many times in the past he had been sworn at and occasionally threatened with violence from a bunched fist, but this was the first time that he had felt the fear of a real threat to his life. The shock made him shiver and keep quiet. If only Molly would walk in. It might save him.

"You understand that you don't deserve to enjoy this life?"

Hallett's mouth and tongue were now too dry for him to make any sound other than a groan at the realisation that the threat was real. He continued to stare at the gun near his nose when the jogger's left hand and arm swung round in a flash and the bamboo knife was thrust up to the hilt into his chest. The sharpened point went through the victim's jacket and into the heart. A quick twist of the handle broke it off, leaving the six inch blade embedded in Hallett's chest. There had been very little noise.

Anders put the gun into his rucksack, swung it on to his shoulders and walked to the door. He opened this quietly, listened for a moment, and then calmly closed it after himself as he crossed the hallway and walked out of the front door of the Grange. He could hear some noises of typing and chatter as he left but there was no sound of panic. He was soon out of the gate, jogging steadily down Field Lane on his way back to Barnsley.

Another job well done. He believed that it had gone smoothly mainly because he had dominated the victim at every stage. He had known exactly what he was going to do at every step, whereas Vince Hallett had been almost paralysed with shock and he had not given him an opportunity to recover. The only thing he had not been able to avoid was being seen as a jogger in the locality. He did not know that Helen Fagin, the woman in the cottage who had seen him the previous day, had also noted his presence here again today. Police enquiries could possibly lead to the true nature of his mission if they became aware of his description.

He had plenty of time to think about this hobby as he made his way back to the red Cortina. His age was beginning to show, not only with his thinning grey hair but also with his health. One sign was the increasing need he experienced to pee more frequently and it was starting again now. He thought he would just about make it to the car park where there were some toilets. It had started to rain before he reached the car but that was really a benefit for him. People tended to keep their heads well down under their umbrellas, and not notice silly old men running for pleasure in the rain.

An hour later Anders had left the Cortina in Sheffield, changed his clothes into his usual business suit, and regained his own car for the journey back to his flat. "Yes," he thought, "I think that I'll make that my last one. I can wind up the business, sell the rest of the rubies and spend the next few years travelling to those places I have always wanted to visit, Australia, New Zealand and the Pacific islands to start with."

Chapter 20

# *April 1982*
# *Police Intelligence*

DI Harry Bennet came to his office each morning these days in a state bordering on euphoria. He had played his hunches many times before his move to Barnsley, but this time he was absolutely sure that he was on to a winner.

His visit to the Sheffield Police Computer Centre had given him access to the Crusoe File (Computer Record of Unresolved Serious Crime of Europe). This recent result of the European National Police Forces' co-operation in sharing their records of unresolved crimes was very informative. It reduced the need to make frequent contact with Interpol to ask for the favour of advice and, at the same time, it reduced the time required to make that contact. Harry had merely to feed into the system the two parameters "bamboo" and "13th April" to be given an instant list of unresolved crimes throughout Europe associated with these headings.

His first surprise was to receive a list of suspected murders on 13th April for most of the thirty-six years since the War, which showed that each one had apparently involved a single person and the weapons had been of bamboo! All were in the United Kingdom.

His Chief Inspector had, admittedly, given him a little prompting on the various stages of his investigation. He had nudged him into withdrawing the word 'bamboo' and checking only the date of 13th April. That had clinched it. There had definitely been a murder on that date each year since the World War II involving a male victim who could be described as anti-establishment – someone denigrated in the popular press and who could be described as a 'thorn in the flesh' of the generally honest British public. Sometimes the weapon had been a handgun, a relic that could have been taken home by a demobilised soldier. On one occasion there was the report that the victim of a train accident could have been pushed under a passing express train in Motherwell station. Harry was convinced that his own local murder, on 13th April this year, was just the latest of a series committed by some 'nutter' who must be quite an old man by now.

His witness, Helen Fagin from Field Lane, would prove invaluable, if only she could identify this jogger. He did not really believe that it could be Jimmy James, but eventually that would be sorted out one way or the other. Tina James appeared to believe that Dusty Miller was a more likely suspect, but he had disappeared from the face of the earth in 1946. The coincidence of her thinking that she had seen him in Sheffield only recently was the best hope he had of identifying that elusive man, once he had been found.

Harry's boss, DCI James Ackroyd, had been extremely helpful in more ways than one. By arranging for them both to have an evening together with an old soldier contact named Alan Fenner, they had learned the story of the $3^{rd}$ Carabiniers' activities in Burma in the $14^{th}$ Army, sometimes called the 'Forgotten Army'. B Squadron of that mechanised cavalry regiment had been very successful when the Japanese $15^{th}$ Army had invaded India in 1944, after pushing the British out of Burma the year before. The eight tanks of B Squadron had climbed a mountain named Nunshigum, near Imphal, capital of the state of Manipur in North East Assam. Alan Fenner had been in that battle and had also continued to fight in the Squadron Leader's tank for the next twelve months. It had been a long and difficult part of the War in the Far East, in which our Forces had had to contend with disease, shortages of food, water and medicines, as well as a determined enemy who did not give up the fight until he was killed. Under those conditions was it possible for a man to become so disillusioned with the government and the lack of effectiveness of the system of justice that, on his return to peacetime, he could decide to take the law into his own hands? And to commit a murder on the same day each year for thirty-six years?

Harry Bennet had decided that it was possible and, having heard Alan Fenner's story of the Forgotten Army, that it was a very likely theory. He could almost understand the frustration of the killer.

What he needed now was help from the general public. This

would require some planning and extra expenditure. It was time to ask the boss.

---

Immediately after lunch Harry presented his suggestions to DCI Ackroyd, who listened without interruption.

"You see, sir, everything points to a solitary man aged about sixty, who has all his wits about him but who is really as mad as a hatter. He has kept it all a secret from his nearest contacts and he has stuck to his plan to kill one person on 13$^{th}$ April each year. This one victim has probably had his name picked out of the newspapers with a pin. The media condemns so many strong characters because they are successful in whatever they do – financiers, con men, politicians, and Union men. The list is endless. Some of them are really 'bad hats' and don't deserve any sympathy when they come to grief, but they are all entitled to a fair trial to answer any charges that we might bring against them."

"Agreed," butted in Ackroyd, "but what are you proposing?"

"There are enough intriguing aspects to this case for the media to whip up a lot of public interest. I have prepared a possible press release and would ask for your approval before I send it out." He handed an A4 sheet of paper to the DCI.

*PRESS RELEASE*
*Further to the reported murder of Mr Vince Hallett, President of the Colliery Workers Union, on 13th April 1982, information has now been received indicating that the man concerned in that attack may also have been involved in up to thirty other murders, dated on or near 13th April in each of the past 30 years.*

*The significance of this date is not yet clear but it could be connected with some trauma in the man's life, probably during the Second World War. It is believed that he spent some time in action, possibly in Burma or the Far East, and that, despite his age of around 60, he has kept fit with regular exercise, including jogging. He was last seen on 13$^{th}$ April this year, wearing a navy blue or black jogging outfit. He is intelligent and dangerous. Anyone knowing a person who fits this description should not approach him but should contact the local police station.*

*The information will be welcomed and treated in confidence. It is vital that he is quickly traced and stopped.*

"You do that, Harry. Copy it to all stations and I'll get approval for all Forces in the UK. This man could be living anywhere. It must become a national hunt for him. We might even be able to stimulate him into making a mistake!"

---

The local and national press made headlines of the murder. With little news coming from the Government recently, they had been delighted to splash the questions posed by Harry Bennet's press release.

> 'SOLO SERIAL KILLER'S 30 YEAR PROGRAMME.'
> 'ONE MAN JUDGE, JURY, EXECUTIONER.'
> 'NUTTER NEEDS NABBING.'
> 'D.I.Y. – THE ULTIMATE DETERRENT?'

Harry realised that he had really started something when he was contacted by numerous reporters from the press and TV. He was able to fill out the limited information given in the press release and stimulate more and more articles, which asked the same sort of questions.

'Is there a solitary fit man in his 60's living near you? Does he disappear on 'business' at odd intervals? Are you living with or near a man like this? If so, tell your local police of the facts and let them eliminate a possible suspect from their enquiries.'

He continued to follow up the local interest, with his men completing the house-to-house calling in an ever-widening circle around the Grange.

He did not have to wait very long. Two days later he had his first contact with the suspected murderer. It came in the form of a facsimile message received during the night.

*'To DI Harry Bennet, Barnsley Police.*
*From the Jogger.*
*You have succeeded in creating a lot of publicity for your case but you are so wrong in your assumptions and you will not succeed in finding me.*

*No, I was not at Imphal nor was I in Burma.*

*No, I was not in the 3rd Carabiniers.*

*Yes, I picked the date of the Battle of Nunshigum, 13th April 1944, for two reasons. Firstly, the 13th sounds unlucky and it was to prove so for the creatures that I have eliminated. Secondly, I was very impressed with the story of that battle in which, when all the officers were killed, the men carried on with the action to wipe out the invader. They succeeded and set an example to the rest of the 14th Army. Kohima was another example of a few determined, ordinary men refusing to accept defeat and clearing the land of evil.*

*Evil people are not all foreign invaders. There are many of them in the British Isles and our government are not going to get rid of them, despite their election promises. They refuse to review capital punishment. They encourage the spreading of cigarette smoking, even when they know it kills thousands every year. They are far more interested in the welfare of the criminal than in helping the victims of crime. They make a criminal of a man who defends his home and property against burglars. It is left to people like me to do all we can to make this country a better place.*

*If you check my list of successes, you will see that they are all child-abusers, rapists, black marketeers, crooks, trade union officials who try to destroy our way of life and who succeed only in destroying their market and the livelihood of their own members. They are all people who use their power for their own selfish ends, whether it is personal gain or extreme left or right wing politics. They do not deserve to live.*

*The press do nothing about it. In fact, at least one of the press barons needs to be studied and, if found guilty of such crimes, he will be punished. When that happens, think of me.*

*You refer to my hobby as a crime, when I am merely doing my bit towards punishing criminals. It has always been the right of any individual to protect himself, his family, and their way of life against any outside threat. We did that in Europe and the Far East in the Second World War and we have done it since in Korea and other places.*

*I shall continue as long as I have the health and strength to do so, but, as you are now aware of my existence, I will increase my output to more than one per year.'*

James Ackroyd read it through twice without comment and then burst out, "What a pompous ass! When did this arrive, Harry?"

"It's recorded as coming in at two o'clock this morning, sir. There is no indication of where it came from and the duty clerk merely found it in the machine when he came back from the loo. This man seems to think he's smart, writing to us this way and eliminating any paper, prints and post marks."

"But, can't we get BT to trace a fax transmission to our number at about that time?"

"We can ask them but there must be a few hundred thousand accounts to check. There's no way of tracing the sender from our end and, knowing how bright our man is, I suspect that he would send it on someone else's machine and telephone line. He might even have used a portable fax, if there is such a machine, and a public 'phone box. He wouldn't make a mistake such as using his own number."

Ackroyd took a drink of coffee. "But he has made a mistake. And he'll make more. He's given us an insight into his mind, and our specialists can build up a profile of the man we're looking for. He may believe that he has the right to act as he does – how arrogant can you get? My first reaction to this message is that he is lying about his not being in Burma. He thinks he is some sort of Robin Hood looking after the welfare of the masses, and he wants to get more publicity for his so-called hobby. He will get plenty of that until we catch him.

Let's keep up the pressure from the public with another press release, quoting from his fax, and it might just encourage him to write some more. We will get him sooner or later, because the general public always come up trumps in the end. They are not daft.

And one more thing, Harry. I believe that the idea of using a portable facsimile machine is so very new that there cannot be many people who have invested in one, if they are available. Contact every possible supplier, manufacturers first, and then the wholesalers (if they have been supplied) and ask for a list of all their customers for such a machine. The lists might be long but I think that they could contain the name of the owner of the machine that sent that fax to this office."

# Chapter 21

# *1982*
# *Media Manipulation*

The questions raised by the newspaper headlines filled the correspondence columns for some weeks after they first appeared. They ranged from the frivolous to the very serious question of the ethics of capital punishment.

*Laughing from Bradford* said, *If we have more vigilantes like this jogger, then perhaps the police will learn to appreciate that the amateur approach to justice is more speedy, efficient and satisfying to the general public. Added to that is the fact that it is very cost-effective.*

*Bring back the rope!* was the theme of many of the printed letters.

*Serious, of Tunbridge Wells,* raised the basic question that had been brought to the attention of the Government and the population. *Sir, The question put before us is an ethical one. After basing our legal system, of hundreds of years, on the principle of innocence being presumed until guilt is proved, are our laws going to be ignored and our citizens killed by a vigilante who has set himself up as a judge, jury and executioner? However much we might disapprove of the activities of some of the victims of this man, his actions are against the law and he should be pursued by the police and brought to justice. Under his own so-called rules he would appear to qualify for the same treatment as his victims. Is he prepared to eliminate himself for that reason?*

The reaction to this type of letter was strong, indicating that the public thought that the police were not effective enough to prove that our legal system was sufficiently popular.

The views of *Old Soldier*, of London, created a record number of letters supporting his opinions.

*I am about the same age as your jogger and I served in the Army throughout the 39/45 War. Like him, I was trained by experts to kill the enemy in a variety of ways. I became very skilled. I put most of the methods into practice and, I hope, helped to win the War in my own small way. When I was in action I was often frightened and occasionally highly excited at the success of the moment. I knew that I had sworn allegiance to the King and no one ever suggested that I might be doing something wrong in fighting for my Country. I still believe that I did the right thing. Whilst I was overseas, I was very aware of the fact that there were many others at home who were taking advantage of the war conditions to make a lot of money. Some of them even took advantage of the frustrated wives left behind. We had plenty of 'hate lists' but we were too busy to do much about it. When we returned to 'Blighty' after the fighting was over, we were mostly too occupied in making a living and feeding our families. I think that this jogger was convinced that the enemy were not only the Germans and Japanese but also some of the 'blackmarketeers' and 'fly-boys' at home. If he is as convinced, as I am, that those who try to destroy our way of life should forfeit their own, then he has a case, especially if the police forces are unable to do their job. When will someone ask the police what powers they need in order to become effective? If and when they find this man they must thoroughly investigate his motives as well as his methods.*

The gist of the majority of his supportive replies showed that there were a large number of people who had survived the War with a wider view of justice than the government appeared to have. Questions were raised in the House about the responsibilities of Parliament to the victims of crime rather than simply the need to give each defendant the benefit of the doubt at every stage. It was made very obvious that many people believed that the judiciary was barely interested in the effect of crime on the victims or the witnesses. The feeling of 'them and us' began to grow more strongly. Some of the more intelligent members expressed their awareness of the dangers of the loss of faith in Parliament. This jogger had certainly made an impression on the philosophy being upheld in the country and expressed throughout the media.

---

Back in his flat in north Cheshire, the jogger was unaware of the plans for police action that could identify him. He was about to receive a rude awakening.

# Chapter 22

# *1982*
# *The Informer*

Mollie Cadell had always been a realist. From the age of eighteen, when she met and fell in love with Alec Cadell, she had been well aware of the fact that life is not for ever. Her mother had died at forty, after a late pregnancy had surprised them all, and Mollie had helped her father to raise her two brothers. Alec had found her to be both lovable and practical. She was the pride and joy of his life when he went overseas with a draft of reinforcements from the 56$^{th}$ Training Regiment, RAC Depot, Catterick.

His six weeks training there had started immediately after their wedding in Sale in 1941. Mollie had moved into a bed-sitting room in the market town of Richmond, Yorkshire, in order to be as near to him as possible during the first few weeks of their marriage. Whilst this was completely against the rules given to Alec when he was called up for service, he knew that he would be permitted to visit Richmond in the evenings after the first week or two. This was officially allowed after the second week of intensive training in drill on the square, and of undergoing a driving course in the lines and on the moors.

Alec could not wait the two weeks before he saw his bride again. On his first day there he made a quick reconnaissance of the boundaries of Menin lines and found that there were many places on the western side of the camp where it was possible simply to walk out. This was due west, heading in the direction of Richmond along what was known as the 'back road'. The only point to watch was to make sure that no officer or NCO saw him doing it. He tried this route on his second night in Menin lines and within one hour he was locked in Mollie's arms in her room.

"Darling," she said, when at last she came up for air, "aren't you taking a risk, coming out of camp without a pass?"

"Don't worry, sweetheart, nobody saw me. They were all having their grub and no one will look for me until 'Lights Out'. We can have three hours together before I need to be back in the barracks".

That short time had been spent in making love and sweet talk, planning their future and arranging for Alec to see her each evening from then on. They were very happy and treasured memories. He was seen illegally returning to Menin lines only once, and that was by another trainee, Jock Cameron, who was in his last week there, expecting a posting to a regiment at any time. Jock told him that he had 'wangled' a sleeping-out pass after two weeks, on the basis that his wife had turned up in Richmond suffering from depression. The only cure seemed to be his company whenever he was off duty! He had approached Captain Fergusson, in charge of training. "Is he reasonable?" asked Alec. "Sure. Never a maither, at a'. But don't tell him ye've met me! You can work on it." And Alec did just that.

Two weeks later, Alec was the proud owner of an official pass, permitting him to be 'absent from his quarters between being off duty each day until 0700 hrs the next day'. Such a permission was known throughout the camp as a 'crumpet pass'. Whatever it might be called, he was delighted to have it and to share those precious hours with his Mollie. "I did feel that those earlier visits, when I was sneaking out without a pass, put an extra bit of spice into those days," he told her in a weak moment. "Perhaps it was the possibility that I could be stopped on my way to or from Richmond." There had been an anxious minute once, when he had foolishly walked out of the camp at a point immediately in front of the officers' bogs. He had been aware of one officer, with his trousers down, glaring at him from his throne, but not in any condition to rush out in order to confront this deserter. He had used a different side of the perimeter after that.

The time at Catterick had passed so very quickly. The two newly-weds had lived for their nights together, and Alec had also been fully committed to learning all he could to become an effective member of a tank crew. The routine was broken once a week when Alec found he was on guard duty at the main gate.

He had passed all his courses on driving tanks and heavy lorries; gunnery, when he fired the 2-pounder and the Besa machine gun; wireless, in which he only scraped through the morse tests at ten words per minute, but he managed to use the huge No1 set reasonably well. He never saw the No1 set again as it was soon replaced with the more modern and efficient No 19 set. In the midst of all this intensive work, he was also given some basic infantry training, to the point where he could strip and reassemble the Bren gun blindfold. He spent time on the ranges, firing the Smith and Wesson .38 pistol, the .303 Lee Enfield rifle from the 14/18 War, the Boyes anti-tank gun, an absolute horror, which pushed him backwards with the first round that he fired. The Mills hand grenade was thrown under very strict supervision. Dummies were used at first. When live grenades were supplied later, some of them proved to be duds, with faulty detonators, or, worse still, long-delayed fuses. They all learned to keep their heads well below the parapet for a minimum of 30 seconds if they heard the word 'missfire'.

From his first day he had made a friend of Gerry Morris, who lived in Cheshire and was training to be an engineer. They shared confidences about their progress, or lack of it, throughout the training period, but Alec did not let Gerry know where he went when he sneaked out of camp each evening. He believed in keeping that as a secret between himself and Mollie. That lasted until the day when Mollie was walking along the road past the camp entrance just as the whole squad was marching out at the beginning of a route march. They had just been given the order to march 'at ease' when the randy young men spotted her leaning casually against the telephone box at the crossroads. Wolf whistles and cries of "Cor! Look at that!" came from many of them. Mollie remained where she was and smiled across at Alec, who was marching next to Gerry. He looked at Alec and said, "That's a lovely bit of crumpet, and she had her eyes on you, you lucky bugger." He was surprised to receive the never-to-be-forgotten answer, "That's no 'bit of crumpet', that's my wife." Alec was smiling to himself, well aware of his wife's attractions.

The six weeks went past too quickly. All members of the squad were passed out as competent tank crew members and the majority of them were posted to a transit camp near Bovington, from where they were sent home for two weeks' embarkation leave. Four of the remainder were sent to other RAC camps for pre-OCTU training, hoping to receive a wartime commission in due course. Although they were rapidly spread around the world, including North Africa and India, many of them were to meet up again in a variety of armoured battalions of the Royal Tank Regiment and regiments of cavalry and yeomanry. Some of them would be happy to be troopers serving in the same squadrons, and even the same tanks, commanded by an officer who had shared the same barrack room and ablutions with them when they were troopers together in the early days of their training. The knowledge of each other's humanity helped to cement the family spirit within the unit.

For Mollie and Alec, the two weeks of leave were bliss, tainted by the knowledge that they would soon be parted by thousands of miles and, possibly, by years of waiting for the War to be won. They had no doubts about the Allies being the winners. They were well aware of the risks of Alec being involved in fighting, although they rarely spoke of the possibility of being parted permanently.

Mollie had moved from Richmond as soon as Alec had left Catterick, returning to the Manchester area, where she soon found a well-paid job in a munitions factory. She maintained her independence from her family by taking a first-floor flat above a chemist's shop in Wilmslow. If she could not have Alec with her, she preferred to be alone and concentrating on accumulating as much money as she could before he returned. She had all the friendly company she wanted from the girls at the factory, sharing many hours of overtime with them each week. As for the flat, she easily kept it tidy and wrote a daily letter to Alec. She received only a brief farewell and love letter from him a few days after they parted. And then nothing for months.

Alec found that the return to a 'man's world', of being with his pals on the same overseas draft, clarified his thinking. He could face up to the fact that he was now ready to join a tank unit and go into action against the Germans, wherever he might find them. The newly married ones amongst them had their quiet moments of thinking about those left behind, but the excitement and chatter were contagious, and the rumours about the progress of the embarkation train from Bovington became wilder as it progressed through the night. Only dim lights were permitted and the blinds had to be kept down. The sergeant's "You'll be on a charge if you even try to look out," did not stop the lads from looking every time the train slowed down. During the hours of darkness there were whispered reports that they had just arrived at Hull, Glasgow, Cardiff and finally Liverpool. This proved to be the only true arrival point and at least six Scousers slipped out of the offside doors to escape into the dark dawn.

All the soldiers were quickly lined up at the side of the train, a roll call identified those missing, and those remaining were marched across some lines and on to a dockside. That started a long, uncomfortable two months on a troopship, in convoy across the Atlantic before turning south to cross the Caribbean. Then they turned east to cross the Atlantic again to arrive in Freetown, Sierra Leone. After refuelling there, the convoy sailed to the south, past Cape Town, without seeing the coastline, and eventually docked at Port Tewfiq in Egypt. They all looked over the side at the mass of locals who were scurrying about doing their various jobs. The sight of the muddy, rubbish-laden water below them raised a pertinent question from Geordie Burn. "Sergeant, why do they call this the Red Sea, when it's been the colour of shit for the last few hours?" Sergeant Kelly gave him a knowing look, making it obvious that he knew all the answers. "You should know by now, laddie, that Tewfiq is the arse'ole of all Egypt, and what comes out of an arse'ole? What you're seeing down there – and I'll tell you this for free – if you fall into any water in Egypt you will have at least twenty-four different inoculations before you die in agony. My tip to you is to be very, very careful."

More rumours started at Tewfiq, from within an hour of docking. Rommel was about to enter Cairo. His armour had been very successful in driving the Allied 8th Army all the way from Tobruk and we were making a stand under the command of General Bernard Montgomery. He was the man to succeed. The only thing he was waiting for was this shipload of trained tank men to fill the empty spaces in a few hundred brand new Matildas.

There was possibly some truth in these rumours. All the men were loaded into trucks and within twenty-four hours they were distributed amongst under-strength units on the outskirts of Cairo. Alec and Gerry were in the group received by the 47th Royal Tank Regiment and quickly welcomed into a squadron. The next week gave them very little chance of sleeping. If they were not on guard duty, they were living in and around their tanks, stowing and re-stowing their own kit, the ammunition and spare cans of petrol. Above all they were learning from the old hands how to survive in the desert. The Desert Rats were survivors. They knew how to drive, using compass and stars, across featureless landscapes, how to cook using a can of sand and petrol and, especially, how to 'muck in' together, to share their rations, cigarettes, and to mind each other's backs.

The newcomers were able to write only a few airgraph letters home, which they did. They could not say where they were and all letters were censored but the sad fact was that none of the mail arrived in the UK. The aeroplane carrying it was shot down over the Mediterranean.

Alec was blissfully unaware of this as he continued his preparations with his new regiment. Two weeks later, the $47^{th}$ RTR were taking their part in the $8^{th}$ Army attack on Rommel's armour near Alamein. They were making good progress until they found that they were exposed to concentrated fire from German tanks and artillery. Alec's tank and crew were hit with high explosive, burst into flames, and none of them survived. Theirs was not the only tank to go in that way.

Mollie had not heard from Alec for nearly four months when the dreaded telegram arrived. " ... regret to inform you that your husband, Trooper Alexander Cadell, has been killed in action".

The first reaction was shock at the brutal way that the news came to her. Despite all the prior knowledge of the risks of war, neither of them had believed that it could happen to them. Other people might be parted and bereaved, oh, yes! But, Alec and she? No! It could not be true. She would soon wake up and find that there had been some mistake. Eventually the horrible truth sank in and she knew that she needed some time back in her father's house, in the company of the remainder of her family. She had a week off work, again looking after her father and brothers, when she decided that she must start to face the future alone. It was the best thing for her to do. Involved in the long hours in the factory, helping to make something that would kill the Germans, she quickly settled into a routine of hard work and saving money.

Nearly four years later she noticed that the next-door flat, above the hardware shop, had been taken by a man of about her age. She guessed that he was a returned soldier. The quiet confidence and air of self-sufficiency as he went about his business convinced her that he might be well worth meeting. Only if the occasion arose, of course. She had a smile to herself when she learned that his name was Phil Anders. "I hope that is not his real name," she thought. "Who could trust a man with that name?" She was not going to find out.

Phil Anders was very soon aware of the cuddly young widow living in the next door flat. He correctly read the signals, that she was unable to suppress, that she was "willing" if approached in a decent way. He knew, without the shadow of a doubt, that he would be an idiot if he became involved in anything other than a casual way with a near neighbour. He did not want to antagonise her, and, at the same time, he did not want to encourage any close feelings. He settled for the exchange of greetings and the odd comment about the changeable weather. Mollie soon settled for that once she realised that she was not making any progress. She was aware that he received the occasional lady visitor but she rarely saw the same one twice. "Possibly, they were old school friends," she laughed to herself. She still was aware of his continuing presence and the erratic hours that he worked.

The years rolled on. Mollie's employers had switched smoothly from making munitions to designing and producing a range of 'white goods'. The returning members of the Armed Forces had demanded something to make life a little easier for their spouses, and new cookers and washing machines were only the start of it all. Her intelligence and years of long devoted service had brought its own reward. She was respected by all her colleagues in the factory, and the management eventually agreed that she should be given promotion and more responsibility. The increased income and growing confidence helped her to assert herself at work and in her few leisure hours. She even tried to enjoy the company of a very limited number of men who approached her with a variety of intentions, mostly carnal. No. She could not settle for anyone that she had met so far. She still retained an interest in Phil Anders as a 'possible', if he would only show a little more interest in her.

Here she was, in 1982, a widow for nearly forty years and due for retirement next year, still wondering if her neighbour would wake up to her interest in him, when she realised that the whole of the country was looking for someone whose description fitted Phil

Anders. It came as an overpowering shock to her when she read all the publicity that had been gained by that Yorkshire policeman. Slowly but surely she became convinced that he could be the serial killer described in all the national and local newspapers.

He was certainly in the right age group and her milkman had told her that he had been "in tanks in Burma". She had occasionally seen him going out for an exercise run in his dark blue jogging kit, he spent the occasional day or two away from his home and he used his garage as a workshop, tinkering with odd pieces of metal and wood. If he really was the killer, then she must tell the police and let them ask the questions that would either identify him as the man they were all seeking or else eliminate him. But she did not want to have to face him with her accusations.

The police sergeant was very 'matter of fact' when she went to the desk at the Wilmslow police station. "Yes, madam, I'll just get hold of someone who can help you".

Five minutes later she was in an interview room with a bright young inspector named Willett. He listened carefully when she told him that she had been aware of the neighbour, Phil Anders, since the War. "Are you interested in him as a possible 'friend'? Has he rejected your approaches?" he asked the pertinent questions, wondering whether she was only acting out of spite. Mollie coloured slightly, bursting out with, "No! We have merely exchanged the time of day when we passed each other near our flats. He seems to be a decent enough fellow, but there is something about him that keeps him aloof from anyone else, let alone a single woman like me. He always seems to be bright and intelligent but he has little contact with any other human being. He has been like that for nearly forty years. Surely, that puts him into a different category? *You* are the ones trying to find a murderer. *You* have put out the description of the man you want to interview. I'm only trying to do my duty as I see it. It's up to you what you do with him now." She stood up to indicate that she had had enough.

Inspector Willett accepted that he had as much information as she was likely to give him at the moment and thanked her, leading the way out of the station. Within twenty-four hours the details of Phil Anders were included in the list on Harry Bennet's computer list of 'possibles, to be checked'.

Harry was surprised when he received a facsimile message from Wilmslow the same day. "Re Phil Anders, possible suspect. National Insurance Records report that his contributions are fully paid from the year 1946 but they have no records of him before August 1946. No trace of any pre-war work or Forces service. Inland Revenue records show regular payments of Income Tax over the same period, but nothing before 1946. Please discuss asap. D. Willett, Insp."

Harry Bennet could hear the bells ringing as he went into CI Ackroyd's office with the fax in his hand. His smile told his governor that he was on to something. "I think, sir, that the press release has been effective. I suggest that we ask the Cheshire police to get this man in for questioning, and very carefully! He is bright enough to disappear again if they mess things up".

The process was then moved up into the higher ranks before the instructions were issued and Phil Anders' flat was put under observation. As soon as the police were sure that he was at home, a group of ten armed men stormed the premises.

# Chapter 23

# *1982*

# *Arrested*

Phil Anders had just placed the newly cooked meal on the table when the sudden noise of heavy hammering on his flat door caused an immediate loss of appetite. His instincts told him to look out of his rear window and he knew that his day of reckoning had arrived. Three armed policemen were covering his garage and windows and he was left in no doubt that there were more of them at his door. He walked up to it and called out, "Who is it?"

"Police. Open up." He unlocked the door and was instantly rushed by two heavy men pointing handguns at him. He could not have resisted if he had wanted to do so.

The next few days became a mixture of hours of questioning, broken up with hours of boredom waiting in a cell. He was told that he was being detained for questioning in regard to a murder committed in West Yorkshire on 13th April that year. He refused to comment. He was not told that he had been 'shopped' by his neighbour, Mollie Cadell.

The questioning became much more probing and effective after he had been taken by police van to Barnsley and when he came in front of Detective Inspector Bennet, who was in charge of the investigation into the murder of Vince Hallett. Anders knew very well, from his own work experience, that he had only to refuse to answer all questions, other than those about his name and address, to make it essential for the police to find some proof of his involvement in a crime. If they failed to do that, they would have to release him. He was soon told that he was required to appear in an identification parade that afternoon.

Harry Bennet had had no difficulty in finding the necessary number of men of similar height and appearance and Anders joined the parade dressed, as he had been when arrested, in his business suit with his hair smartly brushed down. His was as unlike a sweaty jogger as he could be. He wondered who the little lady was who was walked along the line of 'possibles' for identification. Was she the one who had seen him in the lane the day before he attended to Vince Hallett? After the years of being a private eye, and having a secret hobby, he found it quite easy to appear 'dead-pan' and he did not even look closely at Helen as she paused in front of him. She was unsure and moved on to the end of the line.

"Sorry", she said to a disappointed DI Bennet, "I could not be sure about any of them". She was thanked and taken back to her cottage in Field Lane.

Harry Bennet had another string to his bow. He told the parade to stand fast whilst he replaced Helen with another lady witness. This time Phil Anders caught sight of her out of the corner of his eye and felt a very nasty shock in his gut. He saw the dusky features of the Burmese wife of Jimmy James, 'Tina'. He had remembered the name after he had seen her at that wholesaler's office. "Blast it, she might recognise me under the old name". He must keep calm and try to bluff it out if she pointed to him.

It was no good. Tina walked slowly down the line, looking into the eyes of each man and then moving on. That was until she reached Anders. She touched him lightly on the chest and continued down the line to the end. Harry Bennet looked intently at her as she completed the job and she nodded. "Yes, Inspector, that is Sergeant Andrew Miller of B Squadron. I can never forget him after that time he came to my room in Myinga. He is the man I saw recently at the wholesalers, the one I told you about." Harry could have kissed her, he was so excited about her as a witness. "Thank you so very much, Mrs James, you have given us that link with his past that will help us to convict him of a whole string of crimes that he has committed over many years. The whole country is indebted to you."

After seeing Tina James out to her car, Harry went to CI Ackroyd's office with the good news. "We must charge this man and keep him inside until we can prove that he committed the Hallett murder or any one of the others." His boss was not quite so effusive. "You slipped up by having him dressed for the parade in a suit. You knew that the Fagin woman had seen him twice in his jogging kit. You'd better arrange another parade with him properly dressed, and give her a chance to make the right decision. Only then can you charge him with that murder. Something that will help to prove the other murders is the fact that the Cheshire police have not been sitting on their bottoms. They have had a good search of his flat and garage and there is a mass of things that will link him with your list. They have found papers and bamboo daggers, even a crossbow that he had modified so that he could carry it in a haversack and assemble it quickly when he wanted to use it. What we have to do now is to ensure that he cannot escape. Tina James' life would not be worth a jot if he could get to her. And more than that, we need to find out how he changed his name so successfully. Surely some organisation has slipped up in not noticing that he had no past, that is in the early days. He has since built up a history over the last forty years. You have plenty of work there. Don't delay before we get a psychiatrist's report. We are not going to let him off the hook by claiming that he was mentally damaged by that War of his. You will need more men to cover all I've given you. Think around your needs and let me have your report. You'll get some help but don't be greedy!"

# Chapter 24

# *1982*

# *Trickcyclist*

The Police machine was quickly put into a forward gear and the so-called 'routine enquiries' continued to bring in the missing facts and confirmation of any that required being re-checked.

Harry Bennet knew that his superiors were watching him and he made sure that all the suggestions from his DCI were carried out in detail. He arranged for another identification parade, with all the men wearing dark blue or black jogging outfits. Miller, as he was now known, was wearing his own kit, which had been brought over from Cheshire together with all the other relevant evidence. Harry had spent some time examining the items that might be needed for evidence, especially the crossbow and the bamboo projectiles and knives.

The parade was an immediate success. Helen Fagin had been advised not to rush the job, and she made some attempt to consider each man standing there in front of her, but she was very convincing in her approach to Miller when she almost hit him with her hand. "That's him. That's the man I saw in the lane!"

Miller now accepted the fact that he was not going to be released and that he would eventually be taken to court to face the charge of murder. He told his recently appointed solicitor that he was prepared to plead guilty in order to reduce the length of that ordeal, but that brought the reaction that the defendant should fight the charges and make the police bring all their evidence out into the court for scrutiny. Miller was already coming to the conclusion that he had personally spent far more time in his life actually in court and being involved in the legalities of cases than this young solicitor had done. He did not put it into words, but he was aware of the financial benefits that could arise from a lengthy trial and the young man must have noticed his disdainful look.

Harry Bennet was able to arrange to be the police presence during the psychiatrist's assessment interviews with Miller and he found the time to be well spent. He had always thought that he was a reasonably capable interviewer and that he was a fairly good amateur psychiatrist himself, but his eyes were opened to many nuances practised by this professional man. He could understand that the questions were designed to probe deeply for reasons, but whereas the policeman was hoping for answers that would prove guilt, the doctor was seeking motivation and an indication of how the prisoner would react under any slightly different circumstances. He really needed to know if the case could be thrown into disorder, if the man could plead 'insanity' and succeed in being sent to a hospital rather than a prison.

Dr Roberts started the questioning in a quiet, friendly voice that might have given the average man a false sense of security. "Tell me, Miller, you are accused of an intriguing list of crimes, mostly committed on 13$^{th}$ April each year since the War. Have you any idea of how the general public are reacting to the news that you are in custody?"

Miller looked at him with one eyebrow raised. "I have read a few of the papers and they seem prepared to print anything if it will help to increase their sales. I have a very cynical opinion of the press. I have seen too many court cases reported by journalists who were obviously not in court at the time. I would guess that the public is enjoying the thought that they will soon have a lot of their questions answered. Perhaps some of them will appreciate exactly what I have been doing to introduce a little justice into this country since the War." He shrugged his shoulders indicating a lack of interest.

"You certainly sound as though you have a poor opinion of the British system of justice. Is that what started you on this path of removing men that you consider to be evil? Most of us can feel that way at times, but we don't carry it out. Would you like to take your time and tell us how you started, and what made you go to all the trouble of changing your identity in order to lead this life of solitude. It shows an amazing determination as well as skills in concealing your purpose." The doctor sat back and gave the floor to Miller, who only hesitated for a minute.

"It all seemed so logical to me," he started, "and it is really very simple. My parents taught me the difference between right and wrong and I have applied the final sanction to only a few of those who deliberately try to damage others. There are plenty more around the country, still trying to feather their nests at the expense of the masses. Some of them are politicians, which makes it even worse.

"It was the politicians who started the Wars. On one side or the other, sometimes on both sides, they decided that it would pay them to go to war, especially in both 1914 and in 1939. They did it, knowing full well that many people, most of them innocent, would die under horrible circumstances. Then they realised that they could make vast profits as long as there was the need for a flow of armaments, so the Wars continued longer than necessary. We were all brainwashed.

"I was young, fit and eager to learn all the various ways to kill the enemy, with guns, knives, ropes and my bare hands. I had chosen to go into a tank unit, mainly because I would be able to carry a few more of the comforts of life with me, and to me it seemed a very efficient way of attacking the enemy. This proved to be the case, especially in India and Burma.

"We were doing quite well in B Squadron of the Carabiniers, the lads were getting over the worst of their illnesses from Imphal and we were heading south, chasing and eliminating a beaten Japanese army, when that sod Benton went berserk. You know what he did. To my mind he was just as bad as a Jap and he needed the same treatment. I know that Jimmy James suspected that I had dropped a grenade on him when I had sent him out of the tank and he was right. I had. He deserved it. If he had been arrested and charged with rape, he would have been sent out of the line to comparative safety. He would have missed any more action and had a few cushy months awaiting court martial. Then he would have spent the rest of the War inside, well away from flying lead. He got justice. And all the others did, too.

"When the fighting finished in Burma, we suddenly realised that we would soon be going home to a changed Britain. I had no wife or family waiting for me to go home to then. The old country was full of lefties and liberals who would make excuses for all the criminal activity. The trades unions would be taking the blinkered view of demanding more and more concessions for their members;

shorter hours and longer holidays were only a catchphrase for ever-increasing attacks on the management. Most of their activity was inspired from Moscow with the intention of proving that capitalism was a failure. This was added to the fact that the country was led to believe that the best future was with the Labour Party and the Conservatives, including Winston Churchill, were ejected after he had led us to a tremendous victory. I suppose that we deserved all that we got after dumping Winston like that.

"We've seen years of frustration and corruption since then. When we've elected a Conservative government, they have been so weak that they have made little progress, until now. It looks as though Maggie Thatcher has the making of being tough enough to get rid of the threats from the Unions, but she has a problem with a lot of nasties in her own party. I wish her well.

"Whatever the party, all the politicians seem to be obsessed with helping the criminal rather than their victims. They openly support any member of their own party who has been seen misbehaving, to put it mildly. Such people give meaning to the famous statement that there was only one honest man who went into Parliament – Guy Fawkes. Bribery, corruption and sleaze seem to be the order of the day. And now some of them are even trying to encourage us to agree to hand over the government of the United Kingdom to some bunch of unelected foreigners. There are plenty more targets for me or my successor."

The doctor butted in here.

"Do you mean to tell me that you have already organised a successor?"

"No, of course not. But when the full story of my efforts, results and reasons is read, I am sure that you will find that there will be a few more willing to follow me in applying justice. You might think that I am mad, but the logic of it all will soon be appreciated. The main essential is that the man must be a solitary and totally dedicated. He will soon be starting in business – you can be sure of that! And he might not be the only one."

"I don't think for a moment that you are mad, or that you will be able to plead insanity as your defence. In fact, you impress me with the logic of your argument. The Inspector here appears to be equally impressed." Harry nodded gravely at this point. He was beginning to understand the logic of the man. "But he is here to uphold the law of the land and he will be handling things from that point of view. There is one question that I must ask you at some time during this interview and I might as well ask it now. You appear to have been brought up in what is known as a 'typical middle-class family', knowing what is right and wrong. Tell me, how do you reconcile all your activities with the usual basic standards of the pre-war Yorkshire family?"

Miller was quiet for nearly a minute.

"I've told you why I killed Benton. He was as bad as the Japs that we were fighting. We knew that we were all likely to be killed in the months, and possibly the years, ahead. Remember, at the time, we were faced with chasing the remainder of the Japanese army and destroying them, even if it meant fighting our way to Rangoon, then on to Bangkok. There were more of their armies between where we were in Burma and Japan. We could even have to fight our way across the whole of China and Korea before we could invade the Japanese islands. I was aware that Benton could have been killed in action at any time but he sickened us all by boasting about his rape as a 'conquest'. I have never regretted what I did.

"As for the religious aspects, that is not one of my strong points. I am prepared to concede that there is a 'heaven' of some sort and that there could be a survival of a form of life after death, but I don't profess to understand it. I'm quite sure that there is no such place as hell, with devils waiting to torture the baddies when they arrive there. I've seen enough of this life to know that we create our own hell on this earth. You've seen it in the photographs of Belsen and such places. And it is still going on in some part of the world or other. I went to the local C of E church with my family, when I had one, until I went into the Army.

"Some of the Army padres were fine men, who would be up there in the fighting area, taking their chances with the rest of us. They were the same mixed bunch of what we recognised as 'officer material'. Some of them were conscientious objectors who would risk their lives to help bring in the wounded. Others were willing to use weapons to defend their position during a Jap attack. Most of them gained a lasting respect from the ranks. None of them even tried to convince me that I would go to some sort of hell because I was involved in killing thousands of other so-called 'humans'.

"After doing just that for more than a year, with all the authority and training of my elected government, I still can't see any reason for not continuing to remove the enemies of the state, those who are trying to destroy all that we have fought for over the five years of the War. Everyone has to die at some time. It is the only true fact of life. If the government were true to their pledges, there would be no need for someone like me. The police would catch the rogues and the courts would put them away for a long time. The deterrents would be effective. That simply does not happen. The public want a return to hanging, but it is not allowed. I can see no end to the weakening of attitudes to criminals. The authorities are obsessed with wanting to help the 'poor criminal' and 'to hell with the innocent victim'. Sooner or later, there will be such a strong reaction from the silent masses that the government of the day will be caught unaware of the problems that they face. There is always the danger that the reaction will be excessive and that we will end up with a police state, with the forces of discipline dominating our lives. It could be refreshing to see the weak liberal attitudes being swept away, but there would be the danger that this would be followed by another swing of the pendulum, back towards the present sloppy mess. The successful politician is the one who can assess the mood of the public correctly. The greedy, self-motivated one reacts, as usual, by doing what he can to chase votes.

"You must be aware of the growing trend for many people to be weakening their interest in saving all human life, at whatever cost in cash or effort. We can often read in the press about the attitudes to old people. Younger members of the same family cannot be bothered to look after their parents. They prefer to have them put into old peoples' homes where they can be maltreated to the point of death, without anyone giving a damn. These trends will continue to worsen until there is an outcry in the media. Why should there be so must fuss about my activities? No one appears to shed any tears over the deaths I cause. The general comment in the press is that the targets had caused much grief and hardship with their nasty ways. I can go on about this for a long time, but I think I am wasting my time."

The doctor was smiling rather wistfully. "Not at all, Miller. You give it a certain logic and I can understand your motivation more clearly now. You still have to face the problem that your actions, however well intended for the safety of the country, are against the law and that the police will be taking whatever steps are required by the law. From the discussions that we have had during the past few days, I can only come to the conclusion that you might expect. In my opinion, you are perfectly sane. You have had a traumatic experience similar to those experienced by the many thousands of others in the 14$^{th}$ Army, but you appear to be the only one who has been affected in this way and acted as you have done. I want you to know that that will be the gist of my report on your mental condition to the court. You will have other medical examinations by other doctors, but this could be the last time that you see me before you appear in court. Do you have any questions that you would like to ask me?"

Miller simply shrugged his shoulders and shook his head. "No, doctor, I agree with your findings and accept them."

"Then I can only wish you well and leave you with DI Bennet here."

He spoke into the microphone to terminate the official record of the meeting and switched the machine off at the mains, taking the tape with him as he left the room.

Harry Bennet was silent for a full minute after the psychiatrist had left the room. Then he stood up and checked the recording equipment, switching the machine off on the box and re-checking that there was no tape in position. "You can't be too sure, these days," he smiled.

Dusty Miller was watching him very carefully, suspicious of the new attitude of the policeman. Was this some sort of trap? He made no comment, waiting to see what the DI was going to ask him.

Harry Bennet picked up one of the chairs and carefully placed it at Miller's side so the he could sit down facing the prisoner with their heads only three feet apart. They could now talk without the possibility of being overheard by anyone outside the room.

## Chapter 25

# *1982*
# *Another Volunteer*

Harry Bennet was in a quandary. He decided to play things step by step. Here he was, sitting beside a confessed serial killer, feeling a strange and unexpected warmth towards the man. Perhaps it was based on the attraction that he had felt towards the other members of the 3$^{rd}$ Carabiniers whom he had met in recent months. The strong sense of belonging, the family feeling, seemed to emanate from each one of them. There must be something in the cavalry esprit de corps that had continued through the shocking loss of horses in the thirties and into the noisy, oily world of the mechanised modern army with their lumbering tanks.

When CDI Ackroyd had introduced him to the Squadron Wireless NCO, Alan Fenner, his eyes had been opened to the way of life in that tank regiment in the villages and jungle fighting in India and Burma. The later interviews with another wireless operator, Jimmy James, had given him a further insight into the lives of those men, fighting for their country against the Japanese Army in 1944 and 1945. He had found Jimmy's Burmese wife to be a delightful person, now married and living in this foreign land, so far from home. When living in her uncle's village in northern Burma, she had been approached by a sex-starved Miller, only to be repulsed in a never-to-be-forgotten incident. That stupid mistake had cost him his freedom because she had never forgotten him and had recognised him more than thirty years later in Sheffield.

He decided that he would start the next session of questioning in a more indirect way.

"Well, Miller, there is not a lot more to say at this stage. This is, as you know, entirely 'off the record'. There is no tape running and I will deny anything that you might report about the conversation at a later date. Understand?"

Miller frowned. "What sort of game are you playing?"

"This is not a game. It is deadly serious. You realise, don't you, that you convinced the trickcyclist that you have a logical approach to the treatment of wrongdoers?" Miller's eyebrows came together again.

"And, what's more, you have sown seeds of ideas in my own mind that do not square with my training and responsibilities. I am feeling inside me that I want to help you to have as easy a time as possible. Do you understand what I am saying?"

Miller was quiet for a moment. Then he laughed, quietly.

"You are the first 'Bobby' that I have ever met who wanted to help a criminal. Come off it, Inspector, I've spent too much time in various courts to believe that! But carry on. I would like to understand your motivation."

Bennet swallowed carefully before he started to speak again.

"To start with, you are not yet a criminal, Miller. There is little doubt that you will become one after your trial, but not yet. The doctor was not the only one to be impressed with your logic. I am already thinking that I should work out an action plan for how your successor might continue the 'capers', as you call them. It would be a very interesting exercise. He would need to have the intelligence and the knowledge necessary to evade police investigation. He would also need to be a solitary person and I can already see that a policeman could combine both jobs and enjoy a great deal of satisfaction."

Miller closed his eyes in order to exclude the sight of Bennet's eager face and to concentrate on the words and possible honesty of this young man. He began to believe what he was hearing.

"This will take a lot of believing. How do I know that you are not winding me up? Carry on, Inspector".

"I hope that you will soon begin to believe me. Let me ask you the next question. When you hear it, you will know that I am not trying to trap you into confessing to any of your recent crimes. You have indicated to us on more than one occasion that you have plans to destroy a well-known industrial tycoon who has been stealing large sums of money from the pension funds of his employees. Is this the famous, or should I say infamous, Robert Wexmall? He has had plenty of publicity in the press, with implications that he is up to those tricks. If it is so, can you tell me how far advanced you are with your plans?"

Dusty Miller took the plunge. He had nothing to lose.

"Yes, you are right. Wexmall is the man. Only this time I have already met him a few times. It was during those meetings that he convinced me that he is not merely what the press implies, but he is in the shit far more than anyone could guess. It will all come out in the next few weeks.

During the past three years I have been given a number of routine jobs to do for him, checking references, reporting on meetings between various members of his staff at many levels. It was all fairly simple stuff that could have been done by any competent investigator but it happened to come my way. Anyway, he was pleased with my 'efficiency' and paid me well with his compliments. Since then, he met me at a secluded hotel and sounded me out to do something that smelt to me as being really illegal. He probed me about my Army life and my knowledge of small arms. When he heard my account of experience with pistols, knives, garrottes and bamboo weapons, to say nothing of unarmed combat, he became very persuasive. He admitted that he had a business contact who must be removed permanently. Without my agreeing to do the job, he gave me £10,000 on the spot and promised another similar bundle when the work had been completed. He would tell me the name of the target when I met him on his yacht in Marbella Marina thirty days later. He also gave me precise details of how I could board the yacht at night without being seen by anyone ashore or on the boat. With that information I accepted the invitation and the cash. It gave me the perfect method of contacting him secretly and eliminating him at will. And, more than that, he had paid me for my expenses.

As you know, I have been prevented from making the journey to keep the appointment. He has lost his ten grand and now has to find some other willing agent to remove his problem. It could be too much to hope that he finds another man like me who would like to rub him out instead of one of his rivals. I simply don't know the name of the proposed target so I can't help you there.

I will be glad to have a friend in the police force and I hope that you will be able to follow your instincts in your future activity. Mine tell me that we must keep every conversation on a very formal level, using surnames and not being too obvious. Agreed?"

"Agreed!" And the two men shook hands.

Harry Bennet went back to his desk knowing that there would be at least one successor to the 13$^{th}$ April serial killer.

# Appendix

# The Battle of Nunshigum

Extract from the order of Ceremonial at the Fiftieth Nunshigum Anniversary Parade of the Royal Scots Dragoon Guards held at Stanley Barracks Bovington, 13th April 1994.

On April 13th, 1944, was fought one of the most crucial actions in the great battle for IMPHAL, the most fiercely contested battle of the Burma campaign.

In March of that year, the Japanese 15th Army, moving swiftly through the jungle and crossing the mountains of the North East frontier of India, cut the land communications of the British and Indian troops of 4th Corps. Thereafter, the only link between this large force, amounting to nearly one hundred thousand men, and the outside world, was by air. All the supplies, petrol and ammunition to enable it to fight had to be flown into the airfields on the Imphal Plain.

NUNSHIGUM, a dominating hill standing almost four thousand feet above sea level and rising abruptly from the parched fields, lay six miles from Imphal, around which, besides the airfields, were all the dumps, the hospitals, the workshops and the 4th Corps Headquarters controlling the battle. The loss of this base could have been disastrous.

On 6th April, part of the Japanese 51st Regiment attacked NUNSHIGUM, the hill was lost and won again and again until finally, on 11th April, the enemy firmly established themselves upon it. Now, only scattered defences, largely manned by administrative troops, lay between the enemy and the hub of the defence. The security of the whole Corps was threatened and the recapture of NUNSHIGUM was imperative.

The troops allotted for the operation were 1st Battalion The Dogra Regiment supported by the tanks of B Squadron the 3rd Carabiniers, with the artillery of the 5th Indian Division and three squadrons of the Royal Air Force in support.

The plan involved an advance on two separate company axes up neighbouring spurs of the hill. Each company was supported by a troop of tanks, with two troops in squadron reserve, and half squadron headquarters with the left-hand company. The attack began at 1030 hrs on 13th April, without prior reconnaissance by those taking part, due to shortage of time. Known enemy positions were shelled by the artillery and attacked by aircraft as the attackers climbed the hill.

The enemy occupied strongly defended bunkers on the twin peaks of NUNSHIGUM, one behind the other. Most of the advance was screened from their view by a series of false crests and involved a climb of a thousand feet above the plain.

After an hour the first peak was reached and action joined. The only feasible tank route was astride the crest of a razor-backed ridge along which the tanks had to move, perforce, in single file. So steep were the slopes that one tank, overbalancing, fell a hundred feet but ended its fall on its tracks and the crew survived. The hill was covered with scrub and bushes, affording good cover for dug-in infantry and the attackers came under fire at ranges of a few yards. Tank commanders could not close down if they were to guide their drivers and retain control in these circumstances. The first officer casualty was Lieutenant Neale, shot through the head. Shortly after, the Squadron Leader, Major Sanford, whose father commanded the Regiment twenty years before, was similarly killed.

About this time the commander of the left-hand company, Major Jones, was wounded. The commanderless tanks were withdrawn with difficulty and Lieutenant Fitzherbert, now in command, continued the attack with the remaining tanks. Within fifteen minutes both he and the commander of his leading tank, SQMS Branstone, were killed, as was Sergeant Doe. Other crew members attempting to take over in these tanks became casualties also.

At this moment B Company Commander, Major Alden, was wounded while directing the fire of a tank. All the British officers in the two companies of the Dogra Regiment were now casualties. It became clear that a relieving commander would have to be sent up the hill to take command of the operation, now apparently leaderless.

Meanwhile, deterred by neither casualties nor confusion, Squadron Sergeant Major Craddock assumed command of B Squadron. He and Subedar Ranbir Singh, the senior surviving Viceroy's Commissioned Officer, together replanned the attack. They closed once more with the bunker positions, were forced back, repositioned the tanks, notably Sergeant Hannam's, directly above an enemy bunker, finally destroyed the bunkers and their occupants and gained the day. By 1400 hrs the peaks were in friendly hands. The enemy fled leaving over 270 dead. An hour later the relieving British Officer arrived to find, in his own words, 'The position entirely satisfactory and consolidation nearly complete.'

Thus, as a result of this supremely gallant action, the very serious threat to 4$^{th}$ Corps was removed.

Never again did NUNSHIGUM fall into enemy hands.

This citation continues to be read to the assembled Nunshigum Parade on 13$^{th}$ April each year by the Chaplain of the Royal Scots Dragoon Guards.